SPY FOR HIRE

A MARK SAVA THRILLER

DAN MAYLAND

THOMAS & MERCER

The characters and events portrayed in this book are fictitious. Any similarity to real persons, living or dead, is coincidental and not intended by the author.

All maps by XNR Productions

Published by Thomas & Mercer, Seattle

www.apub.com

ISBN-13: 9781612183374
ISBN-10: 1612183379

Cover design by The Book Designers

Library of Congress Control Number: 2013911339

Printed in the United States of America

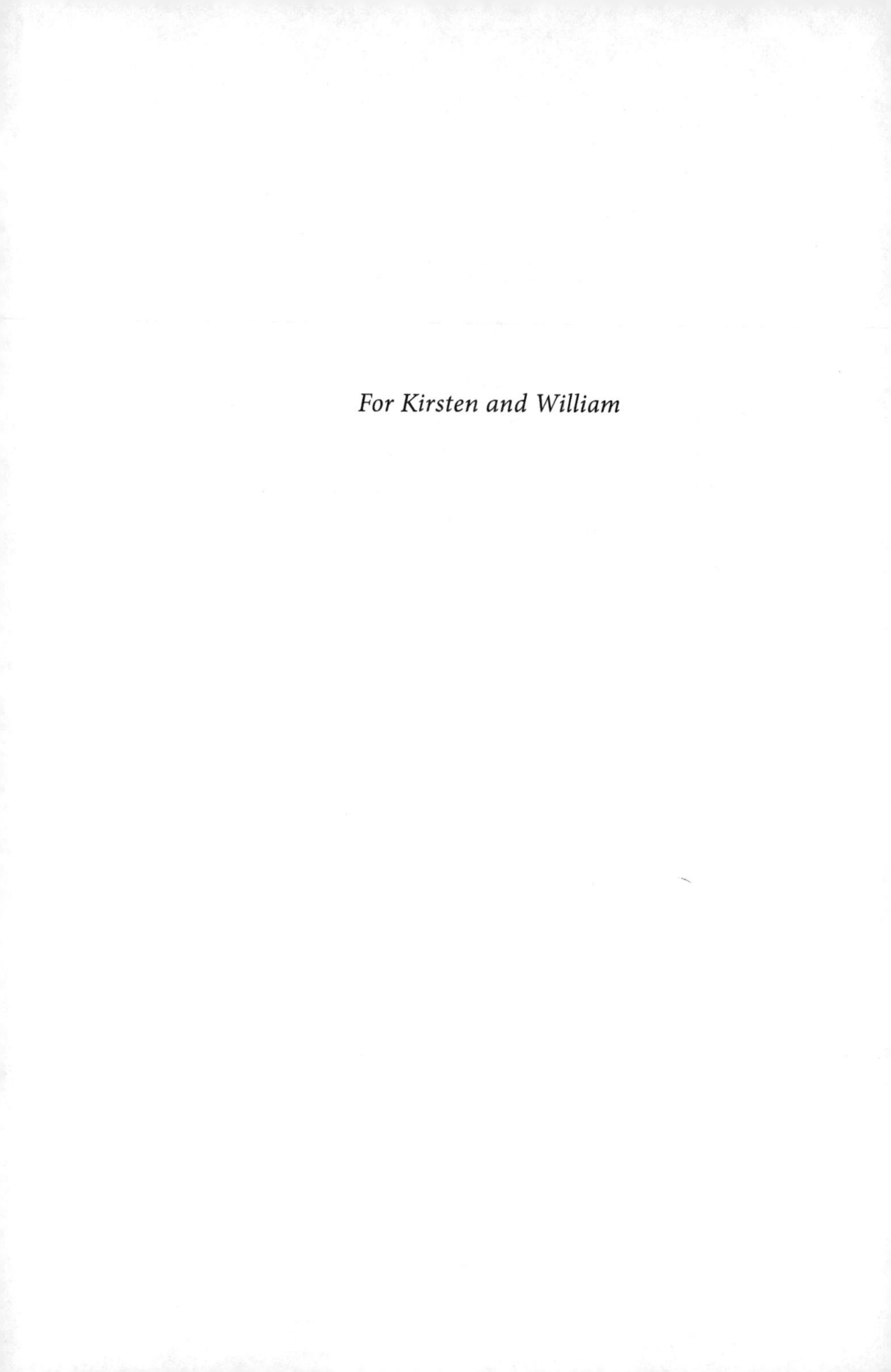

For Kirsten and William

Author's Note

At danmayland.com, you'll find extras that might be helpful or interesting to have when reading *Spy for Hire* or other novels in the Mark Sava series—maps that may be downloaded or printed, my own photos of places featured in the novels, lists of characters, an annotated bibliography, and a glossary.

DM

PART I

CENTRAL ASIA, SOUTH ASIA, and the MIDDLE EAST

KYRGYZSTAN

KAZAKHSTAN
ALMATY
Chu River
MANAS AIR BASE
BISHKEK
ALA ARCHA NATIONAL PARK
CHOLPON-ATA
BALYKCHY
Lake Issyk Kul
KYRGYZSTAN
OSH
CHINA
TAJIKISTAN
N
0
50 MI
0
50 KM

1

Bishkek, Kyrgyzstan

Former CIA station chief Mark Sava opened the door to his two-bedroom condominium, hung his black nylon windbreaker on a coatrack, and cast a disapproving glance at the outdoor balcony off his living room.

His condo was upscale for Bishkek—oak floors, new Chinese appliances, tile countertops—and in a safe part of the city, on a treelined street near several foreign embassies. But the balcony was a sad affair, barely three feet wide by eight feet long. The metal balusters were rusting. The concrete floor was cracked. And positioned as it was on the second floor of a three-story building, it was too close to the street to provide any real privacy.

Mark was in a good mood, because he'd just beaten a Kyrgyz friend at narde, a backgammon-like game he'd grown addicted to of late. But that lousy balcony was a constant irritation.

It was one o'clock in the afternoon on November seventh. The leaves on the trees were beginning to fall. The roadside pumpkin vendors had packed up and left weeks earlier. Soon there would be snow.

For a brief moment, Mark longed to be back in Baku, Azerbaijan—his home until seven months ago, when the Azeris had kicked him out because of an intelligence operation gone bad. In Baku, the balcony of his eighth-floor apartment had been a spacious affair, with more than enough room for a few plastic lawn chairs, a little table, and his collection of tomato plants.

Tomato plants . . . they'd freeze here in the winter, but maybe in the spring, he'd buy some. He looked out to his rump of a balcony again, imagining where he'd put a few pots, but instead his eyes fixed on what was going on just outside the Soviet-era hospital building across the street.

"In November?" he said out loud, speaking half to himself and half to Daria Buckingham, an Iranian American former CIA operative who was also his live-in girlfriend.

"What?" called Daria.

Mark stepped into the kitchen, where Daria was frying chicken with onions and carrots in a large cast-iron pot. She turned, and smiled at him. It was a wide, easy smile that reminded Mark why he'd fallen for her.

"They're bringing the mattresses out again."

Every so often, orderlies would drag out the frayed, red-striped, futon-like hospital mattresses and air them out in one of the building's courtyards. It always depressed Mark to think that a human being, a sick human being no less, had to sleep on one of those things.

"You know, you could volunteer to help."

"Yeah, and after that I'll volunteer to help Sisyphus push his rock up the hill."

"Maybe figure out a way to get them some good mattresses."

"It's not like, if there's piss on them, they're going to dry out. It's too cold. What do they think they're doing?" When Daria didn't answer, Mark added, "Remind me never to have a heart attack here. I take it the chicken's for the kids?"

"Yeah." Daria used the back of her wrist to wipe a strand of her long dark hair out of her eyes.

Mark took a moment, as he always did upon entering a room, to analyze the situation. Daria was wearing an apron over a nice black skirt and a green blouse, which told him she'd come from a meeting, probably in Bishkek, and that she had more meetings planned for later in the day; her phone was on the counter, and turned on, so she'd likely been trying to conduct business while she cooked; onion skins were scattered all over the countertop cutting board, which suggested she was rushed because she typically cleaned as she cooked; and her large brown eyes looked happy but tired.

He'd be tired too if he worked as much as she did, he thought. Her work helping orphanages throughout Central Asia—work funded by an intelligence operation she'd made a killing on—was what motivated her. She was constantly meeting with wealthy supporters of her cause, traveling to orphanages, making dinners . . .

He admired her dedication. Not so much that he wanted to join her cause, but he was relieved that, after going through hell while working for the CIA, she'd lived to find her true calling.

"Smells great." Mark put a hand on her waist and leaned into her for a kiss. Daria surprised him with a more passionate response than the perfunctory peck he was expecting, given that he hadn't shaved or showered yet that day. The feel of her smooth warm cheek as it brushed against his own was a comfort.

"It's for the orphanage in Bishkek," she said. "One of the kids is being adopted, it's his last night. Remember?"

Mark didn't. "Oh, yeah." He started cleaning up the onion skins on the cutting board, but then he felt Daria's eyes on him and he turned to face her. "What?"

His first thought was that she was annoyed at him for claiming to have remembered the dinner, when in fact he hadn't—she was perceptive that way—but her expression looked more intense than that. He couldn't tell whether she was holding back laughter or tears. They locked eyes for a moment.

"Nothing." Daria turned back to the chicken.

Between the kiss and now this, Mark wondered what was up, but he figured that if it was important, he'd find out soon enough—probably that night. They often saw each other only in passing during the day, but they always made a point of catching up before going to sleep.

"Hey, another deal came through this morning," he said. "The Agency's subbing out an intel job they want done in Almaty."

In his teens, Mark had worked his butt off after school and on weekends as a gas station attendant in Elizabeth, New Jersey. In his twenties, he'd served as a CIA case officer and paramilitary operative in the CIA's Special Activities Division. In his thirties, he'd been one of the youngest officers in the CIA to be given his own station. But now? Now he was pretty much just loafing, cashing in on his CIA experience by drumming up business for a privately owned spies-for-hire firm that operated out of the nearby US air base. Every time he brought in work, he collected fifty percent of the profits.

"What's the job?" she asked, sounding less than enthusiastic.

"Intel op on a Chinese construction firm that's upgrading the oil ministry building. We'll have to put a couple officers on TDY in Almaty."

TDY was short for temporary duty.

"Is the job already cleared with State?"

"Seems to be. I talked to—"

The phone started ringing.

Mark didn't feel like talking to anyone, so he didn't move to answer it.

Daria flashed him a look that said, *Listen, I've been working like crazy all day trying to help impoverished kids while you've been sitting on your ass playing that silly narde game with your old geezer buddies down at that filthy Chinese restaurant and making money hand over fist by selling your reputation. The least you could do is shuffle a few feet to the phone.*

"I'll get it," said Mark, but he was a second too late.

Daria picked up the phone. After listening for a minute, with the handset held a little ways from her ear because the person on the other end was talking so loudly, she said, "Hold on, slow down. No. Tell them they need to go through the normal channels, no exceptions." And then, "*No*, they can't do that. Absolutely not. *Do not* let them take that child." And then, "OK, I'll be there as soon as I can. Stall them until I get there."

She turned to Mark, looking frustrated. And tired. "Any way you can finish the *paloo*?"

"Yeah, sure." *Paloo* was what the Kyrgyz called meat and rice mixed together in a big pot. Mark figured he could handle it.

"And drop it off?"

"No worries. I got it covered. What's up?"

Daria had already left the kitchen and was putting on her coat. "Problem in Balykchy with one of the kids."

"What problem?" asked Mark, but Daria was already on her way out the door.

2

The road to Balykchy, a town of forty thousand people about one hundred miles east of Bishkek, shot straight through a fertile valley that was one of the few flat places in all of Kyrgyzstan. Mountains rose up from the northern and southern edges of the valley.

As Daria pushed the limits of her Volkswagen Jetta, trying to make good time before she hit the part of the highway the Chinese hadn't fixed yet, her thoughts turned to Mark. And to the fact that her period was a week late. Was it possible?

Yes. Unlikely, but possible.

Neither of their efforts to prevent conception had been heroic. Birth control pills made her feel bloated, and besides, she didn't trust the quality of the locally available brands. So instead they'd relied on the rhythm method and the occasional condom. She'd known the risks, and had accepted—maybe even welcomed—the possible consequences. But could the same be said for Mark?

She exhaled and gripped the steering wheel a little tighter, wondering what his reaction would be if this wasn't just a scare; she hoped the news would bring them closer, but worried he would pull away from her.

Truth be told, though they'd been living together in Bishkek for more than seven months now—ever since Mark had gotten kicked out of Azerbaijan—she still sometimes felt as though she didn't understand him. She certainly didn't understand the rationale behind what he was currently doing with his life.

During their first month living together in Kyrgyzstan, she'd sympathized with him wanting to take it easy for a while. He was more than ten years older than she was. He'd already seen, and done, plenty with his life. Running away from home at seventeen, putting himself through college, joining the CIA and rising quickly through its ranks . . . It had been nice to see him just relax in a way that, she suspected, he'd never done before.

Maybe the fact that he'd gotten kicked out of Azerbaijan had been a blessing in disguise, she'd thought. She'd continued to feel the same way during the second month. He just needed time to unwind.

By the third month, she'd started wondering just how long this unwinding business was going to last. In Azerbaijan, after leaving the CIA, he'd taught international relations at a university in Baku. She'd figured he'd try to land a similar teaching position here in Bishkek. It wouldn't have been hard, given his credentials.

Instead he played narde. Every day. And worked halfheartedly for that spies-for-hire outfit. She couldn't understand how someone as bright and capable as Mark was could be satisfied with that kind of life.

Balykchy was a wretched place.

During the Soviet era, the town had been a thriving factory center, a rail hub where wheat, corn, tobacco, cotton, beef, and wool had been consolidated and then shipped out across the Soviet Union. Situated on the far western end of Lake Issyk Kul—the tenth largest lake in the world—it had also been a big fishing port. But when the Soviet Union collapsed, Balykchy collapsed with it. The factories had closed. The trains had stopped. The orders for trout and whitefish had dried up. And most of the Russians had gone home, taking most of the jobs with them.

Twenty years later, what was left was a scarred and abandoned relic, a place that had sunk low and was still sinking.

Daria turned onto a rutted road that cut through the center of town. Along the roadside, women wearing tightly wrapped headscarves sold ten-kilo sacks of flour and round—to represent the sun, said the locals—loaves of *lepeshka* bread. Men in wool sweaters sat on their haunches in front of collections of used hardware equipment, or beside piles of salt- and mineral-rich boulders that would be used as cattle licks.

It was getting cold out—snow was visible on some of the distant peaks. She shivered, turned up the heat, and took a left off the main road. As she headed down toward the lake, she passed a few abandoned factories and horses grazing in marshy fields.

The local orphanage was in a converted one-story home that had been enlarged to serve its current purpose. It sat behind fencing made of corrugated-metal roofing panels, and the building's exterior white-stucco walls had been repeatedly patched with gray mortar. A telephone pole leaned against the roof. The bright-blue wooden shutters on the front windows had been closed tight.

As Daria pulled up to the entrance gate, a gray Volkswagen police car, its red, white, and blue lights flashing, pulled up behind her.

"Shit," she said. The police car could only mean one thing. She was too late.

3

Mark had grown to love the Shanghai, a Chinese restaurant in Bishkek.

The wine-red carpets were stained, half the plexiglass lids on the buffet-station dishes were cracked, and the ceiling had cobwebs in the corners. The fancy coffee shop next door—which offered free Wi-Fi and pricey double espressos to diplomats and government types—only made the Shanghai appear all the more shabby by comparison. But the Shanghai had both cold beer and an owner who tolerated daily narde games, and that was more than enough to make up for its faults.

At the moment, two narde boards were in play, both of which were set up on a long, cigarette-scarred laminate table in the back of the restaurant. Two players sat across from each other at each board. A Kyrgyz with a round brown face and perpetually flushed cheeks was up against a bald and bearded Uzbek. Mark sat across from a heavily jowled Kyrgyz-born Russian. All the men, save Mark, were in their seventies.

Each man's face registered total concentration. Four open half-liter bottles of Arpa, a local beer, sat on the table. The loud smacks of narde pieces hitting the wooden playing boards created a steady staccato din that could be heard all around the room.

Mark rolled the dice, came up with a four and a six, and then slapped down his pieces in a way that set him up to start bearing them off in a turn or two. That was the ultimate object of the game—start off with all your pieces in one corner, circle them around the board, and then bear them off the board entirely. The first person to remove all his pieces won. Though luck played a role, it was also a game of strategy and skill.

At the adjacent board, the Uzbek looked as though he was about to roll his dice. But instead he leaned in toward Mark and, as if sharing a confidence, said in Kyrgyz, "Always so lazy."

Mark got a whiff of sour old-man beer breath. He turned away.

The Uzbek lifted his eyes slightly from the board and briefly made eye contact with his Kyrgyz opponent. "He worships his pieces like his relations worship their sheep. Ha!"

The loser of the round-robin tournament had to pay for the beer, and the second-to-last player had to cover the gratuity—an easy burden to bear, especially if you were the Uzbek, though the Russian and Kyrgyz were not known for their big tips either.

Lately the Uzbek had been buying a lot of beer and he wasn't happy about it. So he'd taken to insulting his opponents, after which he'd claim he'd just been joking. That wasn't what bothered Mark, though. It was that he did it during the game.

Mark exchanged a glace with the Russian. The Russian then shot the Uzbek a look that simultaneously managed to convey aggression, boredom, and pitiless disdain. The Kyrgyz almost certainly *did* have extended relations who still herded sheep, and who likely still believed in at least some aspects of paganism. So the insult, on top of disturbing the game, was also a bit of a low blow.

"Play," insisted the Kyrgyz.

Suddenly Mark's cell phone rang. He was supposed to have turned it off before the game started, but he'd forgotten to do so.

His Russian opponent threw his hands up in the air. The implication was clear—first the insufferable Uzbek and now this.

"I'm sorry," said Mark. "I'll turn it off." But when he pulled his phone out of his pocket, he saw the call was from Daria. "Actually, I have to take this."

"*Chert poberi*," said the Russian. *The devil take you.*

"Hey," said Mark to Daria.

"I need your help."

Mark could hear kids crying in the background and a woman talking loudly, about what he couldn't tell though.

"Now?"

"Yes, now. There's been—"

The Kyrgyz slapped down a narde piece, clearly frustrated by Mark's behavior.

Daria asked, "Are you playing narde?"

"I dropped off the *paloo*."

"I thought you said you played narde this morning?"

"I did." He took a sip of his beer. "What's up?"

"Someone took one of the kids from the orphanage. I think they're headed your way, and I need you to intercept them."

"Back up. Who took a kid?"

Mark's Russian opponent groaned and with both arms gestured to the breach of narde protocol that was taking place in front of him.

"Two guys," said Daria. "One of them claimed to be the boy's uncle."

Mark figured this was just some family custody struggle gone bad. After all, this was the same country where wannabe husbands occasionally just kidnapped their future brides rather than proposing to them. It wouldn't shock him to learn that someone had circumvented the law to speed up an adoption process. "Well, was he?"

"I don't know. Either way, he can't just take a child from an orphanage. That's kidnapping."

"OK. But now you want me to . . ."

"Intercept them. Stop them. I need your help."

Mark recognized that passionate tone of voice in Daria. He'd heard it before—whenever she believed that some grave injustice had taken place, or was talking about what a morally bankrupt monstrosity the Iranian government was.

He knew that arguing with her would be pointless. "All right." He paused, but just for a moment. "I'm on it." As he stood up, he downed what was left of his beer in one long swig, then, cupping his hand over the phone, said, "I lose, beers are on me," and left a thousand Kyrgyz soms—about twenty dollars—on the table.

The Uzbek shook his head, disgusted. Even the Kyrgyz looked appalled.

Mark walked out of the Shanghai, trying to hear Daria over the angry complaints of his narde partners. "What do we know about this boy?"

"I didn't know him. Nazira says he's only been here a day."

"Who's Nazira?"

"She's the director of the orphanage. I've told you about her."

"Oh, yeah."

"This is all kind of weird. She told me the child only speaks Arabic."

"What's a kid who only speaks Arabic doing in Kyrgyzstan?"

"Like I said, it's kind of weird."

"This just happened?"

"Well, they showed up two hours ago and tried to give Nazira ten thousand dollars in exchange for her releasing the boy to them."

"What the hell?" Ten thousand dollars was a small fortune in Kyrgyzstan.

"Yeah, I know. Nazira managed to stall them for a while—"

"She didn't just take the money?"

"No, she's honest, and, frankly, I think it was a large enough sum that it scared her. A couple hundred dollars and we might have had a problem. Anyway, she said they needed to wait until I got here with the adoption papers, but they got impatient and just took off with the boy. One of them had a knife and threatened Nazira with it. She said they left here twenty minutes ago, so I probably won't be able to catch up to them, but they're headed your way so you might be able to intercept them."

"How do we know they're coming *my* way?"

"Nazira tried to follow them on a bike," said Daria. "She says she got far enough to see that they turned toward Bishkek. It's worth a shot."

One main road led all the way from Balykchy to Bishkek. For the first half of the drive, there were virtually no turnoffs or alternate routes.

"Did you call the cops?" he asked.

"They were pulling up when I got here."

"And?"

"And what do you think?"

"That bad?"

"They say I need to go down to the station to file an incident report before they can take any action."

If Daria hadn't been so damn honest, thought Mark, she would have just handed the cops a couple thousand soms to cut through the red tape. But it probably wouldn't have made any difference. Even with a bribe, the cops' reaction time would have been too slow.

"All right. I'll see what I can do," he said.

By this time, Mark had reached his Mercedes, which he kept parked on the street near his condo. As he climbed into the driver's seat and inserted his key into the ignition, he asked, "What kind of car am I looking for?"

"Tan Toyota Camry."

"The two guys inside?"

"I think."

"Kyrgyz?"

"No. Foreign, but they spoke Turkish well enough for Nazira to understand them. They spoke Arabic to the boy. The younger one claimed to be the boy's uncle."

"Guns?"

"Not that I know of, but be careful."

"Always."

"Thanks." Daria sounded relieved. "You'll call?"

"As soon as I know anything."

4

Mark's Mercedes clattered loudly as he hurtled down Route 365 at ninety miles an hour, feeling a little buzzed from the two half-liter beers he'd downed at the Shanghai.

His car, he'd come to realize, was a Potemkin village—nice to look at, especially with the Mercedes hood ornament, but pretty crappy on the inside. He'd bought it used upon arriving in Kyrgyzstan, before he'd started making any serious cash.

Which meant he'd saved a couple thousand dollars, but now had to deal with no power windows, a cheap plastic interior, a fickle heater, and a steering wheel on the wrong side of the car because the used first-world cars that got shipped to places like Central Asia to be driven into the ground included those from Britain.

He passed a turnoff for a border crossing to Kazakhstan, where soldiers were standing in front of a gate that blocked access to a two-lane bridge that spanned the Chu River. He saw no tan Camry, so he kept going.

What had been a wide, newly paved road transitioned abruptly to a much older, narrower one hemmed in by low mountains. Along this stretch, Chinese laborers were building big stone retaining walls to contain landslides, preparing to widen and repave this section of road the way they had the previous one.

The damn Chinese were everywhere, thought Mark as he drove. He knew that they were building this road, which would run from Bishkek to the border with China, at no cost to Kyrgyzstan, in an effort to help pry open the Kyrgyz market. He didn't blame them; the Americans were also trying, with limited success, to get good transit routes running from Central Asia to Afghanistan. But he found it unsettling to see just how much faster the Chinese were getting the job done.

A minute later, he came to a bumpy transition between the old asphalt road and a patch of dirt road, which caused the Mercedes to bottom out.

No Chinese workers were in sight, so he parked behind a huge pile of gravel and grabbed the Russian-made sport version of a Dragunov rifle—he'd bribed the appropriate bureaucrats to qualify for a rare hunter's license—from where he'd hidden it underneath the trunk of the Mercedes. He took ten cartridges from a box of ammo that he'd wedged in next to the rifle, loaded them into the magazine, then jogged over to a half-built stone retaining wall. Standing on a little rockslide that had accumulated behind the wall, he practiced aiming his rifle at the point where the road switched from old asphalt to dirt.

As he was waiting, he thought of the narde game he'd been forced to forfeit. That would cost him with the guys. Thanks to his abrupt exit, his moral position was now even worse than the Uzbek's. What really bugged him, though, was that he'd been beating the Russian when Daria's call had come through.

A cold breeze started to blow and he shivered. He'd been too rushed to think about grabbing a coat, but he wished he had one now. It was only November, but out here in the country, way above sea level, winter had already long since arrived. Though the mountains were too dry, treeless, and windswept to hold much snow, their tops were covered with a light dusting of white. All the roadside yurts that had been stocked with fresh apricots, blackthorn berries, and smoked trout during the summer had been taken down for the season. The tourists from Russia and Kazakhstan, crammed into cars overstuffed with beach umbrellas, towels, and inflatable rafts, had stopped coming through months ago. No fishermen stood on the banks of the Chu River.

Now the Chinese were the only ones in the area. And crazy people, like his do-gooder girlfriend. And himself.

What the hell are you doing out here, Daria? What the hell am I doing out here?

Kyrgyzstan wasn't his home. Baku was. His buzz had worn off, leaving him just tired.

In truth, though, he knew perfectly well why he was here—because of Daria. Things had actually been going pretty well between them, mostly thanks to her. She put up with his narde games; she was rarely in a bad mood; she'd hooked him up with a LASIK doctor in Almaty so he could finally see without glasses; she'd made him get a physical so he was now taking Lipitor to control his cholesterol; and despite working as hard as she did, she often came home with a healthy libido. She did all that and more—Mark sometimes wondered where she got the energy—without expecting much in return.

But that didn't mean she didn't expect *anything* in return.

They'd never talked about it, but he knew that she needed for him not to cheat on her. Which he didn't. She needed for him to love her. Which he did, even if he didn't always express that love particularly well. And when the shit hit the fan, like it had this afternoon, she needed for him to be there for her.

Which, Mark noted, he was. But he still wished he'd brought a jacket.

A tan Camry appeared. One man was driving. Another sat in the back, next to what appeared to be a small boy.

Mark sighed, brought his cheek down to the worn leather riser that was clipped to the stock, and stared down the iron sights. He wasn't a fantastic shot without a scope, but at this range—less than a hundred feet—he figured he didn't need to be. As the Camry hit a big bump where the road transitioned, bottoming out with a loud smack, he fired two quick shots.

The rear tire didn't immediately deflate, but by the time the car was almost out of sight, it was riding on its metal rim. The driver would almost certainly believe that he had suffered a flat as a result of lousy road conditions.

Mark jogged back to his Mercedes, reloaded the Dragunov, laid the rifle across the passenger seat, and threw the car into drive. A minute later, he was pulling up behind the Camry.

Two men stood outside the car, looking wary and frustrated as they stared at their flat rear tire. The older of the two—Mark guessed he was in his fifties—was bearded and wore a dark blue suit, shiny black dress shoes, and a bright red tie; the younger twentysomething had just a hint of a mustache and wore dark gray slacks and a white dress shirt. Both men glared at Mark as he pulled up behind them. The one in the suit gestured to the road, indicating that Mark should continue on his way.

Mark rolled down the window of his Mercedes, leaned out, smiled, and with great enthusiasm, yelled out to them in Kyrgyz, "You have a flat tire! I will help you!"

The man in the suit said something that Mark recognized as Arabic but couldn't understand.

The younger man replied in Turkish, "We are not in need of assistance."

Mark understood Turkish perfectly well. Indeed, most Central Asian languages were Turkic-based, including Azeri, a language he'd learned to speak fluently years before. But there were big differences between all the regional dialects, just as there were big differences between Latin-based languages like Spanish and French and Italian. So he knew he was on safe ground pretending not to understand Turkish.

Mark repeated in Kyrgyz, "I will help you!"

He saw the tousled black hair of a child poking up above the rear seat of the Camry.

In Turkish, the younger man said, "Leave us, sir. I tell you, we are not in need of assistance."

Mark climbed out of his car. "Do you have a spare tire?" He eyed both men, looking for odd bulges that might indicate one of them was carrying a concealed firearm. He saw none, but something about the way the older man in the suit carried himself—a hint of arrogance that Mark had found to be common in people who were confident in their ability to defend themselves—raised his hackles.

"Sir," said the older man in Turkish. "I must insist that you leave us."

Mark glanced up and down the road. No cars were visible in either direction. He stuck his hand through the open driver's side window of his Mercedes, grabbed his rifle, and pointed it at the older man.

"Both of you on the ground, hands clasped behind your necks." He spoke in Turkish now too. His tone and expression had changed from that of village idiot to one of bored, steely competence.

"We are guests in your country, sir. This is no way to treat guests."

Muslims were known for showing deference to guests. Given that Kyrgyzstan was a Muslim country, it wasn't a bad angle to work, Mark thought. In theory, that is. If a random act of highway robbery was what you were trying to avoid.

Mark pointed to the shoulder of the road. "This isn't my country, neither of you are my guests, and I'm not here to rob you. Both of you, on the ground. You can use your hands to lower yourselves but keep them in sight at all times and once you're down I want them clasped behind your necks."

The two men glanced at each other, then at Mark. Inside the car, the child was quiet.

"What is it you want?" said the younger man. "If it is money—"

"I just told you what I want," said Mark.

"There is a child in the car."

"I'm aware of that."

"I cannot leave him alone in the car while you—"

Mark was getting tired of this conversation. "You're not in a position to make demands."

The older man in the suit glared at Mark with an unyielding stare as the younger man rushed forward. Mark backed up, aimed quickly, and shot the younger man in the foot. It all happened in less than a second.

The older man didn't even so much as flinch, or show any concern whatsoever, as his colleague began hopping on one leg, howling in pain.

"Both of you on the ground." Mark watched as they awkwardly lowered themselves into the dirt. He hadn't wanted to use the gun. Not with the kid in the car. Not without knowing the full extent of what was really going on. "Spread your legs wide."

"I have a wallet," said the older man. "Inside is over three thousand dollars, US bills. Take it, and leave us."

"Hand it over." Mark noted that the older man wore a watch on his right wrist, which meant he was likely a lefty. "Reach for it, slowly, with your right hand. No sudden moves."

The man did so, then began to open his wallet and extract the money.

"Hand the whole thing over."

Mark grabbed the wallet when it was offered up and flipped it open. It was stuffed with cash—US hundred-dollar bills.

But what Mark really found interesting was the driver's license. It was green and white, with a photo of the man in the lower left-hand corner, and was covered with Arabic script—except in the top right section, where, in English, it read KINGDOM OF SAUDI ARABIA, MINISTRY OF INTERIOR, DRIVING LICENSE.

"Huh," said Mark, eyeing both men. "You both Saudis?"

Neither man answered.

"Is the kid a Saudi?"

Still no response.

Mark used his phone to snap a photo of the driver's license, and then tossed the wallet, and the cash inside it, back to the older Saudi.

He pointed to the younger man. "Hand yours over."

After confirming that the younger man was also a Saudi, and taking a photo of his driver's license, Mark walked back to the Camry and pulled open the rear door. Sitting behind the passenger seat was a boy Mark guessed was about two years old. His black curly hair was in need of a trim, and his dark brown eyes were wide with fear. A seat belt was tight around his waist.

The boy wouldn't look at him.

Mark searched his limited knowledge of Arabic. He settled on *sadiq*, which meant *friend*. He pointed at himself as he said it.

"Don't you dare touch that boy!" called out the Saudi that Mark had shot. "You know not what you do."

Mark had a bad feeling about this. But he'd promised Daria. "Who is he? Why did you take him?"

"He is my nephew. He comes from a powerful family. He was kidnapped."

"From Saudi Arabia?"

"That is not your business."

"What family?"

"That is not your business either. But I can tell you I am here on behalf of the boy's family."

Mark sighed. "You can't just steal a child from an orphanage."

"We only stole what was stolen from us."

"If he really is your nephew, and he really has been kidnapped, then you need to go back to the orphanage, apologize, file the appropriate paperwork, and wait for things to get sorted out. That's the way it's done, even in Kyrgyzstan."

Mark turned back to the car and unlocked the boy's seat belt, causing the boy to flinch. Mark extended his hand. When the child didn't respond, Mark leaned inside, wrapped his left arm—the one that wasn't occupied with the rifle—underneath the boy's armpits, and gently lifted the child to his chest.

As he walked back to his Mercedes, the boy began to cry and squirm. Not a good situation, thought Mark. Not a good situation at all. He saw the boy turn and look back toward the Saudis. Screw it, thought Mark. Regardless of what he'd promised Daria, he was going to let the kid decide.

He put the boy down on the ground and stroked the child's head while keeping the rifle pointed in the direction of the Saudis.

"Hey buddy, I'm not going to hurt you. We'll sort this all out." Mark spoke Kyrgyz because he didn't know how to console the boy in Arabic. "If you want to stay with these men, you can." Turning to the Saudis, Mark said, "Talk to him. If you guys are his family and I think he wants to go with you, I'll let him."

Though Mark was no longer holding the boy, the child made no move to approach the Saudis. Instead, he stood there crying, looking more desperate and scared than ever.

The Saudi with the shot foot called out to the boy in a soothing voice. Mark couldn't understand what was said, but the boy didn't appear to be persuaded. If anything, he leaned in closer to Mark. Then the Saudi spoke more rapidly in Arabic. The boy remained unconvinced. When the Saudi's tone grew harsh, prompting the boy to cry even harder, Mark leaned down, picked the kid back up, and walked to his Mercedes.

Before setting the boy down in the car, Mark opened the trunk. Inside was a first aid kit that Daria had bought him a few months ago. She'd put it in his trunk along with a wool blanket and a spare flashlight. Mark, while appreciating the kindhearted gesture, had thought it a little overkill. The hunting rifle was the only emergency item he'd packed.

Now, however, he was glad for the first aid kit. He dropped it to the ground.

"Stay down until I'm out of sight." Looking at the Saudi with the shot foot, he said, "When you do get up, you'll find some bandages in this kit. I'm going to take the child now, but if you really are here on behalf of his family, I suggest you make your case to the orphanage. The people who run it won't know where I am, but I'll check in with them. If you're telling the truth, then I'll make arrangements for a *legal* transfer."

5

"It was Holtz!" said Daria. She called as Mark was pulling away from the Saudis. Bruce Holtz was the owner of Central Asian Information Networks—or CAIN, for short—the spies-for-hire firm that Mark had been working with for the past seven months. "*He* brought the boy to the orphanage. Yesterday. He just dumped him at the front desk."

"Why?"

"You tell me."

"Ah . . ."

"What's that noise?"

"I have the boy. He's crying—"

"Why didn't you call me?"

"I was going to—"

"I told you to call me as soon as you—"

"Two minutes, that's how long I've had him. Two minutes. And you know, I'm trying to be nice to him, but he's upset and . . . Daria, I don't like this. I really don't like this."

Mark explained how he'd taken the child away from the Saudis. At gunpoint. He had to speak loudly so that he could be heard over the boy's crying. "Wasn't a good scene. And, you know, maybe the reason the kid only speaks Arabic is because he's a Saudi. Maybe those guys really were here to take him back to his family."

"Is he OK?"

"He's not happy, but he doesn't seem hurt. He's right next to me. I'm looking at him now." Mark glanced at the child sitting next to him. He was a bit pudgy, in a baby-fat sort of way, with cheeks that were healthy and full. His baby teeth were straight and white and he had a cute round nose. Though scared and confused at the moment, he appeared well cared for. Mark tried to muster a friendly smile, but the boy was looking down at his clenched fists as he cried. "We're headed back toward Bishkek."

"You have him in the front seat?"

"Yeah."

"Is he wearing a seat belt?"

"Ah, no."

"He should be in the back seat at least."

Daria sounded flustered.

"You know, I'm kind of trying to prioritize what I worry about right now."

"If you get in an accident—"

"I'm not gonna get in an accident. Talk to me about Holtz."

"When I asked Nazira how the boy—"

"Does he have a name?"

"Muhammad."

"Great, that should help us identify him."

Muhammad was the most popular boys' name in the world.

"When I asked Nazira how Muhammad came to the orphanage, she told me a big American dropped him off yesterday. She said he was wearing a belt buckle in the shape of a football helmet. And that he had a goatee. And—"

"OK, that's Holtz."

"One of us has to call him."

"Maybe I should handle it," said Mark. Before starting her orphanage project, Daria had worked briefly for Holtz, and it hadn't gone well. "I'm kind of headed his way anyway."

CAIN's headquarters was located at Manas, a major US air base just north of Bishkek.

"I don't want Holtz anywhere near Muhammad."

"Then hustle back to Bishkek, and you take Muhammad while I meet with Holtz. Besides, the boy needs someone who can understand him and I'm not doing so well on that front."

Daria wasn't fluent in Arabic, but Mark was certain she could do better than he was managing to do. He glanced at Muhammad again, who was now twisting his shirt up into his fists.

Mark didn't connect with kids the way Daria did. He had no experience with them and had no idea how to put them at ease. But he wanted *someone* to put Muhammad at ease. No little kid should be scared; no little kid should have to get shuffled from an orphanage to a cynical middle-aged spy with a beat-up car, a two-day beard, and a gun.

"All right," said Daria. "I'm already halfway there, probably just a little bit behind you. Meet at our place?"

"I'll be there."

6
Kyrgyzstan

Muhammad started crying when he was handed off to Daria, but Mark was pretty sure the boy would warm up to her. Either way, he figured Daria was the child's best option at this point. After making the transfer, he drove to the White House because he'd been told Bruce Holtz would be there.

The White House in downtown Bishkek was similar to the White House in Washington, DC, in that it housed the office of the president, was open to anyone willing to make a large political donation, and was, in fact, white. In the Kyrgyz version, however, it was because the Soviets had glued white-marble tiles all over its clunky concrete frame.

While waiting for Holtz, who evidently had stopped by to make a strategic political donation, Mark sat outside on a low wall stained with pigeon droppings, across from a long line of thick blue spruce trees. The nearby guards who were manning the west-side service entrance were dressed in army-green camouflage and teal berets. They ignored Mark, and he ignored them.

One of the few good things about Bishkek, Mark thought, was that it was a pretty easygoing town. Sure, they had an occasional political riot here and there, but for the most part, the city had an open, leafy Midwestern-college-town feel to it. The cops and soldiers didn't bother people much unless they wanted bribes.

Holtz walked out of the building ten minutes after Mark got there. He was a tall man, well over six feet, with broad shoulders that had grown even broader over the past year—the result of fine dining rather than time in the gym. But in a custom-made suit and a tightly cinched belt, Holtz looked like a guy to be reckoned with as he strode confidently across the brick pavers in front of the White House. His goatee, which he'd started growing a month earlier, made him look mean. Which he pretty much was.

Holtz shook Mark's hand enthusiastically as they met outside the gatehouse.

"Sava! You stalking me, dude?"

"I called the office. Jana told me you had a late meeting here. Figured I'd wait." Jana was the suspiciously attractive secretary Holtz had recently hired. "Listen, we need to talk."

"We're talking now."

"Tell me about the kid."

Holtz tried to keep the grin that had been on his face fixed in place, but he couldn't quite manage it. "You don't have to speak in code, Sava. There's no one around us that can hear."

Mark started to walk toward Panfilov Park, a weedy Soviet-era amusement park located behind the White House. "Tell me about the kid, Bruce. The kid you dropped off at the orphanage. The orphanage Daria's been helping."

"Oh. That kid."

"Yeah. That kid. Muhammad."

"Why do you ask?"

Mark explained what had happened with the Saudis.

Holtz looked stricken.

"That's how I feel too," said Mark. "What's going on?"

Holtz exhaled. His jaw was set in a hard frown. "Fuckin-a. I knew this was gonna come back to bite me in the ass. I knew it. OK, bring him to me, I'll deal with it."

"Oh, yeah. Daria will agree to that, I'm sure."

"Daria has him?"

"She does now. And you're the last person she'd turn a child over to."

"I know you guys are tight, but she can go stuff it."

"Believe me, she returns the sentiment. Now, what's up?"

"I'm sorry you got involved in this. I didn't think—" Holtz shook his head. "Well, what's done is done. I can't go into details, but I promise I'll figure out a way to make it right."

"You gotta fill me in on this one, Bruce. We're partners."

Holtz made a face. "You're the figurehead executive vice-president of a company I own. We're not partners."

"Close enough."

"No, not close enough. I bust my ass running the company, you collect a check for sitting on your ass. That's not partners."

But they were, in a way, thought Mark.

To be sure, Holtz had been doing pretty well on his own—despite his light résumé—before Mark had come on board. With the war in Afghanistan winding down, the CIA had been cutting down on personnel in Central Asia, and the air base at Manas was seeing a lot less traffic. CAIN had been in the right place at the right time, one of the few reasonably reputable private intelligence firms in the region for governments and energy companies to turn to.

But getting Mark on board had resulted in an avalanche of new business for CAIN: evaluating security procedures at oil installations in Kazakhstan, supplying the CIA with a steady stream of capable bodyguards, helping the NSA set up and maintain listening posts throughout Central Asia, helping to translate phone or electronic communications that the CIA or NSA had intercepted. . . The work was coming in at a frenzied pace. Mark had served in the Caspian region and Central Asia for the better part of twenty years. Azerbaijan, Turkmenistan, Kazakhstan, the war in Nagorno-Karabakh, the war in Abkhazia, the buildup of Manas Air Base in the run-up to the war in Afghanistan . . . He had the kind of résumé, and the kind of connections throughout the region, that attracted both good clients and good employees. Holtz, by contrast, had only served as a CIA officer for five years before starting CAIN.

Initially, Mark hadn't been especially enthusiastic about the prospect of entering into a business relationship with Holtz; he didn't really like Holtz, and he thought it was at best stupid and at worst corrupt the way the CIA bureaucrats in Langley were willing to pay private contractors—often former and maybe future colleagues—ridiculous amounts of money to execute ops that should have been done in-house for a fraction of the cost. But once the money had started to flow his way, he'd gotten over his qualms. And besides, he'd reasoned, as long as the CIA was the dysfunctional, sclerotic bureaucracy that it was, they needed the private contractors.

He'd also come to realize that he liked keeping his feet wet when it came to the intelligence business.

"Call our relationship what you will, Bruce. Bottom line is that I'm not giving the kid back to you until I learn what's going on."

And maybe not even then, Mark thought.

They stared at each other for a long moment. Mark was reminded that the history between them hadn't always been good.

"It was a CIA contract," said Holtz.

"Who was your contact?"

"Val Rosten."

That bit of news gave Mark pause. Val Rosten was the highly-regarded deputy chief of the CIA's Near East and South Asia Division, better known simply as Near East—the bureaucratic fiefdom that covered hot spots like the Middle East, Afghanistan, and Pakistan; any Agency op in Kyrgyzstan should have been handled by the CIA's Central Eurasia Division, or maybe the CIA's counterterrorism center in consultation with Central Eurasia.

"I didn't know you knew him," said Mark.

"I didn't, at least not personally. I mean, I'd heard the name of course. But I've worked with people who work for Rosten. That's how CAIN got the recommendation." Holtz let his last sentence hang there, as though waiting for Mark to say something.

"Ah, yeah . . . so anyway, Rosten calls, tells me that he's got a problem. He says he's got this kid on his hands. Son of a Jordanian couple who died in a car accident while doing work for the Agency. The kid was in the car, but survived. So now, because Langley had promised the parents that if anything like this ever happened, they'd make sure the kid—"

"Muhammad."

"Muhammad," agreed Holtz. "They'd make sure that Muhammad was cared for."

They'd come to a roller coaster. The electric-green metal track was rusted, and there were big patches of dirt in between stands of unmowed grass—the Kyrgyz, originally a nomadic people, rarely bothered to waste time on an endeavor as stupid as cutting grass; that's what cows were for.

All the rides in the park had been shut down for the winter.

"Muhammad didn't have any other family members in Jordan?"

"Guess not."

"Huh."

"That's why Rosten figured finding someone to adopt him was the best option."

A string of lights, haphazardly joined together with wire and black electric tape, hung across the brick-paver path. Holtz ducked his head to avoid hitting them.

"Two thousand miles away in Kyrgyzstan?" said Mark.

"Rosten said he wanted the kid out of the region altogether, so that Muhammad could start a completely new life. He didn't want to take the chance that someone would recognize him and ten, twenty years from now, tell him what happened to his parents."

"The kid speaks Arabic. He couldn't have at least been brought to an Arabic-speaking country?"

Mark thought of Muhammad and wondered whether the boy would like this amusement park. Probably. Having walked through the park during the summer months, Mark recalled that most kids seemed to. They appeared to like all the cheerful rip-offs of Disney characters, the bouncy music, the candy . . . Adults might compare it to the real Disneyland and find the place terribly wanting, but young kids didn't care.

"I don't know. Rosten didn't say anything about that."

"And you didn't ask."

"My asking a lot of questions wasn't part of the contract."

7

After eating two bowls of vanilla ice cream and then getting his pull-up diaper changed—Daria had stocked up on food and toddler supplies at a local supermarket—Muhammad appeared to be feeling much better.

Better enough, at least, that he was comfortable roaming around Daria and Mark's condo, sucking on his new pacifier, playing peek-a-boo with a felt sheep's-wool carpet that hung on the wall, playing drums with a kitchen spoon and an assortment of pots, and sitting on Daria's lap as she paged through a Kyrgyz version of *The Very Hungry Caterpillar.*

Neither Mark nor Daria had invested much effort into furnishing their place—Mark because he viewed their time there as temporary, and Daria because she had been too busy with her orphanages—so most of what was there was fair game for Muhammad to climb on or play with. After pulling the cushions off an uncomfortable Russian-made couch in the living room, smearing mucus on the bottom half of the television, and bouncing on the queen-sized bed in the bedroom, he toddled into the office Daria and Mark shared and wreaked havoc by pulling many of their books to the floor.

She did prevent him from chewing on a stack of papers that Mark had been reading and marking up—a former colleague of his had taken a sabbatical year to get his master's at the John Hopkins School of Advanced International Studies, and had asked Mark to review the thesis he'd written on the conflict between Armenia and Azerbaijan. Muhammad wasn't happy about having the thesis taken from him, so as a consolation prize, Daria let him grab a brass Iranian vase off the coffee table, and when he discovered the narde set Mark had brought with him from Azerbaijan, she let him pull it down from a shelf in the living room.

She reasoned that the least she could do for Muhammad—a child who had already borne more than any two-year-old should have to bear—was to make him feel comfortable and loved while he was in her home.

"Careful," she said in Arabic. "No mouth, OK? Please?"

Daria's Arabic was limited. But she had three things going for her: the first was that she'd taken an entry-level language course in Arabic when she'd first joined the CIA; the second was that she spoke fluent Farsi, which helped because even though Farsi and Arabic had different roots, Farsi used the Arabic alphabet and had adopted many Arabic words; and the third was that she'd loaded a translation program onto her smartphone.

"No mouth," Muhammad agreed, in Arabic.

Daria felt a little guilty when Muhammad started banging the circular narde pieces on the board, whacking them down as hard as he could. The narde set was one of the few things Mark had salvaged from Azerbaijan. She felt even more guilty when he threw a couple of pieces across the room, but she figured keeping the boy happy was all that mattered for now. Besides, Mark always smacked the pieces down hard on the board when he played. How much more damage could a two-year-old do?

She sat down cross-legged on the floor, next to Muhammad, pointed at him, and said his name.

"Muhammad," he agreed, as he brought a narde piece to his mouth.

"No mouth." Daria gently took his hand away, then pointed to herself and spoke her name. After a few rounds of this, Muhammad figured it out, pointed at Daria and spoke her name, only it came out as *Dara* instead of Daria.

"Yes! Daria. My name."

Muhammad started scraping the narde board with one of the black pieces.

Daria typed a question on her phone, then read the translation: "Where are you from, Muhammad?"

The boy appeared to consider the question for a moment, then stood up. "I go to Anna now."

"Anna is where you're from?"

"I go to Anna."

The boy began to walk around the house, as though searching for something. Not finding what he wanted, he grew increasingly agitated and began to call out, "Anna, Anna, Anna!"

Daria knelt down in front of him, so that she was at his eye level. "You want Anna?"

"Yes, Anna!"

"Why Anna?"

Muhammad thought for a second. "Anna plays."

"Anna plays with Muhammad?"

"Yes."

"Anna is a person?"

"Anna pretty."

"Anna is big like Daria or small like Muhammad?"

"Big."

"Does Anna feed Muhammad?"

"Yes."

"Anna is your mommy?"

"No."

"Where does Anna live?"

"My house."

"Where is your house?"

"Ba-bay."

"I don't understand ba-bay."

"Anna in ba-bay."

8

"Did you at least ask Rosten why he wasn't using CIA assets here in Bishkek, or anywhere else throughout Central Asia, to place the kid?" asked Mark.

They'd reached Frunze Street, a wide road that bordered Panfilov Park. A white garbage truck, spewing black diesel smoke, drove by. Behind it was a pickup truck that stank of raw meat, a result of all the beef carcasses that had been stacked high in the open bed. Mark kept walking on the sidewalk.

"Well, I didn't ask, but it seemed pretty obvious that Rosten was trying to do right by Muhammad's parents without making the Agency look like it was running a baby-trafficking op."

"And it's OK for CAIN to run a baby-trafficking op?"

Mark had always known Holtz was aggressive when it came to his business. He'd known Holtz wasn't afraid to cut a few corners, maybe make promises he wasn't sure he could deliver on. But this was breaking new ground.

"Hey, man. If the CIA could do everything CAIN was willing to do, we'd be out of business. Rosten wanted to keep the CIA's hands clean with this deal. I thought, fine—I'll take the risk *and* their money. And it's not a fucking baby-trafficking op. I placed the kid in a decent orphanage and paid to grease the adoption wheels."

"Does Central Eurasia even know Rosten is running an op in their territory?"

"I don't know. You'd have to ask Rosten."

"Was Kyrgyzstan station given the heads up?"

"Again—"

"Ask Rosten."

"Yeah. *I* didn't ask about that stuff because I didn't want to know. It's not my business to play referee between Near East and Central Eurasia."

"Central Eurasia's going to be pissed if they find out Near East was running a black op in Kyrgyzstan, behind their backs."

Holtz threw his hands up. "So they're pissed. Not my problem."

"Ninety percent of our contracts with the CIA are run through Central Eurasia, Bruce. If we piss them off, it's definitely our problem."

Mark thought of all the cash he'd raked in over the past seven months. He'd been trying to pull off a delicate tightrope act—to profit from his association with Holtz without getting dragged down by it.

He had a sense that he'd just fallen off the rope.

"Which is why I thought doing a job for Near East would be a good way to grow the business, broaden our reach a bit. Anyway, I agreed to fly down to Jordan and pick up the kid. I brought him back here because I knew Daria's been involved with that orphanage in Balykchy and I figured it was as good a place as any to keep him while I lined up some reasonably normal parents to adopt him."

"You didn't think Daria would find out?"

"I didn't care if she found out. Or if you found out. We're all on the same team, remember?"

"Daria's not on your team, Bruce."

"Once I brought the kid here, I figured the decision would already have been made and that the solution would be obvious to everyone—to find some decent adoptive parents for him and move on."

"I think you might have misjudged the situation."

"Well, what the hell else are we going to do?"

"How much is CAIN getting for the job?" asked Mark.

"A hundred K. Which covers picking the kid up and watching over him until he gets adopted. I left a donation at the orphanage to make sure they took *good* care of him. And the orphanage gets another ten K bonus when they line up good parents for the kid. It was a no-worries deal."

"You didn't think that a hundred thousand for a couple days' work might not come with a few worries attached?"

"You're not one to talk, Sava. Everything we do at CAIN comes with a few worries attached. That's why we get paid. I'm vulnerable to blowback from the jobs you bring in, and you're vulnerable from the jobs I bring in."

"Yeah, but I tell you about the jobs I bring in."

Holtz laughed. "Dude, you negotiate deals behind my back with your old CIA contacts, and then pretend that you're actually considering my input after the deal is already done. You tell me as little as possible about whatever it is you do. Besides, my not telling anyone else at CAIN, or the CIA, was part of the contract. Rosten made me agree to personally handle the placement and adoption of the kid."

"He mention anything about the possibility that a couple of pissed-off Saudis might show up?"

"No, he sure as hell didn't."

"Call Rosten," said Mark. "Tell him what happened. See how he reacts. Ask him why a couple Saudis would want the kid."

"And when he tells me to bring the kid back in and stonewalls me on the Saudis, then what do I tell him then?"

"You tell him it's not up to you. It's up to me."

"He's not going to like that."

"He doesn't have to like it. Tell him I'm being a dick about it."

"You kind of are. Hey, where are you going?"

Mark kept walking away without looking back. "Call Rosten. I'll be in touch."

9

To prevent the Agency or anyone else from tracking him, Mark powered down his cell phone and removed the battery. Then he hailed a cab and got dropped off at a pharmacy, where he bought three cheap cell phones that came with prepaid SIM cards.

The pharmacy sat across from Victory Square, in the center of which stood a three-pronged granite arch that was supposed to be suggestive of a yurt and which had been erected to honor the Kyrgyz soldiers who'd died fighting for the Soviets in World War II. Under the arch was an eternal flame, which Mark was surprised to see was burning—he'd heard it had gone out recently because of a dispute over the gas bill. As he'd hoped, there were enough people milling about the square that he didn't stand out.

He took a seat on one of the chestnut-red granite steps leading up to the flame, activated one of his new phones, and called Ted Kaufman, the division chief for the CIA's Central Eurasia Division. Kaufman, a tired bureaucrat who was nearing the end of a forty-year career with the CIA, answered his personal cell phone on the fourth ring.

"I need you to run a couple names for me," Mark said as soon as Kaufman picked up.

Kaufman didn't speak for a moment, prompting Mark to consider the eleven-hour time difference between Bishkek and Washington, DC. He did the math in his head, then envisioned Kaufman swinging his spindly legs off the bed, his paunch hanging out over his boxer shorts, shaking off sleep.

"Sorry if I woke you," Mark added.

"I've been well, Sava. Thanks for asking. And you?"

"Listen, I'm going to text you two files. They're both images of Saudi driver's licenses. The names are in Arabic, so I couldn't read them. I need you to figure out who these guys are."

"First, I'm not your secretary, Sava. Second, you shouldn't have called this number—I don't recall ever giving it out to you."

"Ever hear of caller ID? You've used it to call me."

"Third, apparently you've forgotten that Saudi Arabia is part of the Near East Division, so go bug them. Fourth, it's six thirty in the damn morning. And my alarm is set for seven."

Kaufman had been Mark's boss at the CIA for seven years before Mark had finally quit. For better or worse, they knew each other pretty well.

"This is important, Ted."

"OK. But why call *me*, Mark?" Kaufman spoke with a tone of unenthusiastic resignation; Mark imagined that Kaufman's wife heard that tone a lot.

"I just told you. I need you to run some names for me."

"Is this for one of your CAIN projects?"

"In a way, yeah."

"A project Central Eurasia currently has open with CAIN?"

Mark looked around Victory Square. Dusk was approaching. All the flowerbeds, which in summer had been a riot of color, were now empty save for the broken vodka bottles. The Kyrgyz really knew how to do flowers right, Mark thought. Seeing the place so barren now made him think of the fast-approaching winter again. He knew it wouldn't be long before the cold from the mountains descended into the city. As he scanned the crowd, he felt a fleeting pang of claustrophobia.

"I don't know. You tell me." Mark didn't want to stab Holtz in the back, but if Holtz had tried to run a Near East op in Central Eurasia on the sly, then Holtz had stabbed himself in the back.

"What's that supposed to mean?"

"It means it's related to a Near East op."

"Super. Then you know who to call."

Kaufman was a by-the-books bureaucrat. He stuck to his turf and expected others to do the same.

"A Near East op that's being run in *your* area of operations. An op they hired CAIN to execute."

Silence. Then, "Are you pulling my leg?"

"Wish I was."

"What op?"

"Well, here's the thing. When CAIN takes on these jobs, we sign confidentiality agreements."

"Don't give me that crap, Sava. What is Near East up to?"

"Like I said, I need you to run the names of a couple Saudis for me. I'd remind you that my top-secret security clearance was renewed when I joined CAIN. I'm an approved Agency contractor. You help me out, I might be in the mood to share with you what Near East was up to in your backyard."

Kaufman let a few seconds pass. "Deal."

Mark briefly powered up his old cell phone, texted Kaufman the images of the driver's licenses, then shut his phone back down and removed the battery again. As he was walking away from Victory Square, he called Daria on one of his prepaid phones.

"Get your iPod," he said. "I'm going to call it."

Though an iPod Touch was typically just used as a small digital tablet device—it was pretty much an iPhone, minus the phone part—Daria had rigged hers in such a way that it could be used to make calls over the Internet. The downside was that it had to be connected to a wireless network for the phone function to work. The upside was that when it did work, the call was untraceable.

Mark rang Daria's iPod, filled her in on the details of his conversation with Holtz, then asked about Muhammad.

"He likes ice cream," said Daria. "And banging pots."

"Is he talking about his parents dying, or Jordan?"

"No, but I asked him where he's from. He says he lives in *babay*. I haven't been able to figure out what that means yet. And I think he misses someone he calls Anna. He says she's an adult, pretty, plays with him, feeds him, and isn't his mother. I'm guessing it was someone who helped raise him, like a nanny. He's been calling out for her, walking around the house looking for her."

"All right. See what else you can find out. I'm working a few angles on my end."

"When do you think you'll be home?"

Mark hesitated. He could make calls from their condo, but his gut was telling him that it would be better to keep his distance. The last thing he needed was for Holtz or Kaufman to hear Muhammad crying in the background.

"I don't know," he said. "As soon as I can."

As he was walking through a narrow alley that ran between two massive *khrushchevka* apartment buildings—old housing units built during the Khruschev era—Mark called Holtz. His prepaid cell phone crackled.

"Listen, I talked to Rosten," said Holtz. "He's pissed to hell and insists you release the kid to me. Like now."

"Well, that's not going to happen."

"I'm telling you, Mark—he's livid. He's flying into Bishkek ASAP. He wants you to meet him at the embassy."

"He's pissed that I saved the kid? From being abducted by two Saudis?"

"No, he's pissed that you won't tell me where the kid is now."

"Well, he can stay pissed. What did he have to say about the Saudis?"

"That the op has been compartmentalized and that we're not cleared to know about the Saudi compartment."

"Yeah, we'll see about that."

Mark called Kaufman back.

"They're both GIP intelligence officers. Both were in our database." As Kaufman recited the real names of the Saudi kidnappers, Mark committed them to memory. The GIP, he knew, stood for General Intelligence Presidency, which is what the Saudi equivalent of the CIA called itself. "The older of the two has been with Saudi intelligence for twenty years. The younger guy, just three."

"Are they working with the Agency?"

"I don't know."

"You don't know or won't say?"

"Don't know. Which, in my book, is a serious problem. What's Near East up to in my division, Sava?"

When Mark had told Kaufman everything he knew, Kaufman broke in, "That peckerhead Rosten's really flying into Bishkek? And I don't know about it?"

"You do now," Mark pointed out.

"Rosten had better have been acting on orders from on high on this one. Because if he made the call to run a Near East op in my territory without telling me, I'll skewer the bastard. As for Holtz, did he really think he could get away with this?"

"I don't think the slight was intentional. So you're going to confront Rosten on this?"

"Damn right I am."

"When?"

"Now."

"I'll call you back."

Mark hung up, reasonably satisfied with the way things were going. And content, he realized, to be back in the field—even if it was only a temporary thing.

He'd never regretted leaving the CIA—he hadn't been cut out to be a station chief. He realized that now. All the cables from Langley; the obligation to suck up to a parade of desk-jockey bureaucrats full of ideas completely divorced from reality; the need to kowtow endlessly to the ambassador and by extension the State Department; trying to motivate risk-averse ops officers who liked to spend more time in the embassy than in the field; constantly worrying about covering his ass and the asses of people who worked for him because he could never be certain that the bureaucrats in Langley had his back . . .

No, he didn't miss any of that. But he did miss being in the field. He missed the satisfaction of running actual operations.

10

Twenty-five miles south of Bishkek, former Navy SEAL John Decker was enjoying the view of Ala Archa National Park almost as much as he was enjoying the view of the buxom Australian woman who was pinned, missionary-style, beneath him.

She was twenty-three years old, almost six feet tall, strong, rubber-band flexible, and had this beads-woven-into-her-hair thing going on that Decker thought was just fantastic. Her fingers were calloused from rock climbing and felt good on his chest, which she was rubbing to the rhythm of their lovemaking.

A little over seven months earlier, Decker's six-foot-four frame had taken a serious beating—the result of an ill-fated excursion into Iran. The German physical therapist who'd treated him at a high-end medical center in Almaty, Kazakhstan, had been into yoga and rock climbing. After beginning a one-month fling with her, Decker had decided he was into yoga and rock climbing too. And that was how he'd healed.

Even after that relationship had ended, he'd kept stretching—that was what he preferred to call his yoga—and climbing. And climbing had led him to Jessica.

They'd met two weeks earlier at an expat bar in Bishkek and had been together ever since. Last night, they'd camped out at an old Soviet hut frequented by climbers; today they were climbing a mixed ice-and-rock route up the north face of Free Korea Peak, a nearly three-thousand-foot wall. They weren't in any rush, though, and had stopped early to set up camp and have a little fun.

Decker tried to reposition Jessica, causing the portaledge—a platform that ice and rock climbers slept in when ascending huge rock or ice walls—to rock back and forth.

"Careful!" she said.

Decker wasn't worried. He'd personally attached the portaledge to a bomber anchor—a big rock nose, over which he'd draped a long sling—ten feet above them. And then he'd backed that up with another anchor. And if those anchors failed, it *still* wouldn't matter because he and Jessica were both wearing climbing harnesses that were affixed to well-placed cam anchors above them.

Granted, they'd both unsnapped the leg loops on their harnesses, so that they could remove their pants, but the leg loops weren't essential. Worst-case scenario, Decker figured they would just be left hanging by their waist belts.

That was a risk Decker was more than willing to take. His knees sank into the nylon floor of the portaledge, his right shoulder kept hitting the rock wall on one side of the tent wall, and the whole contraption was swinging back and forth. Through an open air vent, he could see the rock wall and a little picturesque silver thread of a stream cutting through the valley far below them. Jessica laughed and so did Decker. Life just didn't get much better than this, he thought.

Then his cell phone rang.

He ignored it. From the ring tone, he knew it was a call from home—almost certainly his mother or father, the last people he wanted to speak to right now. Talk about a buzzkill.

"Why are you stopping?" said the Aussie. She reached around and smacked his thigh as though taking a crop to a lazy horse.

"Who's stopping?" said Decker—though he had slowed down. He loved his parents, but they weren't exactly an aphrodisiac. When his phone stopped ringing, he flipped Jessica into a doggie-style position, smacked her rear, and got back to business.

But a few seconds later, his phone started ringing again. It was the same ring tone. Which meant it was almost certainly his mother—if he didn't pick up the first time, she always tried again. His father would have just left a message.

"Shit, Mom."

Jessica gave a little huff of disgust. "I'm not your mom."

No, she most certainly wasn't his mother, Decker thought. He forced himself to ignore both the ringing and the image of his mother standing impatiently—phone in hand—in the kitchen of the New Hampshire home he'd grown up in. But before long, he'd gotten one of his knees wedged painfully under one of the metal bars that formed the frame of the portaledge. Time to finish this off, he thought.

His phone started ringing again.

"You gotta be kidding me. I'm sorry, I have to answer this."

"Shut up."

"Something's wrong."

"I'll really scratch you this time, you fruit loop."

"I have to take this. No joking, Jess. Three calls means there's a problem."

Jessica sighed as he pulled out of her, then she flipped to her back, and patted him gently on the chest.

Decker fished his phone out of the pocket of his Gore-Tex shell jacket, which he'd wedged in a corner of the portaledge.

"Hello?"

As expected, it was his mother. "John," she said. "How are you?"

"Ah . . ." He detected a quiver in his mother's voice.

"I've got some bad news, honey."

Decker felt his stomach rise up to his throat. His mom was a call-it-as-she-sees-it tough army wife who'd raised three huge boys in northern New Hampshire, all of whom had entered the military. Overly sentimental, or dramatic, she wasn't. If she said she had bad news, it was bad news.

"What is it, Mom?"

Jessica unzipped another air vent in the portaledge. Decker

felt a cool breeze on his bare schlong. In the distance he could see a line of snow-capped, glaciated mountains. Pine trees grew in the canyon below. He loved it here. The lakes in the valleys were pristine, the streams filled with trout. People called it the Switzerland of Central Asia and he thought that was about right. In between jobs for CAIN, he'd taken to exploring the countryside, often hooking up with expat women looking to explore the world. He'd been pretty damn happy over the past six months.

He had a feeling all that was about to end.

"It's your father."

"What happened?"

His mother began to cry. "He . . ." It sounded as though she'd pulled the phone away from her mouth. A moment later, she came on again. "He got up real early like he always does, to load the stove, and he was out back at the wood shed, when . . ."

She started crying again.

Decker glanced at Jessica. She looked up at him with a worried expression. He shook his head.

Over the phone, a distant voice Decker recognized as his younger brother's said, "Let me tell him, Mom," and then his brother was on the phone, saying, "He had a heart attack. When he was splitting wood."

"Is he . . . dead?"

"No, but he's in the ICU. I don't know, Deck."

"When did this happen?"

"An hour ago. We're at the hospital."

"Is he going to make it?"

"I don't know, man. They're running tests now. We should know more soon."

"I'll come home."

Decker did the calculations in his head. There was still a little light left. On the way up, they'd climbed a mixture of ice and rock, but if they packed up quickly and rappelled down now, avoiding the ice as much as they could and sacrificing gear to the mountain to speed things up, he figured they could be on the ground in under an hour. Once on the ground, they'd have a decent hike back to the car ahead of them, but it was mostly downhill and they were both in good shape. They could run it. Getting back to Bishkek tonight was doable.

"I think mom would appreciate it."

11

“So I talked to Rosten,” said Kaufman. “The son of a bitch turfed me up.”

“How high?” asked Mark.

“High enough.”

“To the top?”

“No.”

Mark figured that meant Rosten had sent Kaufman to the deputy director of the CIA.

“And?”

“And I’m to tell you that you’re to proceed immediately to our embassy in Bishkek, wait for Rosten to arrive, and then turn the child over to whoever Rosten tells you to. The Bishkek station has already been given the heads up. They’re expecting you. You’re to say nothing more about this to anyone except Rosten, including Bamford.”

Serena Bamford was the chief of the CIA’s Kyrgyzstan station.

“Huh. Did you get any answers as to why Near East was running an op in Kyrgyzstan behind your back?”

“No. Nor did they tell me what the op was. Apparently Central Eurasia’s role now is to provide support services for Near East.”

Kaufman’s sarcasm was evident.

“What happens if I don’t turn in the kid?” asked Mark.

“Beats me. I wouldn’t want to find out, though.”

"Well, I appreciate your helping me with this, Ted. And I tell you what—I'll let you know how it all works out. I don't answer to Langley anymore."

"I'd be grateful."

Mark sensed that Kaufman wasn't being the slightest bit ironic. Back during the Cold War, when Kaufman had joined the CIA, Central Eurasia—which included Russia—had been a powerful division. That's part of the reason why Mark too had been so eager to be a part of it. But after the Soviet Union collapsed, much of Central Eurasia's power had shifted to Near East. That shift had accelerated tenfold after 9/11. Now Near East was a division on steroids—they were heavily militarized, ran drone missions 24-7, were deeply integrated with the CIA's counterterrorism center, and were the best funded of all the CIA's divisions. Central Eurasia, meanwhile, had become a bit of a backwater.

But it was Kaufman's backwater, and Mark was certain his old boss hated being pushed aside on his own turf.

The US embassy was located at the southern end of Mira Avenue—a perfectly straight road lined with huge white poplar trees. The actual embassy building wasn't visible from the road, nor was there even a sign announcing its existence—which meant a lot of visa seekers wound up overshooting the place and asking directions from the constantly put-upon Kazakhs who had built their new embassy just down the street.

Those fortunate enough to find the US embassy were greeted by a large parking lot walled off by waist-high red-and-white concrete blocks designed to deter truck bombers. Beyond the parking lot, a tall black fence mounted on a thick concrete base encircled a low-slung, unobtrusive bunker-like building.

The only break in the fence came in the form of a silver, bulletproof gatehouse, which was marked with a United States embassy seal and manned by Kyrgyz security guards.

Mark had been to the embassy plenty of times. First, just as a courtesy, to let the CIA know he was operating in Kyrgyzstan, and later to negotiate contracts the Agency was considering awarding to CAIN.

He checked in with the Kyrgyz guards at the gatehouse—because he was on a list of pre-cleared visitors, he was allowed to keep his phone—and went through the metal detector. Minutes later, he was met by a tightly wound young brunette who claimed to be an economic officer working for the State Department. In reality, Mark recalled, she was a CIA operations officer, one that Mark's friend John Decker had been assigned to guard on several occasions. She escorted him past the marine security guard checkpoint and then to a sterile, utilitarian room deep within the bowels of the main building.

An oval conference table had been set up in the center of the room. Sturdy metal office chairs with hard-plastic back rests had been arranged around the table.

The room also had a self-locking door, which clicked shut when the last of Mark's minders departed.

12

Daria printed out full-size reproductions of the flag of Saudi Arabia, the flag of Jordan, and then the flags of a dozen more Arabic-speaking countries in and around the Middle East.

Muhammad looked on as she arranged the colorful printouts on the floor in a large semi-circle. When she was finished, she sat cross-legged on the floor next to him, smiled, and said in Arabic, "Which is Muhammad's flag?"

The boy said he wanted his Anna.

"Which is Muhammad's flag? This one?" Daria pointed at the flag of Saudi Arabia.

Mohammad approached the piece of paper, looked at it, then kicked it angrily. He did the same to the next flag, only he didn't appear as angry. By the time he kicked the third flag, he had a smile on his face. After kicking wildly at all the flags on the floor, then throwing some of the papers in the air and trying to bat them with his hand as they fluttered to the ground, Daria said, "Hey Muhammad, want to watch TV?"

Mohammad gave an enthusiastic one-word answer—yes.

"And what does Muhammad want to watch?"

The boy said something that sounded, to Daria, like *Cap Kareem*. So she said, "Let's try to find that, OK? Can you help?"

Muhammad nodded.

Daria took her iPod, showed it to Muhammad, loaded up Google, and searched for *Kareem tv Arabic children*.

The first result was for Kareem Abdul-Jabbar's Wikipedia entry. The second was for an animated Arabic children's show entitled *Captain Karim Qitar Al Hekayat*, a program that claimed to introduce children to "the wonderful world of storytelling and reading."

"You want to watch Captain Karim?" asked Daria.

Muhammad did.

After another Google search, Daria learned that *Captain Karim Qitar Al Hekayat* was produced by a children's television network based out of Qatar.

Now we're talking, she thought, hoping that it was a network with limited distribution throughout the region. If she was lucky, it would be exclusive to Qatar, and that would tell her where Muhammad was from.

A few more quick searches, however, told her *Captain Karim Qitar Al Hekayat* was distributed throughout all Arab countries. And Europe.

She pulled up YouTube, found a few *Captain Karim* videos, selected the longest one, and handed her iPod to Muhammad. Then she stood up, intending to use the laptop computer in the spare bedroom to print out copies of the outlines of various Arab-speaking countries. As a young girl, even as a preschooler, she imagined she might have recognized an outline of the United States.

Muhammad pushed something on the phone that made the screen go dark, then screamed in frustration.

"No problem, Muhammad." Daria took the phone back and stroked the boy's hair. "We watch in the kitchen. OK?"

Muhammad said he wanted his Anna.

"I know you do, baby, I know you do," Daria said in English. She picked up Muhammad and settled him on her hip as she carried him into the kitchen. Switching back to Arabic, she asked "Muhammad hungry?"

He'd had some ice cream not long ago, but Daria knew that little boys ate a lot and that a hungry kid was an unhappy kid—

though she also realized that Muhammad had a lot more to be unhappy about than just being hungry.

She opened the pantry door and saw a box of butter cookies on the top shelf, the kind that Mark liked.

She pulled them down and was about to ask Muhammad whether he wanted a cookie when the boy pointed enthusiastically at the package and said, "*Bistoog! Bistoog!*"

"*Kalweki?*" said Daria, using what she thought was the Arabic word for cookie.

Mohammad said no, he wanted *bistoog.* He pointed again to the package, so she opened it and gave him a cookie.

"*Bistoog,*" he said again, taking the cookie and eating it.

She took another cookie out of the package. "*Bistoog?*"

Muhammad grabbed the cookie. "*Bistoog,*" he confirmed. That gave Daria an idea.

She set up her iPod on the kitchen table, propped it up against a cookbook, sat Muhammad on a pillow in one of the kitchen chairs, got the *Captain Karim* video going again, poured him a glass of milk, left him with the open pack of *bistoogs*, and then headed to her computer.

Within ten minutes, she was pretty sure she'd figured out where Muhammad was from.

She knew Arabic was like English, in that the various Arabic-speaking countries had their own regional accents, or slightly different words for things. Just as a truck in the United States was a lorry in Great Britain, she'd learned that in parts of Kuwait, and on the island nation of Bahrain, a cookie was commonly called a *bistoog*, a variation on the English word *biscuit.*

The *Captain Karim* video ended. Muhammad called out for her, and she came to him. He was still sitting at the kitchen table. Half of the cookies were gone and crumbs were scattered all over the table and floor.

"Where are you from, Muhammad?"

"*Ba-bay.*"

Daria thought of how, for many English-speaking toddlers, *library* became *liberry*, or *spaghetti* became *sgabetti*. "Muhammad is from Bahrain?"

"Yes."

"Bahrain is your home?"

Bahrain was a small island in the Persian Gulf connected to Saudi Arabia via a long causeway. Although it was an independent nation, it had been a protectorate of Great Britain for many years—hence the use of the word *bistoog*.

"Yes."

"Where is your Anna?"

"In ba-bay."

13

The first thing Decker did when he got down off the cliff was call Bruce Holtz, his boss at CAIN.

"Dude," said Decker. "You got a minute?"

"Yo, Deck . . . hold on," said Holtz. Then, "This about Mark?"

"No. What's up with Mark?"

"Ah, nothing. Gimme a sec."

Decker heard Holtz typing away at a keyboard.

Jessica, who was coiling their climbing rope, gave him a look that said, *Hurry up already.* She and Decker were both wearing headlamps—the last light of day had disappeared ten minutes ago.

"Listen," said Deck. "I'm going to have to bail on next week's job."

Holtz stopped typing.

Decker added, "Something's come up," and then he told Holtz about his dad.

After a lengthy pause, Holtz said, "All right. I understand. No problem."

Though he didn't sound sympathetic, he didn't sound angry either.

"Sorry, I know that screws you over."

"Shit happens. I got family too. You do what you have to do, man."

"Well, what I have to do right now is get a flight out of here pronto. I'll fly commercial if I have to, but if CAIN can hook me up with a military transport, that would rock. The sooner the better."

"I'm busy as hell, I got this fucking thing going on with Mark."

"All right."

"But I'll put in a call. It'll just take a second."

"I appreciate it. What's going on with Mark?"

"Oh, he's busting my balls on this CAIN situation that's going down. It's confidential, so I can't say more, but give me a heads-up if he calls you, would you? And if you could *not* let Mark know that you're keeping me in the loop, I'd appreciate it."

"Ah, yeah." Decker wasn't about to sandbag Mark, not after all Mark had done for him, but he didn't see any point in telling Holtz that. "Anyway, you'll let me know about the flight?"

"I'll put in a call to the air base, see what I can do."

14

Daria called Mark, and when he didn't pick up, left a message for him about the Bahrain connection.

Then she loaded up another *Captain Karim* video for Muhammad. Halfway through it, the boy's eyes began to droop, so she took the seat cushions off the couch and made a sleeping area for him in the bedroom—on the floor, because she worried he might fall off the bed.

She let him watch the rest of the *Captain Karim* video on his new bed, rubbing his back as he sucked on his pacifier. By the end of the show, Muhammad's eyes had closed. She looked at him for a moment, marveling at his smooth skin, his lips pursed so sweetly around the pacifier that it almost made her physically ache to look at him. His black hair curled around a tiny, perfectly formed ear, and his shallow, steady breathing was as beautiful a sound as she'd heard in this world.

What happened to you, Muhammad?

One thing was certain, she wouldn't tolerate seeing this child thrown back to the wolves.

She sat with him for a few more minutes, until she was sure he was fast asleep, and then walked to the living room and sat down on the cushionless couch. She called a potential benefactor she was supposed to meet in Almaty the next day and asked to postpone that meeting until a week from now. A flight to Tashkent, Uzbekistan, that she'd booked for two days from now, she canceled altogether.

And then she closed her eyes. God, she was tired. This pace was killing her. If her period wasn't just late, then she had to start taking better care of herself, and soon.

Her mind swirled as she started worrying about child care, and preschools, and the lousy health care system in Kyrgyzstan, and how she was going to swing it all . . .

Four hard, sharp raps jolted Daria out of her sleep. Someone was knocking on the front door.

Her instincts told her that it wasn't just a neighbor coming to ask for a cup of sugar, that it was some sort of law enforcement, or—

They were here for Muhammad. She couldn't let them inside.

Daria stood up, took a half second to come up with a plan, then raced silently into the bedroom. Muhammad was still fast asleep. She gently closed the bedroom door just as four more loud knocks sounded.

On her way to the balcony off the kitchen, Daria grabbed her iPod and headset from the living room coffee table. As she eased open the door to the balcony, she brought up the last call she'd made, pushed dial, put on the headset, and slipped the device into her back pocket.

On the left side of the balcony, an old rope had been affixed to a rusted bolt that protruded from the exterior of the building. The makeshift fire escape lay on the floor in a tidy circular coil.

Daria took the rope and tossed it over the side of the balcony just as Mark answered her call.

"God, I was afraid I'd get voice mail again. Pick Muhammad up from our condo." She spoke quietly as she slid gracefully down the rope. "Now." The second her feet hit the pavement, she tied a quick knot in the end of the rope.

"I can't. Complete cluster on this end. Holtz got involved in—"

"No time. They're here for him, I have to draw them away. I can't take him, it's on you. "

"Who's they?"

"I don't know."

"Are you OK?"

With urgency, Daria whispered, "I'll be fine, just pick up Muhammad!"

She tried to heave the knot, and the length of rope that was attached to it, back up to the balcony. She succeeded, but a several-foot-long loop, too high for her to reach, hung down over the side.

"OK, I'll figure it out," said Mark.

"Be quick about it. By the way, I left you a message—he's from Bahrain. He says the woman he calls Anna, and who's probably his nanny, is from there."

Daria ended the call and ran to the stairwell entrance to her condo. As she opened the door, she heard more knocking coming from the hallway.

She climbed the creaky stairs, her footsteps heavy and loud on the oak stair treads. When she reached the second-floor landing, she turned into the hall and feigned surprise when she saw the two men—one a gangly schoolboy redhead with a razor-burn rash on his neck, the other an older man with Asian features—standing outside her door. The redhead held a crowbar in his hand and was in the process of wedging it between the doorframe and the door.

She took a wary step back. As she did so, she noted that the redhead was wearing leather shoes imprinted with the Timberland logo. Bishkek wasn't like Baku, which had long ago been invaded by Western stores. An American, she figured. Backing away, she said in English, "What are you doing?"

"Miss Buckingham?" asked the older man. He had a long neck and straight black hair that had been parted to the side, and his hairline was slightly receding, resulting in a prominent widow's peak. He spoke with an American accent, and carried himself like an American—head thrust forward, more overtly aggressive than most of the Chinese intelligence agents Daria had encountered.

"What do you want?"

"We need to talk to you," he said, adding, "We're from the US embassy here in Bishkek."

That she believed. "You're Agency."

Neither man denied it.

"Why were you breaking in?" she asked.

"We knocked first. Where are you coming from?"

"That's none of your business."

"Your prior ties to the US government require that you cooperate with us now, Ms. Buckingham."

That much was true, Daria allowed. Just because she'd been kicked out of the CIA didn't mean all her obligations to the Agency had ended. Her original contract had made that clear. There were restrictions on what she could say and do that would apply for the rest of her life.

The young redhead maneuvered himself so that he was between Daria and the exit. Daria didn't move to stop him.

"I'm fully aware of my obligations," she said. "What does that have to do with you breaking into my home?"

"We've been told you have a child. Not a child of your own. An orphan."

"And what of it?"

"The US government has an interest in this boy and believes he's in danger. We've been sent to protect him."

"By breaking into my home?"

The Asian opened his palms. "We were simply searching for the boy. As we were ordered to do."

"He's not here. I just returned from dropping him off with friends. And you don't have to worry about him. He's safe."

"Others don't see it that way. Listen, we don't have much choice in the matter. We'd appreciate it if you didn't fight us on this. All we want to do is recover the boy and bring him back to the embassy, where he'll be safe. Can you help us?"

Daria pretended to consider the matter. "If I take you to the boy, can I go with him to the embassy? He's young, and scared. No offense, but neither of you guys looks like the mothering type."

"I don't have a problem with that," said the Asian.

It was clear the redhead didn't get a vote.

Daria paused again, as though hesitant. "OK. I just brought him back to Balykchy."

"*Back* to Balykchy?"

"Yeah. He was taken from an orphanage there."

"We haven't been briefed. Is he at this orphanage now?"

"No, I left him with friends who live near it. I wasn't sure it was safe to bring him back to the orphanage itself. I was afraid someone might try to take him again."

The Asian sighed. "Then let's get going."

Daria led the way down the staircase. When they got to the street, she began to talk rapidly about what had transpired earlier in the day, drawing the attention of the two CIA officers away from the rope dangling from her balcony.

15

After getting off the phone with Holtz, Decker took off his climbing harness, put on his hiking boots—which he'd stored in a bag near the base of the cliff—shouldered his backpack, cinched it tight, and began to jog down the trail that would eventually lead him to his Ford Explorer.

Jessica had already packed up, and was running a few steps ahead of him, stepping from rock to rock as she rapidly navigated the steep, narrow trail. Her pack was strapped tight to her back, her dirty-blond hair tied back with a blue bandanna.

She'd been a good sport about having to abort the climb, Decker thought. And supportive, without being overly doting, after he'd told her about his father.

Decker's phone rang. The normal ring tone told him it wasn't his mother, but he figured it might be one of his brothers.

Still jogging, he pulled out his phone and pushed Talk, wondering as he did so whether this was *the* call—one of his brothers telling him he was too late.

"Deck, it's Mark."

"Oh. Hey."

"What are you doing?"

"Ah, climbing. Actually, I'm descending. Had to stop the climb, something's come up."

As if he hadn't heard the bit about something coming up, Mark said, "You in country?"

"Yeah, just south of Bishkek."

"Great. Listen, I need you buddy."

"You know, this is kind of like a *really* bad time."

Decker was still jogging. He kept his eyes on the trail.

"We're talking emergency."

"I'm hoping to catch a flight to—"

"Delay it. I'll cover any costs for the switch. We're talking five-alarm fire."

"It's not the money . . . "

Decker was about to tell Mark about his father, but then he stopped himself. When had Mark ever called him for help before? When had he ever used the word *emergency*?

Never.

Dammit, he thought. Mark was his friend, arguably his best friend.

Mark didn't like to climb. Or hike. Or pound beers at the expat bars and talk about football, or do a lot of the things Decker liked to do. But Mark was a friend in the sense that he was a guy Decker had been able to rely on in the past—if Mark hadn't bailed him out of a tight spot in Iran last spring, he'd be dead—and knew with absolute certainty he could rely on in the future.

Mark said, "I wouldn't need you for long, I hope. Maybe for just a few hours, maybe for a day or two."

"Damn, Mark, it's just that . . ."

Mark didn't say anything.

"OK," said Deck. "I'll make this work."

What are you saying? You can't make this work.

"Thanks. I need you to power down your phone, remove the battery, then get rid of any other electronic devices you might be carrying. Go to the place where I taught you to play narde. Take extensive SD measures before you get there. When you arrive, you'll find a package."

SD was short for surveillance detection. Which told Decker that Mark was mighty worried about something. "What is it?"

Tell him you can't do this.

"Not over the phone. I can't be sure yours is secure. You'll know it when you see it. Just be gentle, remove it immediately from the site, hide it, and protect it. We'll communicate through our mutual account. Check it every two hours. I'll deliver more intel as soon as I can."

By mutual account, Decker knew Mark was talking about an anonymous Gmail account to which they both knew the password. It was their backup way to communicate—by saving draft messages to it—just in case normal lines of communication became compromised.

"When—"

"Now. Go there right now."

"It's gonna take me some time, buddy. I'm not far miles wise, but it's a hike to the car and then roads are shit. I mean, I'll rush, I'm rushing now, but—"

"Just get there as soon as you can. I have to sign off."

16

Mark hung up on Decker, exhaled, and stared at his phone—hoping to see a text message from Daria. Then CIA station chief Serena Bamford opened the door to the conference room.

A heavyset woman in her mid-forties, Bamford had a full head of wavy dark-brown shoulder-length hair, a pale complexion she'd inherited from her Estonian grandparents, and an unflappable, perpetually cheerful demeanor that masked her considerable intellect. After graduating with a master's in Russian studies from the University of Michigan, she'd been tapped by the Agency and had gone on to serve as an operations officer in Kazakhstan, Kyrgyzstan, Moscow, and Uzbekistan before being given her own station in Bishkek two years ago.

Mark liked her. The occasional compliments she tossed his way suggested the feeling was mutual, but with former ops officers you never really knew; he figured she could have just been trying to manipulate him.

"Coffee?" said Bamford, sitting down. She wore a navy-blue pantsuit and just a little bit of makeup.

"Do we have time?"

"More than you'd probably like."

"Sure."

Bamford pushed an intercom button on the conference table and placed an order with her assistant.

Mark added, "Have him grab a few of those butter cookies they keep next to the coffee machine, would you?"

A regular diet of lousy meals at the Shanghai and too many snacks in between hadn't done much for his physique, but Mark figured now wasn't the time to turn things around. Especially since he knew the embassy was partially supplied by the Base Exchange at the Manas Air Base. The coffee was Starbucks, the cookies Pepperidge Farm.

Bamford's assistant soon showed up with two coffees, several sugar packs and stirrers, and a pile of cookies heaped on a paper plate. He set it all down on the table. Mark took a bite of a butter cookie and leaned back in his chair.

"So," he said.

Bamford smiled. "So." She arranged three packs of sugar together, ripped them all open at once, dumped the sugar in her coffee, mixed it slowly with a stirrer, and then took a sip.

"I take it Kaufman called?" asked Mark.

"Yep." Bamford added, "Sorry about Daria, by the way."

Mark eyed Bamford before asking, "Why should you be sorry about Daria?"

"We had to pick her up. Kaufman's orders, but he was just acting on orders himself. Something about a boy from one of her orphanages. Langley wants him here at the embassy for protection. Apparently she's cooperating."

Concealing his relief that it was the Agency who'd come for Daria, Mark said, "Good luck with that."

"You know something I don't?"

Mark declined to answer the question. He wasn't about to tell Bamford that John Decker was on his way to pick up Muhammad, but he didn't want to lie. Bamford wasn't the enemy.

"Anyway," continued Bamford, "I know you're here to see Rosten, but he won't get here for at least an hour or so. In the meantime, I thought I'd be social. See if you needed anything."

Mark pointed at the coffee and cookies. "I'm good now, thanks."

"Or if you wanted to tell me what the hell CAIN was doing running a Near East op in my station without telling me? Or the ambassador, for that matter."

Mark stared at Bamford. Her friendly expression hadn't changed, but her tone of voice had.

She was pissed.

Mark didn't blame her. A chief of station was supposed to be informed of all intelligence operations going on within her station, and for good reason—in addition to private contractors, the army, navy, air force, and the State Department all had the ability to run intelligence ops. If the chief of station didn't know what everyone was up to, the potential for overlap, or for one operation to unwittingly interfere with another, was high. Though employed by State, the ambassador, as the representative of the president, was also supposed to be kept in the intelligence-op loop.

"Listen, Serena. I just found out about it this afternoon, so it's not as though I personally was running some kind of black op in your station without letting you know about it."

"But Bruce Holtz was. Wasn't he?"

Mark didn't answer. He didn't need to. Bamford already knew.

She said, "You want to tell me what that op was?"

Mark told her. The way he figured it, keeping Central Eurasia happy was more important than not pissing off Near East. Always prioritize existing friends over potential friends. Holtz had broken that rule when he'd taken the job from Near East.

After Mark had finished, Bamford shook her head, exhaled, and said, "What the hell."

"I know."

"So what happens to the kid once he gets to the embassy?" she asked. "Should I be looking for babysitters?" She turned up her nose. "Like I don't have anything better to do. Or is Near East just going to deal with him? This whole thing stinks."

"I don't think you're going to have to worry about that. At least not in the near future."

"What's that supposed to mean?"

"It means Daria's going to do what she thinks is right for the boy, Near East be damned."

Sounding both resigned and defiant, Bamford said, "And you're going to help her."

"Hey, I'm trying to work with you on this, Serena. Don't shoot the messenger. You want my advice—"

"I don't."

"—just let this play out."

"Any chance you could take this fight with Near East elsewhere? Like anywhere other than *my* station?"

Bamford leaned back in her chair. One of the things Mark liked about her was that she was calculating. If she thought she could win, she'd fight; if she thought she was going to lose, she'd back off. Or in this case, if she saw a bunch of idiots fighting in her station, she'd do what she could to get rid of them.

"I'm hoping I don't have to fight at all."

"Yeah, I don't think Rosten got the memo."

17

John Decker sped into a curve on the narrow, twisted dirt road that led out of the mountains south of Bishkek.

"Christ, Deck," said Jessica. She'd pushed herself back into her seat, and was bracing her legs against the floor, as if preparing for a crash. "Would you slow down?"

Decker hadn't realized how fast he was going. He braked.

"Do you want me to drive?" asked Jessica.

"No."

"This friend who called you. I still don't get it. Why didn't you just tell him about your dad?"

After Mark's call, Decker had told Jessica he needed to pick something up in Bishkek, as a favor to a friend, but he hadn't been any more specific than that. He could tell she thought he was nuts, but was too polite, or unsettled, to say much about it. They hadn't known each other for that long, after all.

"I didn't have a chance to tell him about my dad. He hung up before I could mention it."

Decker looked in his rearview mirror. Mark had mentioned taking surveillance detection measures. Decker had been doing so inadvertently just by hauling ass as fast as he had been, but he told himself he should start checking for tails.

"He hung up on you?"

"That's just how he is."

"Some friend."

"He's actually a pretty good guy."

"What kind of favor?"

"I just have to pick something up and hold on to it for a little while."

Maybe he could just bring whatever Mark wanted him to hold on to back with him to the States, Decker thought. Hell, that might even be the safest course of action. Get whatever it was out of the area of operations.

"John, you've got bigger things to worry about. Call your friend back." She put a hand up to Decker's cheek. "Tell him about your dad."

"I can't, Jess. You just have to trust me on this one. Listen, I gotta try reaching my brother in the States again."

Decker flipped on the overhead light and started drifting to the side of the road as he searched for his phone in the compartment under the armrest between the driver and passenger seats. He'd tossed it in there amid the old soda cans and tins of chewing tobacco and random keys and wrappers from his favorite shawarma place in Bishkek.

"Really, honey, why don't you let me drive?"

Decker found his phone. "I got it." He pulled his Bluetooth earpiece out from under a wet napkin, stuck it in his ear, and dialed while keeping one eye on the road.

"What's the latest?" he said, when his brother picked up.

"I don't know, man. We haven't gotten the test results back yet."

"What tests?"

"They're running this line or something from his arm to his heart."

"Is he getting better?"

"He's not getting worse. At least his heart is beating OK now."

"Thank God."

"There was something wrong with the rhythm before."

Decker thought his brother sounded seriously stressed.

"Listen, tell Mom I might not be able to catch a flight till tomorrow morning. I'm working on it now, but things here are a bit of a cluster. I'm in the serious boonies, and even when I get out of here, it'll be a day of travel. I'll figure it out, but it might take a little longer than I'd hoped."

"I'll tell her."

"OK, I'll check in later. I gotta go now."

He'd bought himself a little time, Decker thought, relieved to no end that his father wasn't getting worse. He'd deal with Mark today. Come tomorrow, he'd have to make a decision, but there was no use worrying about that now. His only concern right now was what to do with Jessica.

He glanced at her as he tossed his phone back into the armrest compartment. The problem was, she'd moved out of the climber's hostel a week before and had been crashing with him ever since. He'd feel like a jerk saying "see ya" and just dropping her off on the street. Besides, he liked having her around.

"So, Jess," he said. "You remember I said I worked as, like, a high-paid security guard?"

"You're a SEAL, honey. I know."

"Was a SEAL. But it's because I was a SEAL that I have the job that I have. Anyway, point being, I have special skills. It's cool because I get to take off and climb with you and stuff, but sometimes, man, duty calls."

"And you're telling me this is one of those times."

"Yeah, this is one of those times. That's what the favor is about. It's a job, but it's a job for a friend. Kind of an emergency deal."

"What about your dad?"

"I've got to pick up a package and guard it for a while. It shouldn't be long, maybe just a few hours, maybe a little bit longer. After that, I'll fly straight home. My brother's there anyway. There's nothing I'd really be able to do at home other than try to be nice to people, whereas here . . . Ah, shit, I don't know . . ."

"What kind of package?"

"I don't know."

"Is it dangerous?"

"I don't know, but I figure there's a reason they needed someone like me."

"They don't bring in the big guns for nothing, huh?" Jessica gave him a playful punch on his tree trunk of an arm.

Decker loved her Australian accent, and the way she said *big guns*. She was like a young Nicole Kidman.

"Anyway, if you want, if you're worried, I can drop you off somewhere before I pick this thing up."

"I'm not worried. I figure you can handle it."

"All right. We'll stick together then."

"Done."

"You're a hell of a good sport, Jess."

"Just let me know if I'm getting in the way of you being able to do your job. If I'm a burden, I'll leave. Where is this package, anyway?"

Decker was about to answer when his phone rang. This time, it was Holtz.

"I'm hooking you up, buddy," said Holtz. "Found you a spot on a C-17 that's flying crap from Afghanistan back to Fort Bragg. Leaving tonight, twenty-two hundred hours. Refuel stop at Ramstein. Get your ass over to the air base by eight, have the gate crew give Colonel Greene a holler—I think you know him?"

"Yeah, he handled transport for the job we did for DoD this summer, but—"

"Good. Just check in with him and he'll handle getting you where you need to be."

"Only thing is, it turns out I can't blow tonight. I have something I have to do. I completely blanked about it when I talked to you earlier."

A long pause, then, "What do you suddenly have to do that's more important than flying home to be with your dad?"

"Well, nothing that's *more* important than that, I'm just talking about a brief delay. It has to do with Jessica."

"Who's Jessica?"

"The Australian girl. You met her last week."

"You two still together? I thought she was just a—"

"Hey."

"I'm just saying."

"I promised her I'd drive her up to Almaty. I completely blanked."

"Have her take the damn bus."

"She's not going to downtown Almaty. It's one of the towns outside. She needs a ride for this wedding. I'll catch a flight to the States from Almaty tomorrow morning."

"You're going to pay a couple extra grand just to drive a chick you hardly know to a wedding?"

"We actually know each other pretty well by now." Decker gave Jessica a look and winked. "She's a great gal."

Holtz didn't respond right away. When he did, he sounded suspicious. "Have you been talking to Sava?"

"Actually, no."

"Don't bullshit me, Deck."

"I'm not bullshitting you."

The line went silent. Finally, Holtz said, "All right. I'll tell Colonel Greene you're bailing."

"I'm sorry to have put you out."

"Yeah, whatever. Call me if Sava calls you."

"Roger that."

It took Decker an hour to get to Bishkek. After a ten-minute high-speed surveillance-detection run down half the side alleys in the city, he parked his Explorer a few blocks away from Mark and Daria's condo.

"Wait here, OK?" he said to Jessica. "This shouldn't take long."

He popped open the back hatch of the Explorer, lifted up the mat covering the cargo area, and pulled out a metal box that had been fitted into a custom-made slot. Inside was a tactical chest rig, a Sig Sauer P226 9mm pistol, five spare twenty-round magazines for the Sig, an assortment of holsters, a set of compact night-vision goggles, a body armor vest with spare plates, a SOG SEAL Team knife, a Sig Sauer Mosquito pistol with a threaded barrel, a suppressor that could be screwed onto the barrel of the Mosquito, a short version of an M4 rifle, a box of ammo for the M4, three yards of detonation cord along with a few blasting caps, a thousand dollars in cash, a Leatherman tool, an LED headlamp, a compass, a tin of Skoal Straight dip, and a first aid kit.

Deck considered what to bring. He was just there to pick up a package; better to travel light, he thought.

He strapped on a shoulder holster, glanced around for cops—except for the M4, all the guns were unlicensed—slotted the Sig Sauer P226 into it, put on a nylon jacket that had been on the floor of the cargo area, zipped it up so that his gun was hidden, and slipped two spare, fully loaded P226 magazines into each pocket of the jacket. Recalling that Mark and Daria's condominium had appeared dark when he'd driven past it, he grabbed his night-vision goggles and slid them into an inside pocket.

After packing the rest of his gear back up, he climbed out of the car, walked down a few alleys, and then ducked in and out of the hospital on the opposite side of the street. Finally, when he'd convinced himself that no one was following him on foot, he walked across the street to Mark and Daria's condo.

He let himself into the open stairwell, climbed one flight of steps, and knocked on a new metal door, expecting—with some trepidation—that Daria would answer.

Before Daria had quit the spy business, he'd worked with her on a job. A couple weeks into it, he'd taken her out to dinner. His advances, he recalled, had gone nowhere. They weren't right for each other, he knew, but he still found her distractingly attractive.

Which, since she was with Mark, sometimes made him feel awkward around her.

He knocked again. No one answered, so he tried the door. It was locked. The light in the hallway was dim, but it was even darker along the crack between the door and the floor—which told him that the lights were off inside.

Well, damn, he thought. He knew Mark and Daria had a pretty sophisticated alarm system. Breaking down the door would set it off. If that was what it took, that was what it took, but Decker thought it couldn't hurt to look for an open window. So he trudged back down to the street. That was when he noticed the loop of rope hanging off the balcony—and that the balcony door was cracked open an inch.

Bingo.

He waited a minute until the sidewalk was clear of pedestrians, and then ran at the exterior wall of Mark and Daria's building. When he was close, he leaped several feet in the air, pushed up with his right foot when it hit the wall, and grabbed at the dangling rope with his left hand.

Two seconds later, he was standing silently on the balcony, his hand on the grip of his pistol, listening for sounds inside. All the lights still appeared to be off. He heard nothing, so after a minute, he slipped on his night-vision goggles, gently eased the balcony door open, and ducked inside, drawing his gun as he did so.

"Someone's been having a party," Decker said to himself.

The cushions had been removed from the living room sofa. Crumpled pieces of paper, a vase, and narde pieces were scattered all over the floor. A glass of milk and an open box of butter cookies sat on the kitchen table. Then Decker noticed a big box of what looked like diapers—he couldn't read the Cyrillic letters, so he couldn't be sure—on the coffee table in front of the couch.

Huh, he thought.

Gun still drawn, he started looking for a package. Mark had said he'd know it when he saw it. And to be gentle. Which had made no sense to Decker at the time and made no sense to him now.

He inspected the living room and kitchen, then ducked his head into Mark and Daria's office. When he got to the bedroom, and saw that the sheets had been pulled from the bed onto what looked like the couch cushions, his confusion only mounted. He took a quick look under the bed.

Then Decker saw something move, something inside the pile of sheets next to the bed.

What the hell?

He caught a glimpse of what—with his night-vision goggles on—looked like fur. His first thought was that it was a rat, or a mouse. He swung his gun around and lifted the sheets up with his foot.

"Oh, no," said Decker. "You have got to be kidding me."

18

It was nearly nine p.m. by the time Daria and her two CIA minders reached Balykchy. The air had turned cold, hovering around the freezing point, and smelled of wood fires and marshland.

At a dirt alley that intersected the main road just past the town center, Daria said, "Turn here."

They drove past a cluster of abandoned houses—crumbling, roofless structures with tree-sized weeds growing out of them. The decay stretched as far as the glare from the car's headlights, and beyond. Dogs barked in the night.

"What the hell is this place?" asked the Asian CIA officer, who was driving. The pothole-riddled road was testing the suspension of the beat-up Russian Lada they were driving in. Daria assumed the car was supposed to help CIA officers fit in with the local population when on assignment. Or maybe the Agency had just been trying to save a few bucks.

"It's just Balykchy," Daria said, adding, "It's not far now."

After a half mile or so, a few inhabited houses appeared on the left.

"Stop here," said Daria, when they'd reached the last house on the street. It was a one-story structure, made of dun-colored brick, and topped with a corrugated metal roof. In front of the house, waist-high grass grew around piles of rocks. Electric lights were visible through the single-pane windows. A fence made of scrap wood and barbed wire surrounded three sides of the house; on the right side stood a ten-foot-high concrete wall topped with concertina wire and defaced with graffiti extolling the virtues of a Bishkek-based rock band.

The wall, Daria knew, marked the boundary of an abandoned factory. A rusted metal door—what had once been a back exit from the factory—stood in the middle of the wall. Beyond the door, in the fields surrounding the abandoned factory, were vegetable gardens. Daria knew this because she'd been here before. The house belonged to a handyman who frequently helped at the orphanage; Daria had driven him home on several occasions.

The car stopped.

"I'll have to go inside to get him," said Daria.

"We'll come with you," said the redheaded CIA officer.

"It would be better if you didn't. The people here, they're not used to strangers. Especially not at this time of night."

"We don't have any choice in the matter. Nor do you."

Daria shrugged. "All right, just be careful. And let me do the talking."

All three of them climbed out of the car. It was a starless, moonless night. Daria could hear wind gusting through nearby trees.

She let herself through the makeshift front gate, which wasn't locked. The two officers tried to follow closely behind her, but as soon as she was through the gate, she swung it backward as hard as she could, slamming it into the redhead's knees. She sprinted toward the concrete wall that loomed up thirty feet away to her right.

Behind her, the officers yelled at her to stop. Dogs started barking inside the house.

When she reached the rusted door that led to the factory grounds, she pulled as hard as she could on a jury-rigged handle that had been affixed to the door, slipped through the opening, slammed the door shut behind her, swung a heavy latch into place, and began to run.

19

Jessica's eyes widened in a cartoonish way when Decker opened the door to his Explorer, holding a child in his arms. The boy had a pacifier in his mouth, which he was sucking on hard as he whimpered.

All things considered, thought Decker, the kid was holding up pretty well.

He pulled his keys out of his pocket and tossed them to Jessica. "Here. You drive. I'll sit in back with the kid."

Jessica just stared at him as if he'd lost his mind.

Decker added, "He's the package I needed to pick up."

"He's not a package. He's a child."

"Yeah, I figured that out." Decker slipped into the back seat of the car, still holding Muhammad tight to his chest. "Drive! Please, Jessica. Just drive."

"What's the rush?"

"I don't know. I got a feeling."

"You're weirding me out, John."

"I'm just kind of babysitting, that's all. No biggie."

"Yes, this is a biggie!"

"Go!"

Jessica started the car and pulled out into traffic. "Babysitting for how long?"

"A few hours. Maybe a day."

"Well, whose child is it?"

"I don't know."

"You don't know." Jessica sounded incredulous.

"I know this woman who runs an orphanage, OK? So I'm guessing the kid's an orphan, but evidently there's been some complications."

"This woman who runs the orphanage—is *she* the friend that asked you to do this?"

"No. That's this other guy. But I think he was asking for her. They're like, almost married."

Jessica gripped the steering wheel with both hands, staring with deer-in-the-headlights eyes out the front windshield. She shook her head a few times, as though having a conversation with herself.

Decker added, "The kid's in some kind of danger, some people are after him, and I've been asked to protect him. That's all I know and all I have to know. I'm gonna take him to my place, deal with things there. You don't have to stay if you don't want to."

Jessica took a full minute to answer. "I said I'd stay. We'll take care of him together."

20

Val Rosten, the deputy director of the CIA's Near East Division, showed up at the US embassy in Bishkek just after nine.

Mark had met Rosten years before at Langley, when they'd both been station chiefs. Rosten had just given an intense, one-hour, head-spinning sixty-slide presentation on Jordanian economic policies. In the years since, Rosten had made short work of climbing over colleagues to get to his current position.

He took a seat across from Mark at the conference table in the room where Mark had been kept waiting. He was rail thin, short, and dressed in a navy-blue pinstriped suit with a yellow tie. His white shirt looked a little rumpled from travel and his mouth had taken the shape of something close to a smile.

"I'll get right to it," said Rosten.

"Please do."

"The boy."

Mark sat back in his chair and studied Rosten. He figured they were roughly the same age. "What of him?"

"I believe Ted Kaufman spoke to you about the necessity of releasing him to us. So we can place him under protection."

Rosten spoke quickly, but he enunciated each word with studied precision. Mark had heard he'd been recruited from MIT, where he'd double majored in math and Middle Eastern studies.

"He sure did."

"Evidently you didn't feel it necessary to communicate the same to your companion, Daria Buckingham, though."

"Oh?"

"Buckingham promised to lead two local ops officers to the boy. Instead she drew them away from Bishkek and left them standing with their dicks in their hands. I just got the report from Serena Bamford."

"Hmm."

"You knew she was going to do it. Didn't you?"

"I wouldn't be so sure of that."

"Don't be coy with me, Sava. Do you know where the child is?"

As Rosten spoke, he tapped his foot. He struck Mark as one of those guys who had more energy—physical and intellectual—than he knew what to do with.

"Why'd you involve Holtz in this?" asked Mark.

"One of my younger colleagues used to work with him. He knew about CAIN, and better yet, he knew Holtz."

"Knew Holtz probably would take the job without asking a ton of questions. Even if the job involved kidnapping a two-year-old child."

Rosten pointed a finger at Mark. "I asked Holtz to help us find the son of two dead Jordanian agents, a decent family . . ."

The story Rosten began to tell was the same one Mark had heard from Holtz.

Interrupting, Mark said, "Yeah, only problem is, what you're telling me is a load of crap. The kid's from Bahrain."

Rosten's eyes narrowed just a bit. Mark thought he looked as though someone had just insulted his mother and he'd decided that, instead of getting angry, he was going to play it cool and get even. "And what might have led you to that conclusion?"

"Ah, you may have noticed that Muhammad is a person? The kid told us."

"He's a two-year-old. A confused two-year-old. Who speaks Arabic. Maybe you misunderstood."

"Or not."

They stared at each other for a while.

Mark said, "What the hell is a kid from Bahrain doing in Kyrgyzstan?"

Bahrain was the smallest Arab country in the world, just a tiny speck of an island that had been teetering on the brink of revolution for years. But it was also home to the United States' Fifth Fleet, a massive armada that had helped launch the invasions of Iraq and Afghanistan.

"That isn't any of your business, Sava."

"Listen, if you didn't want it to be my business, you shouldn't have stuck the kid in an orphanage run by my girlfriend."

"I didn't. That was Holtz."

"Daria just wants to know we're doing right by the kid. So that's all I want to know. It's not an unreasonable request."

"Let me break it down for you, Sava. This is a legit Agency operation, approved with a presidential finding."

A presidential finding was a decree, issued in secret by the president, that authorized the CIA to proceed with a covert operation.

"Let me guess, though. The part about the two-year-old wasn't mentioned in the finding."

Presidential findings, Mark knew, were often written in an intentionally vague way that allowed the president to approve a general policy, but preserve some level of plausible deniability when it came to the details.

"I have no intention of telling you about this operation, because that information is classified. I can assure you, however, that you're going to find yourself in the middle of a shitstorm you won't believe if you don't hand over that kid. There's a lot going down right now, as we speak, that you could screw up."

"Let me break it down for you, Val. Daria doesn't care whether your operation goes to hell. She cares about the kid. And she's not going to let the kid go until she's certain that turning him over to you is the right thing to do. And you know what, I won't either. So why don't you and the rest of your buddies at Near East go suck on that."

Ignoring the insult, Rosten said, "It *is* the right thing to do for Muhammad. You have my word. The kid's parents got hit and now we're trying to help him."

"He keeps talking about a person named Anna. Apparently she's someone who helped take care of him. He misses her. What's up with that? Is this Anna dead? Is she in Bahrain?"

Rosten took a second to look Mark over before answering.

"If you don't turn over that kid, this is what's going to happen. First, I'm ordering all your assets, domestic and foreign, frozen. Then I'm going to put the word out to DoD and State and every station around the world that you're actively working against the interests of the United States and not someone to do business with. I'll put the word out to foreign intelligence services too. Your mercenary work will come to an abrupt end."

Not with Central Eurasia, thought Mark. And he wasn't too worried about the money either. He'd lose a few thousand or so, but ninety-nine percent of his cash—over half a million dollars, the result of six months of splitting profits with Holtz—he'd stashed in secret accounts not tied to his name. "I'm not asking for much, Val. Just a little reassurance—beyond your word—that we're doing right by the kid. And I'll remind you, as I reminded Kaufman—I'm an approved Agency contractor with a top-secret clearance. If that's not good enough, if this is a compartmentalized op, I'm sure you can ram through the necessary approvals that will let you bring me on board."

As if Mark hadn't spoken, Rosten said, "Then I'm going to go after your fuck-buddy Daria."

Mark smiled at Rosten. It wasn't a nice smile.

"That fund she's been building for her orphanage project. She can kiss that good-bye."

Rosten smiled back. Mark noticed his teeth were kind of yellowed.

"A real stickler for the law, aren't you, Val?"

Mark wasn't all that worried about Rosten going after Daria's funds either. Given her shaky history with the US, Chinese, Azeri, and Iranian intelligence services, she'd taken care to arrange her accounts in such a way that the funds were protected from people nursing a grudge.

"I get things done. Finally, I'll make sure to get you PNGed from Kyrgyzstan and any other country you try to set foot in. You'll wind up either having to come home to the States or hole up in Somalia or North Korea."

PNG stood for *persona non grata*. Once a country PNGed a person, it meant they had to leave. That was why Mark and Daria had been forced to leave Azerbaijan.

"I'm not that fond of the idea of Somalia."

"Think about it, Sava. I'm not playing around here. I'm sorry you had to get involved with this and I don't fault you for your actions to date. They've been perfectly reasonable. My bad for relying on that meathead Holtz. Even though I wasn't going through you, I honestly thought that with you involved with CAIN, this whole thing would have been handled more competently. But none of that matters now. This is it. It's time to give up the kid."

Mark sighed. He tapped his index finger on the table top for a bit, then asked, "If I were to give you Muhammad, what would you do with him?"

"I'd get him to another orphanage and placed with a good family as soon as possible. The Agency's willing to pay to see that he gets to the front of the line with any adoption outfit."

"It might get a little tricky. I wasn't bluffing about Daria. She doesn't care about whatever op you're running. Her only concern is the kid."

"I'm sure you'll be able to figure something out."

"I'd have to retrieve him myself."

"I'm up for a drive. After what happened with Buckingham, we're going to trust but verify from here on out."

21

Decker lived in a dumpy part of north Bishkek, mainly because he was too cheap to pay to live in a better part of town. He figured he was traveling for work half the time, and when he wasn't working, he was usually climbing or traveling for pleasure, so why spend a fortune on a place he was only going to use a couple times a month?

Jessica parked the Explorer in front of his one-bedroom house. Down the street, lights were on in the other tightly packed homes. Decker hopped out of the car, still carrying Muhammad, and opened the steel door with his key. The door led to a little walled-in courtyard in front of his home.

"And here we are!" he said cheerfully to Muhammad.

Decker liked his courtyard—he liked the wild pumpkin vines growing all over the courtyard's cinderblock walls; he liked the little patch of overgrown grass where he'd set up a hibachi; he liked the plastic beer coolers that doubled as benches. He and Jess had sat on those coolers just three nights before, drinking beer around a little wood fire that he'd started in the hibachi.

He recalled that just two weeks earlier, on an unseasonably warm day in October, he'd set up a card table and had played narde outside with Mark. Decker smiled as he remembered how sour Mark had been after losing the first game.

He turned back to Jessica as he stepped through the doorway. "Maybe I'll fire up the grill tonight, make some s'mores, have a little cookout."

"I'm pretty sure a fire near the ground and a two-year-old kid isn't a good combination. Let's just get settled."

It was a tiny place; one room on the ground floor served as a bedroom, living room, and small kitchen. In the minuscule bathroom, the hot-water heater—which looked like a giant cooking pot with a couple of suspicious-looking electrical wires stuck into it—sat on a rickety wooden shelf above the toilet.

On the upside, Decker had bought a sixty-inch flat-panel television, a home theater system, and a desktop computer that he never turned off because he hated waiting for the thing to boot up.

When he set Muhammad down on the floor, the child scrunched up his face, as though getting ready to cry. So Decker leaned over, grabbed all four pillows from his bed, and threw them down on the floor.

"One of those was mine," said Jessica.

Decker held Muhammad and bounced him up and down on the mountain of pillows until Muhammad got the idea and started jumping on them himself.

"We'll have movie night," said Jessica. "Until he falls asleep."

"Movie night," said Decker, liking the idea. "Sounds good. We'll make the best of it."

He sat on the bed, ran his hand through his hair, and thought about his dad. And his brother. And his mom. *Damn.* Jessica sat down next to him and put her arm around his shoulder—as much of her arm as she could, that is. Deck was too big for her to really embrace.

"I'm going to take a shower," she said. "You can handle things until I'm out?"

If he hadn't had to look after Muhammad, Decker would have jumped in with Jessica. "Yeah, I'll go after you."

Then Decker's desktop computer beeped five times. Loudly.

Muhammad stopped climbing the mountain of pillows and looked at the computer.

"What was that?" asked Jessica.

Decker walked to his computer and tapped the mouse. The screen came to life. In the upper left-hand corner of it, three black-and-white video feeds were displayed, each in a separate window.

One of the screens showed the figure of a man.

"Turn on the shower," Decker whispered urgently.

When he'd first moved in, back in the spring, Decker had rigged up a rudimentary surveillance system. Three commercially available exterior video cameras communicated wirelessly with his desktop computer. In addition, the metal door that led to the courtyard had been wired to send a signal to the computer whenever it was opened. Originally, Decker had also set motion detectors on the tops of the courtyard walls, but the red squirrels, who had come to eat his pumpkins, had set off so many false alarms that he'd shut that system down.

"Why? What's that beeping?"

"Intruder. Go now."

Jessica half-walked, half-ran to the bathroom. Decker clicked on the video feed in which the figure was visible.

Bruce Holtz was pocketing a long silver electronic lock pick and walking across the small courtyard.

"A guy's about to knock," whispered Decker. He rushed up to his front door and silently engaged the dead bolt. "Tell him you're taking a shower, you'll get the door in a minute."

"Tell who?"

Decker pointed to the door. A second later, a fist rapped loudly on it.

"Hey, Deck! It's Bruce! Open up!"

The house had four windows—one on each side. Two of the windows looked out onto Decker's small courtyard. The remaining two looked out onto intersecting garbage-strewn alleys, which doubled as a breeding ground for stray dogs. All the windows had heavy curtains pulled over them; the alley-facing ones were protected by metal bars. The same day he'd moved in, however,

Decker had bought a welding torch at a local hardware store and cut an access hatch of sorts through one of the barred windows—so that in a pinch, he'd have more than one avenue of escape.

"Deck, open up! I know you're in there!"

As he grabbed a key from his desk, Decker made eye contact with Jessica and gestured to the door.

"Hold on!" called Jessica. "I'm in the shower, I can't get the door."

"Is Decker in there?"

"Give me a minute, I'm in the shower."

Decker heard the whir of the electronic lock pick engaging. Holtz, you son of a bitch, he thought. Trying to bust in on my girlfriend while she's in the shower. I'll remember that.

Decker opened one of the alley windows and used the key to unlock the access hatch he'd cut through the metal bars. He picked up Muhammad, looked at Jessica, and mouthed the words *follow me.*

Muhammad wasn't happy about being taken away from the pillows, and when Decker hoisted him through the window and set him down on the ground in the alley, he spit out his pacifier and started to cry.

Decker crawled through the window, picked up the pacifier from the dirt with one hand and the boy with the other, and sprinted to the front of the house. He saw Holtz's black Jaguar parked next to his Explorer. Without slowing down, he yanked open the driver's side door to the Explorer and slid Muhammad—who was by now having a full-blown tantrum—into the passenger seat. Pulling a knife out from under the driver's seat, he pivoted so that he was facing the Jag, and then punctured the sidewall of Holtz's front right tire.

That done, he started up the car and pulled out into the road just as Jessica ran up.

She hopped into the passenger seat and lifted Muhammad—kicking and screaming—onto her lap.

Decker took off in a swirl of dust. Just before cutting a hard right down a side street, he glanced in the rearview mirror—Holtz had run out of the courtyard and was looking right at them.

"Ha! Smoked his ass, didn't we!" said Decker.

Jessica was too busy with Muhammad to respond; the kid's tantrum showed no signs of abating.

Keeping one eye on the road, Decker reached down to the floor of the car and retrieved Muhammad's pacifier. It was covered in gray dust.

He tried to blow the dust off the pacifier, but that didn't do any good. So he wiped it on his pants. It still looked dirty, so he popped it in his mouth and sucked it clean.

"Dude, here." He handed the pacifier to Muhammad, who grabbed it eagerly, stuck it in his mouth, and started sucking as if his life depended on it.

22

As Val Rosten escorted him out of the US embassy in Bishkek, Mark announced that he needed to use the bathroom.

"It can't wait?" asked Rosten.

"No." Mark pointed to a bathroom just down the hall.

Rosten nodded.

Mark entered the bathroom, but Rosten followed him in. It was a small space—just two urinals and two stalls, one of which was large enough to accommodate a wheelchair. No windows.

Rosten glanced around, as though looking for possible escape routes. He gestured to the urinals. "Be quick. I got a car waiting."

Mark gestured to the stalls. "It's not going to be quick."

Rosten shot Mark a look that fell somewhere between confusion and revulsion. "I'll be right outside the bathroom door. Don't try my patience."

Rosten left.

Mark entered the handicapped stall, shut the door, fished his cell phone out of his front pocket, and sat down on the toilet seat without pulling down his pants.

He dialed a number. When Belek, the old Kyrgyz he played narde with every day, picked up, Mark said, "I'm going to need a favor."

After the bathroom break, Rosten led Mark out of the embassy, and into the parking lot, where a black Mercedes was idling with its front headlights on. Unlike Mark's Mercedes, which was parked nearby, this was the real deal—a long new S550. Mark recognized it as one of the cars the embassy used for official diplomatic functions.

Two men were already inside. A blond-haired tank of a man in a marine security guard uniform, armed with a waist-holstered pistol, sat in the front passenger seat; a younger guy in khaki slacks and a pinstriped oxford drove. Rosten and Mark got in the back.

"All right, Sava. Where to?"

Mark gave the driver the address for his condo.

It was quiet and warm inside the car, and the leather seats were comfortable. But Mark could tell it was windy outside by the way the people on the dark streets were walking with their heads down and their hands tucked into their coat pockets.

"Turn here," he said, when the black silhouette of the hospital opposite his condo loomed before them. A few patients bundled in heavy overcoats were wandering around the dimly lit park behind the black hospital gates. "Stop at the building up on the left, next to the green door."

"So you had the kid at your place this whole time?"

"No, he's not here."

"Where is he?"

"At a safe house in Bishkek. But I won't be able to get him until I retrieve my iPod from my place."

"What do you need your iPod for?"

"The people I hired to guard Muhammad won't recognize me. But they've been told to release the child to anyone who provides the proper codes."

"Codes that are stored on this iPod?"

"Yeah."

"You don't remember the codes?"

"No. They're numeric."

"Why the iPod? Why not your phone?"

"Because that's the way I did it."

"I'll go up with you." Rosten gestured to the armed marine security guard. "He will too."

"Be my guest."

The Mercedes pulled to a stop outside Mark's place. Mark, Rosten, and the marine security guard climbed out.

"Wait here. We'll just be a minute," Rosten said to the driver.

Mark led them up the narrow staircase, which had recently been painted pale yellow—a color that Daria had picked out. The walls were bumpy, the result of too many bad repairs to the plaster over the years.

He opened the door to his condo with a key that he'd retrieved from his front pocket, flipped on the lights, and approached the digital keypad to the left of the door, intending to disable the burglar alarm. But he saw that it had already been disabled—which told him Daria had fled in a hurry. And likely not through the front door.

"My iPod's in the back."

The living room was still littered with paper printed with outlines of Middle Eastern countries.

"The kid was here," Rosten observed.

"For a while. Dammit."

"What?"

Mark approached his narde board. It was on the coffee table in front of the couch, which wasn't where he'd left it. The pieces had just been dumped on the board in one big pile.

Mark held up a piece that had been chipped. "Look at that," he said. "I brought this from Baku. Inlaid with teak, silver, and camel bone. Cost me a hundred and fifty bucks. Now it's a toddler toy."

Mark tossed the chipped narde piece back onto the pile and walked into the room he and Daria used as an office. Two desks faced each other—his, which he rarely used, was a mess; Daria's wasn't. His was closest to the door. Out of the corner of his eye, he saw Rosten pick up the chipped narde piece and examine it.

Mark opened his desk drawer. He sensed that the marine security guard was right behind him, watching.

With his right hand, he pulled out his iPod Touch and the small headset that was plugged into it; at the same time, with his left hand he palmed a small leather wallet-like case that contained three forged passports. Because he'd positioned his body in such a way that it blocked his left hand from the gaze of the marine security guard, who was focused on the iPod anyway, Mark was able to pocket the passports without attracting notice.

One of the passports was Azeri, one Turkish, and one British; he'd picked them all up recently, as a result of his work for CAIN. Two credit cards accompanied each passport.

All three identities were just notional covers—good enough for commercial travel, but not backstopped nearly enough to withstand any real scrutiny.

Mark walked back into the living room.

"We ready?" asked Rosten.

Mark walked to his balcony door. A Kyrgyz cop car had pulled up a few feet behind the black embassy Mercedes on the street below. "This shouldn't be open," he said. He closed the door and locked it. "OK, let's blow."

After Mark reset the burglar alarm, he and Rosten trudged back down the narrow flight of stairs. Out on the street they were greeted with a blast of wind and the smell of wet oak leaves rotting in the street gutter. The marine security guard opened the rear door of the idling Mercedes for Mark.

Suddenly sirens started sounding.

Two cops piled out of the Kyrgyz cop car and started running toward Mark.

A second Kyrgyz cop car, closely followed by a third, barreled down the one-way street, going the wrong way.

The Kyrgyz cops—both fit older guys—charged Mark. One had his gun drawn. The other carried a set of handcuffs.

The cop with the gun called out Mark's name and ordered him to stop.

"What's going on, Sava!" said Rosten, his voice wary.

Speaking rapid-fire Kyrgyz, the lead cop explained that the police were there to arrest Mark. Rosten couldn't understand a word, so Mark translated while allowing himself to be handcuffed.

"No," said Rosten. "No, Sava. No. I'm not letting you walk off like this."

"I have some outstanding parking tickets. It's probably that."

"You think you're pretty smart, don't you Sava?"

"Parking tickets in Kyrgyzstan are no joke."

Rosten put his hand on the elbow of the man who'd handcuffed Mark. "You're not going anywhere." He turned to the marine guard. "A little help, here?"

As the marine closed in, three more Kyrgyz cops jumped out of the two cop cars that had just screeched to a stop in front of the Mercedes.

Rosten pointed a finger at Mark. "You tell them that if they don't release you now, they're going to have a diplomatic incident on their hands."

Mark turned to the cops and said in Kyrgyz, "This guy is crazy. Watch for weapons, and don't let him get close."

The Kyrgyz with the gun shouted for Rosten to back off.

"I think he's intimating that you're interfering with an arrest," said Mark.

The three Kyrgyz cops who'd just arrived formed a wall between Mark and the marine guard. Rosten stood behind them, glaring furiously at Mark.

The marine pulled out his wallet to show some identification to the Kyrgyz cops, but he was ignored. The cops pushed past Rosten and led Mark to one of the waiting patrol cars.

Rosten pulled out his black diplomatic passport. "I'm a diplomat, get it? If you take him, there's going to be hell to pay." He repeated the same words in Arabic, but the Kyrgyz cops didn't understand him.

"I'll probably be able to resolve this pretty quickly," said Mark. "I'll call you when I know what the deal is."

"Up yours, Sava. You're not fooling anyone." Rosten turned to the marine. "Get in the car. We're following him."

The marine did as instructed, but before the Mercedes could pull out, one of the Kyrgyz cops drove up and blocked it from moving. The guy behind the wheel of the Mercedes laid on the horn and held up his middle finger, but the cop was unmoved.

Another Kyrgyz cop helped Mark into the police car that was pointing the right way down the street.

As they drove away, lights flashing and siren blaring, Mark could see Rosten staring him down. He'd made an enemy, of that there was no doubt. But he also sensed he'd been able to preserve—barely—his position with the CIA's Central Eurasia Division while still remaining loyal to Daria. On balance, he'd done all right, he thought.

"Thanks," he said to the Kyrgyz cop.

As soon as they'd turned onto the busy Kiev Street, the cop tossed a set of keys back to Mark.

"The one for the cuffs is the small silver key."

"I got it."

"Where do you want to go?"

Mark glanced behind him as he unlocked the cuffs. "Here's fine."

23

Mark walked to the Shanghai. The place was empty inside—except for Belek, the old Kyrgyz, who was sitting in the back at one of the narde tables. The buffet station in the center of the restaurant had been cleared of everything except some rice noodles and steamed dumplings; Mark knew they would be recycled for lunch tomorrow.

Mark approach Belek, offered a brief nod of acknowledgment, and sat down across from him. The old man's brown sport coat was fraying at the elbows, and the blue wool sweater he wore beneath it was pilling. He had the narrow and high-bridged nose of a Caucasian, but his dark brown eyes were almond-shaped, with epicanthic folds that made them look Chinese.

A cup of Chinese tea sat before him.

"Thank you," said Mark.

Belek smiled. The last time Mark had seen that happen was when the Uzbek had set the record for consecutive narde losses.

"Your business is always appreciated," said Belek. "Even on short notice."

Mark had first met Belek five months earlier, on the same day a powerful Kazakh senator had requested an emergency meeting with CAIN. Because Decker and other CAIN operatives had been busy at the time, Mark had asked Serena Bamford for the name of someone local who might be able to help.

Bamford had given him Belek's name. The former chief of the Bishkek police department and older brother of the current chief, Belek had brokered a deal between CAIN and the Bishkek police department. That deal had been followed by others.

It was only after working together for a month that Mark and Belek had discovered their mutual interest in narde.

Mark pulled his iPod out of his front pocket. "I'll transfer the funds now." He knew he could pick up free Wi-Fi reception from the fancy coffee shop next door.

"There is no rush."

"Actually, there is. That's why I asked to meet. I need a flight out of the country. I can't go through the military or civilian airport at Manas."

Leaning back in his seat, Belek frowned and cupped his tea with both hands. "This embassy official you wanted to escape from. Will he cause trouble for the police?"

"He'll try to, but he won't know the right people to cause real trouble. He doesn't know Bishkek."

Mark doubted that Bamford, or any other Agency assets in Bishkek, would try too hard to help Rosten. They'd make a show of trying to, but it would be just that—a show.

"When inquiries are made . . ."

"Tell whoever is making them that I was processed for multiple parking ticket violations and released."

Belek's eyes fixed on Mark. They were calm eyes—probing and observant. Eventually, he said, "This flight. When do you need it?"

"Now."

"Where will you be going?"

Mark told him. It was a bit of a crazy move on his part, but he had the money, and the time, and Bamford had asked him to take the fight out of her station. Besides, it would be awfully nice to get out of Bishkek for a while.

He'd think of it as a vacation.

"Can you drive to Osh?" asked Belek.

Osh, the second largest city in Kyrgyzstan, was only a hundred and eighty miles south of Bishkek as the crow flies, but twice that far by road, and the roads were lousy.

"I was hoping for a helicopter. A police helicopter. This is a matter of some urgency."

Belek frowned again.

"The price is negotiable," added Mark. "I'd also consider it a personal favor."

The Kyrgyz were a tribal people. Most were descendants of nomads who used to wander the mountains, moving from place to place as they sought out good grazing grounds for their livestock. Some were still nomads. A culture that prioritized protecting and promoting the members of your extended family and friends had developed as a result; helping your brother meant your brother would help you, and together, with luck, you both might survive.

Mark knew he wasn't—by any stretch of the imagination—a member of Belek's inner circle; they'd only known each other for five months after all. In that time, though, he'd never betrayed Belek's trust. More important, Belek had invited Mark and Daria to his home for dinner two months earlier. They'd broken bread with Belek and his family.

By doing so, Mark knew that he had at least been afforded the status of a respected ally. A request for help would not be taken lightly.

"Will this bring harm to my brother?" asked Belek.

"No. They want me. Once I'm gone, no one will care about the means by which I left. Only that I'm gone."

"You speak of your government."

"People in it."

Belek nodded, then picked up his cell phone—an older flip model.

As Belek dialed, Mark felt a little dirty. When he'd first met Belek, he hadn't known that he'd need to rely on the old Kyrgyz like this. But he hadn't been playing narde every day just for fun either.

He'd been using friendship as a tool, as a way to recruit a potential asset. The truth was, he viewed almost everyone he met as a potential asset. It was a way of interacting with people that had become ingrained in him after twenty years with the CIA.

Still, despite it all, he genuinely liked Belek. And if he'd used the man, well, Belek had used him in return.

24

Kyrgyzstan

"John, baby. Listen to me. We've got to stop soon. He's going to get a rash if we don't change this diaper. It's not fair to him."

Having finally tired himself out from all the crying, Muhammad had fallen asleep in Jessica's arms shortly after they'd pulled away from Decker's house.

"I know."

Decker's phone had been ringing like crazy. All the calls had been from Holtz. Threatening. Bribing. Yelling. Decker had never picked up, but he'd listened to the messages.

Had Holtz really seen him when they'd been pulling away?

It had been dark out. He hoped there was still a chance he could persuade Holtz that Jessica had been the only one at the house.

But how to explain Muhammad's screaming? Holtz had to have heard the child. And then there was the slashed tire . . .

Decker turned to Jessica. "Do you think you'd be strong enough to slash a tire?"

"John."

"You're pretty strong. The knife bounces off the rubber if you don't stab hard enough, but I bet you could do it."

"I'm serious. We have to get food and clean clothes for Muhammad. And diapers."

Jessica spoke quietly because Muhammad was on her lap, asleep, his head resting on her chest. Her cheek was touching

Muhammad's hair. At first she'd seemed awkward around him, but once his tantrum had subsided, it was as though she'd always known him.

"I think he wears pull-ups," Decker said after pausing to consider the matter.

"What?"

"They're like diapers, but for older kids. I remember them from when I had to babysit my nephew a few years ago."

"John."

Damn, thought Decker. He didn't want to lose his job. He had a pretty good gig going with CAIN. "We'll stop soon."

They were speeding east out of the city, toward Lake Issyk Kul. The farther he could get from Bishkek, the better, he figured. He planned to shack up in one of the lake resort towns for the night—Cholpon-Ata would do fine. Given the season, he knew there would be plenty of vacant hotel rooms.

His thoughts turned back to Holtz.

Bailing on the military flight home right when the business with Muhammad was going down—that must have been what tipped Holtz off. But how had Holtz known to come looking for him at the house?

Decker considered the fact that he was using a cell phone that had been supplied by CAIN. And a Ford Explorer that had been supplied by CAIN. And that Holtz was kind of anal about keeping track of his employees. It was entirely possible, maybe even likely, that Holtz had put a tracker on the car or the phone or both.

He glanced behind him in the rearview mirror. No one was behind them. "We'll stop in Tokmok," he said. He put a hand on her knee, trying to be reassuring. "It's a big town. There'll be places to buy supplies."

"How long?"

"A half hour or so."

"OK."

And while they were there, they'd ditch the Explorer, thought Decker. He'd find someplace to park it and leave his phone in the dash compartment. From Tokmok they'd be able to hire a car to take them farther east.

25

Delhi, India

"I'm telling you, this place is driving me *crazy*."

Thirty-three-year-old Rad Saveljic spoke loudly into his cell phone.

"Did you hear back from Sunoco?" asked his fiancée.

"Have I told you about the monkeys?" asked Rad, ignoring her question.

"Ah, yeah. You told me about the monkeys."

"Did I tell you they bite? One started following me last night."

"Weird."

"*Really* weird."

The driver of the motorized three-wheeled rickshaw Rad was in cut off a guy riding a scooter. What the hell, he thought. Even in Elizabeth, New Jersey—his hometown—that would have been a risky move.

"What about Sunoco?" asked his fiancée.

"I talked with the New York office—they won't do a phone interview." Rad was a project manager for the oil company BP. But ever since BP had assigned him to India, he'd been looking for a new job. So he'd applied to Sunoco, hoping he'd be offered a position somewhere closer to home. He missed his fiancée, Mets games, decent cable TV, and his local hot dog stand. He supposed India was fine if you were an Indian, but he wasn't.

"What, do they expect you to fly back to New York just for a first interview?"

"I don't know what they expect. All they said was to contact them when I'm back in the States, so maybe something will come of it eventually. How was your day?"

"It's just started. It's morning here, remember? I figured I'd call before it got too late there."

"Oh, yeah. Sorry, I thought it was later. How was yesterday?"

As his fiancée chattered away, Rad watched in horror as his rickshaw driver passed within a foot of a cluster of women standing over hot vats of road tar. The smoky wood fires under the vats looked eerie in the shadows of the night. Nearby, two other women were digging out a pothole with a single shovel—one of the women gripped the shaft of the shovel, while the other held on to a rope tied to the shovel handle. By the side of the road, women were using hammers to break big rocks into little rocks. Two men who looked like supervisors were standing around doing nothing.

I gotta get out of here, Rad thought.

An orange Tata truck a few feet in front of him spewed a toxic black plume of exhaust into his face. The back of the truck had been painted with bloodred flowers and decorated with strings of shiny beads that were dancing maniacally all around. Everyone was honking their horns.

A few minutes later the rickshaw stopped in front of a three-story, turn-of-the-century British mansion that sat behind a tall wrought-iron fence. The driver announced that they had reached their destination.

"Listen," said Rad, interrupting his fiancée. "I gotta go. They're waiting for me inside. I'll call you tomorrow."

"OK. Enjoy your dinner."

"It's gonna suck."

"Love you. Miss you."

"Love you too, hon."

Rad Saveljic eyed the salad on his plate with suspicion. Rule number one when traveling—*don't eat uncooked greens.* He'd learned that lesson the hard way on a three-day trip to Mexico with his fiancée the year before.

But he was in the home of an Indian member of Parliament. And this MP in particular was a powerful man, with ties to many of the local construction firms. If BP wanted their new offices in Delhi to get built within the next hundred years, they needed the MP on their side. Also, it was a late dinner—Rad was used to eating at seven—so he was starving.

Which is why, instead of pushing his plate away, he reluctantly lowered his fork, skewered a fresh tomato slathered with a dressing he didn't recognize, smiled, and said, "Looks great."

Several of the other guests, including Rad's boss at BP—a fifty-year-old American of Indian descent—concurred and for the next five minutes the room was filled with the sound of silver clinking and people making small talk.

Rad figured they would get down to business after dinner. That was when his boss would bring up what the MP might want in return for helping to smooth the way for the office development BP wanted to build in downtown Delhi. It would be a pretty basic pay-to-play deal, he was sure. Nothing Rad hadn't seen, and even helped negotiate, dozens of times while helping his father manage and expand his gas stations in New Jersey. You buttered up the right people, then you got whatever permit, or waiver from the department of environmental protection, you needed.

"Ah, a vindaloo!" exclaimed Rad's boss as a woman in a sari brought out a big steaming pot of what looked to Rad like a stew. Next came a pot of beef curry, followed by a plate of tandoori chicken.

“Wow, this all smells so delicious,” said Rad. As people began serving themselves, he ventured to ask, “Is one of the dishes less spicy than the others?”

“Oh, the vindaloo is not spicy at all,” said the MP. “I would suggest it to you.”

So Rad scooped a healthy portion of the vindaloo onto his plate. A minute later, he took a big bite of something he thought was pork.

The pain started in his mouth, but then radiated up to his eyes and into the back of his head. His throat burned and started to constrict involuntarily. For a second, he worried he might pass out.

He grabbed for his glass of water, and downed half of it, but that almost seemed to make things worse, so he grabbed a piece of the naan bread and stuffed it in his mouth.

“You like the vindaloo?” asked the MP.

Rad held up a finger as he tried to compose himself. Twenty seconds later, in a low croak that could barely be heard over the laughter that had erupted at the table, he said, “Delicious, but a bit spicier than I expected.”

“Rad’s still getting used to the ways of the subcontinent,” Rad’s boss explained. He gave Rad a patronizing pat on the shoulder.

Rad’s eyes were watering. He heard more laughter. In the center of the table, a lit candle, in the shape of a lotus blossom, floated in a brass bowl that had been filled with water. The candle seemed to be spinning but Rad wasn’t sure whether it was really spinning or he was just losing his mind. He looked up. A wall hanging adorned with elephants was also spinning.

He blinked. “I’m going to have to excuse myself,” he said. “I’ll just be a moment. The bathroom?”

“Just down the hall,” said the MP, pointing. “I’m sorry, I’m afraid I misjudged your palate.”

“No problem, no problem at all,” said Rad. “I just need a minute.”

Rad found the bathroom. The pain was subsiding, only to be replaced by anger. That son-of-a-bitch MP completely suckered me, he thought. *The vindaloo is not spicy at all.* Misjudged your palate, my ass. He knew what he was doing.

Hell of a joke.

26

The Yakovlev jet that was waiting for Mark in Osh was an old Soviet clunker that had originally been built in the 1970s for regional travel. It was now owned by a Kazakh air charter company that the police force in Bishkek used with some frequency.

Mark had flown on similar planes on many occasions and appreciated the facelift that the charter company had recently given this plane; instead of fraying vinyl seats with sharp metal springs poking out of them, he found two rows of reasonably comfortable captain's seats. And whereas the original Yakovlev had almost certainly provided nothing in the way of in-flight entertainment, this one had been outfitted with a single small LCD monitor, along with satellite Wi-Fi throughout the cabin.

The LCD monitor didn't work, but the Wi-Fi did. Mark used it to contact Daria, communicating via a series of near-instant draft messages posted to a mutually accessible Gmail account.

You OK?

Fine. Where is he?

With D.

D?! As in . . .

Yes, that D.

I thought YOU were getting him?

I was at the embassy. Don't worry. He's safe, hidden. It's better this way. They suspected me. I heard you got picked up.

Yeah, but I ditched them.

That's my gal, thought Mark. He wanted to ask where she was now, but thought it better that he didn't know. He read Daria's next message.

Should I come get him from D?

Mark had to think about that. At this point, a transfer from Decker to Daria would just complicate matters, he decided.

No.

Why were you at the embassy?

Ordered there.

Why do they want him?

They won't say.

Then screw them.

That's what I told them. Didn't go over well.

Thank you. Thank you.

Mark smiled as he read those words, struck by a realization he thought was funny.

He liked to think of himself as an adept manipulator, a spy's spy who'd learned the hard way all the various methods that could be used to bend people to his will—bribes, the threat of an embarrassing revelation, an appeal to ego, to a higher calling, or even just to basic human decency. But Daria had proved to be his equal or better in the bending-people-to-her-will department.

He recalled how she'd interrupted his narde game not even twelve hours earlier and had pitched him on a scaled-down mission in about ten seconds. Now here he was, hundreds of miles away, on a mission that had rapidly been scaled up into who knows what.

And the funny thing was, he didn't even mind. At least not now; he'd minded a bit when he'd had to forfeit the narde game. He typed his next message.

Hope to learn more tomorrow. Stay hidden, so you can't be questioned. Maybe they will think you have him, will take pressure off D. I won't contact you again until I have this thing figured out.

Are you still at the embassy?

No.

They let you go?

Define let.

Where are you?

Next question.

Daria didn't respond for a minute, then replied,

OK, I guess it's better I don't know. Be safe.

You too.

PART II

BAHRAIN

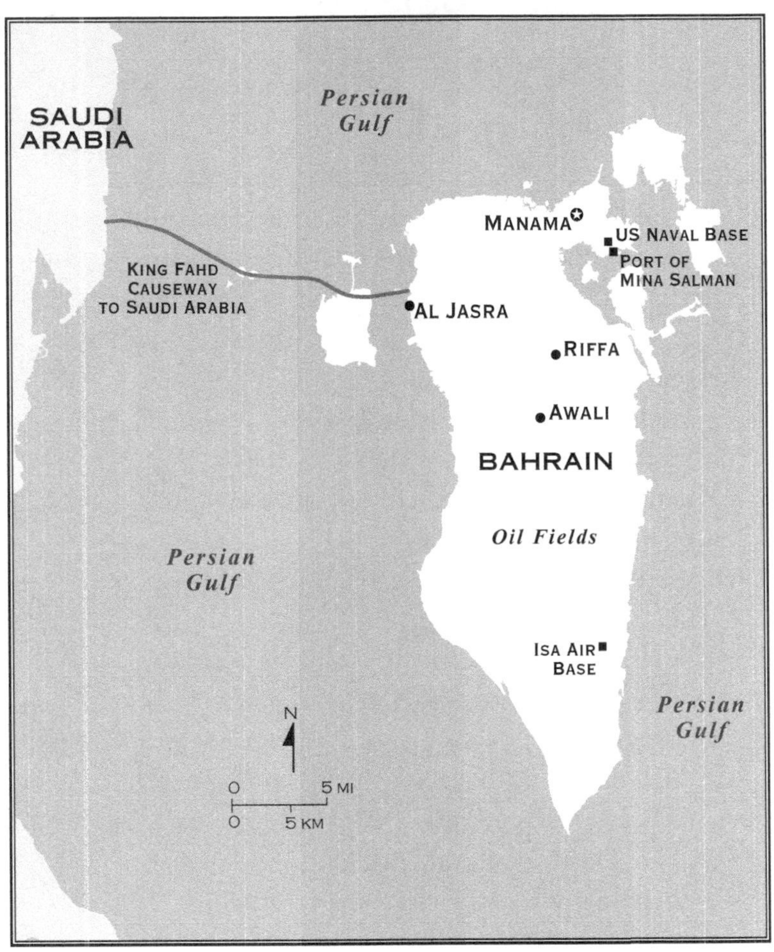
Persian Gulf
SAUDI ARABIA
MANAMA
US NAVAL BASE
PORT OF MINA SALMAN
KING FAHD CAUSEWAY TO SAUDI ARABIA
AL JASRA
RIFFA
AWALI
BAHRAIN
Oil Fields
Persian Gulf
ISA AIR BASE
Persian Gulf
N
0 5 MI
0 5 KM

27
Bahrain

Mark touched down in Bahrain at seven in the morning.

He used his British passport to pass through customs without having to bother with a visa, exchanged money, bought three more prepaid cell phones—though his iPod was rigged like Daria's, he didn't want to be dependent on Wi-Fi—and then called the embassy in Bishkek.

"You'll never guess where I am," he said, after being transferred to Rosten's cell.

"It damn well better be on the way to the embassy. I spoke with Kaufman, and he spoke with the director, and—"

"Bahrain!"

"What?"

"I'm in Bahrain, just touched down. It's nice here, Val."

Mark was standing outside the main airport terminal. It was sunny out. Fellow travelers were milling all around him. He was tired, but he'd been able to sleep for a few hours on the plane. Maybe he'd try to find someplace where he could eat breakfast outside, he thought; take advantage of the good weather.

He wished he'd brought his sunglasses with him.

"You're in Bahrain? Now?" Rosten sounded incredulous, as though he hadn't heard Mark right.

"I figured, that's where the kid was from, so if I wanted to know more about him, why not just come here, show the local cops a picture of Muhammad, and ask them to figure it out?"

"You didn't. Tell me you didn't do that."

"Not yet, but I intend to. And if they can't or won't help, I'll post photos of Muhammad all over Manama myself if I have to."

Bahrain's capital—Manama—lay just a few miles south of the airport, on the largest island of the Bahraini archipelago, which itself was situated on the western edge of the Persian Gulf. The airport was located on the second largest island in the archipelago, and the two islands were connected by a bridge.

"You're determined to flush your life down the toilet on this, aren't you?"

"Calm down."

"Because that's what you're doing."

"I'm calling your bluff, Val."

"I'm not bluffing."

"Well, regardless, I've listened to too much BS to feel comfortable just handing the boy over and trusting you to do the right thing. I need to know what's going on, and then together we can make a call."

"We'll find you down there, Sava."

Mark scratched the three-day stubble on his chin. It was beginning to itch. "I don't doubt you could. But, you know, after the reception I received at the embassy last night, I put a few contingency plans in place. So finding me won't mean you find the kid. Or end this." He listened to Rosten breathe heavily into the phone for a while, then said, "I'm not going to wait around all day, Val. You've got two more seconds to decide."

Rosten told Mark that he'd call him back after conferring with the director of the CIA.

"Actually, how about I call you back," said Mark. "Say in a half hour."

Mark tossed the phone he'd been using into a nearby garbage can. Then he hopped in a cab.

What a relief to be out of Bishkek, he thought, as he was being driven into Manama. The last time he'd been here, some ten years earlier, he'd been working with Near East on an arms trafficking op; it had been the height of the summer, when temperatures of a hundred and twenty degrees Fahrenheit were common. But it currently felt like a balmy eighty degrees or so. How pleasant.

He had the cabbie drop him off in the diplomatic section of Manama. A gentle breeze from the Persian Gulf wafted through the canyons that cut between the gleaming skyscrapers. Mark stuck his hands in his front pockets and began to walk, feeling remarkably relaxed about the whole situation. He'd dealt with CIA crap like this before. All the posturing and bluffing usually didn't amount to much. It would all work out.

In the meantime, he was going to enjoy Bahrain.

The main island was just thirty-five miles long and some ten miles wide. The country's culture had been defined by tact and restraint—at least until the uprising had started. While vulgar upstarts in Dubai built indoor ski areas and goofy islands shaped like palm trees, Bahrainis had built a thriving financial sector. While the Saudis to the west choked their citizens with a repressive religious regime, the king of Bahrain talked of allowing religious freedom, and even followed through on some of the talk. And while the Iranians to the north thrived on confrontation with the United States, the Bahrainis had developed deep ties to the Americans—especially to the US Navy.

Mark recalled that on the cab ride from the airport, the cabbie had actually switched on a real meter! True, the same cabbie had then tried to impose a dubious surcharge over the metered fare, but this was a small insult compared to what Mark had come to expect in Bishkek.

To be sure, he knew the island was no paradise, especially now; in the airport, he'd read that two anti-government protestors had been killed in a skirmish with the police just the day before. But Bahrain, even on the brink of revolution, was still a far cry from the third world.

He walked a few more blocks, then stopped at a Cinnabon, where he ordered a coffee and a cinnamon roll with extra frosting. He took a seat at one of the yellow metal tables that had been set up outside and ate his roll while basking in the warm breeze. After a full half hour had passed, he called Rosten back.

"OK, Sava. We'll deal." Rosten sounded more resigned than angry.

"Good news."

"You're not making any friends at Langley, though."

"What's going on, Val?"

"How familiar are you with the political situation in Bahrain?"

"Familiar enough."

Mark knew that Bahrain was a monarchy, one that had been ruled by the same Sunni Muslim royal family for hundreds of years. The problem was that most Bahrainis were Shia Muslims. The Shias—or Shiites, as they were sometimes also called—weren't happy about that arrangement.

Not happy at all.

"Good. Then I'll make this simple. Muhammad is a Sunni."

"Muhammad is a two-year-old."

"A two-year-old who was born to a Sunni family. For political reasons, he was kidnapped by a group of Shias. We got involved, in a way that—in retrospect—might not have been the best call on our part. But now we want to help reunite the kid with his extended family in Bahrain."

"His parents really are dead?"

"Yes."

"How'd they die?"

"Let's just say it wasn't from natural causes. And no, the Agency had nothing to do with it."

"Huh."

"This is what you wanted, right? To know you were doing the right thing for the boy? Well, here's your opportunity. You get to reunite the kid with his family. So pat yourself on the back, Sava. I've arranged—"

"Back up a bit—kidnapped for political reasons?"

"The specifics involve issues you don't need—and probably don't want—to know about."

"How and when was he kidnapped?"

"I'm going to try to arrange for you to meet with someone who was taking care of Muhammad before the Shias kidnapped him. He should be able to provide whatever proof you need to convince you that the child really belongs with him." Rosten paused, as if expecting Mark to weigh in. When Mark didn't, he added, "The only thing I require in return is that you *not* mention the CIA's role in this other than to confirm that, once we learned you had the child, we immediately worked to facilitate the process of getting Muhammad back to his family."

"You've done nothing of the sort. You were complicit in kidnapping the boy and trying to shuffle him off to an orphanage over a thousand miles away from his homeland."

"It's a complicated situation, Sava."

"I'm sure it is."

"In a complicated part of the world. Bahrain is a tinderbox. We're doing our best."

"I'm sure you are."

Mark wasn't being sarcastic.

He knew that the CIA was capable of doing some pretty awful things—but never just for the hell of it. If they'd helped the Shias in Bahrain steal Muhammad, it was almost certainly because someone at Langley had thought—wrongly or rightly—that a greater good was being served by doing so.

Rosten said, "Listen, I can't go into specifics, but I can say this—we've backed the royal family in Bahrain for years. They've been good to us, and we've been good to them. But the Shias outnumber the Sunnis on this island two-to-one and have shit for power. That can't last forever. They're going to fight it out at some point."

Rosten was probably right about that, Mark thought. The Sunni-Shia split, akin to Christianity's Catholic-Protestant division, was at the heart of why Iraq, and then Syria, had devolved into civil war. Why not Bahrain?

The thing that got Mark was that the original cause of the schism—a disagreement over who would succeed the prophet Muhammad—was a dead issue. Dead, in the sense that everyone involved—all the Sunni caliphs and Shia Imams who claimed they had a right to rule—had died long ago. Granted, the Shias didn't see it that way, but no one had seen their last claimant for over a thousand years, so Mark was counting him as dead.

Now the two groups were mainly just fighting for power in the region.

"Listen," said Rosten. "This is the story I need you to sell: The Shias kidnapped Muhammad. We found out about it and were going to retrieve him ourselves, but then the Saudis beat us to it. At which point you interfered, not knowing that the Saudis were trying to help the kid."

"Were they?"

Ignoring the question, Rosten said, "You're working for us now, just trying to reunite Muhammad with his family."

"I assume, given that the Shias thought it worth their time to kidnap him, that Muhammad is one of the royals?"

"Well, aren't you clever."

"So you and I form an alliance, Muhammad gets to go back to his family, the Bahraini royals are happy, the Saudis are happy. But the Bahraini Shias—and probably the Iranians—are pissed because the plug gets pulled on whatever damn cockeyed deal you tried to cut with them."

Mark knew that any dispute between Sunnis and Shias was never just a local issue. It was inevitable that Iran, a Shia country, would be backing the local Shias, and that Saudi Arabia, a Sunni one, would stand behind the local Sunnis.

"Close enough. Minus the part about anyone being happy. We're all just reacting to a bad situation."

"Must be a really bad situation."

"The Shias are going to rule this island eventually, Sava. The Saudis will try to stop it, they'll send troops, but they'll be fighting a rearguard action. We were just trying to manage a crisis and stay ahead of the curve. Support the local Shias, but fend off Iran—just like we're doing in Iraq. I would think that would make a lot of sense to a guy who's been in the business as long as you have."

"Helping the Shias kidnap a two-year-old doesn't make any sense to me, but I don't have a problem selling your bullshit story to the Bahrainis if it means the kid gets to go back to his family. So who do I meet, and when?"

"I have to line it up—I had to know you were on board before I pulled the trigger. Wait for my call, it won't be long."

28

Delhi, India

Thank God for places like the Connaught Hotel, thought Rad Saveljic as a waiter brought him a late breakfast of French fries and coffee with cream.

After having dinner here last week with his boss and a few BP execs, Rad had taken to coming to the Connaught every day for breakfast. And he always got the French fries. He was especially appreciative of them this morning. Ever since last night's debacle with the spicy vindaloo and the fresh salad, his stomach had been cramping. The fries were just the sort of normal food his digestive system needed to get back on track.

Rad took a sip of his coffee and winced as his stomach tightened. He wished he could just stay here for the day. Conduct business from the lobby. Instead, in an hour, he was supposed to meet both his boss and the owner of a local construction firm at the future site of a new BP office building.

It was peaceful here, behind the high walls that surrounded the Connaught. Hidden away in this elegant refuge, he could watch BBC at the bar, enjoy a quiet dinner while reading the *International Herald Tribune*, or surf the web without being jostled by the sweaty crowds on the street.

He used his phone to check his Facebook account. Back in the States, he'd never been much of a fan of Facebook, but now he loved even the stupid inspirational photos people posted, because they reminded him of home. He pushed the Like button on a friend who'd posted a picture from a New York Giants' game where the Giants were up 21-10 against the Eagles, then clicked on a newspaper article in his feed; the mayor of Elizabeth, New Jersey, had been indicted for corruption. No shocker there, thought Rad, laughing to himself as he forced himself to eat a French fry.

Thinking about New Jersey put Rad in a good mood, and made him temporarily forget about the rumbling in his stomach. Maybe India wasn't *that* bad, he thought.

The day before, they'd driven around the India Gate—which he gathered was Delhi's version of the Arc de Triomphe. They'd eaten lunch at a place where the lattice windows had been sculpted out of marble. Pretty good stuff.

Rad was beginning to think that maybe Delhi was like New Jersey, in that, sure, it was crowded and corrupt, but not without its charms if you knew where to look.

The pollution was unbearable, though. Which, he thought, given that he was comparing it to New Jersey, really said something.

Rad looked up from his phone and out toward the front of the hotel, expecting to see some evidence of that gross pollution just beyond the hotel's tall, wrought-iron entrance gates. Instead what he saw was a man looking right at him; a man of modest stature, whose skin was a shade lighter than that of the average Indian; a man Rad was almost certain he'd seen earlier that morning, as he was leaving his apartment.

His apartment was a half mile away. And Delhi had a population of over sixteen million.

Strange coincidence, he thought.

29

Bahrain

Rosten called Mark back. Muhammad had been living with extended family in the house of his great-uncle prior to the kidnapping, he said. This great-uncle was eager to meet Mark and arrange for the return of the boy.

Mark popped the last of his second Cinnabon into his mouth and washed it down with the dregs of his coffee. "OK," he said, feeling a little sluggish. "Where do I go?"

Rosten told him everything he needed to know.

After he got off the phone, Mark wanted to shoot Daria an e-mail, to let her know where he was and what he'd learned about the boy, but he decided against it. Communicating via draft messages through their anonymous e-mail account was a good way to minimize the risk of being tracked or surveilled, but it wasn't an infallible method; to try to do so now would be to indulge in a personal pleasure at the risk of potentially compromising the op.

"Riffa," said Mark to the young, dark-skinned cab driver who'd pulled up in front of the Cinnabon store. "The Sheikh Isa Mosque."

There were many wealthy enclaves in Bahrain. Well-tended English gardens could be found in many villages on the west coast, and the Americans had all but taken over the eastern

Manama district of Juffair—but Riffa, located ten miles south of Manama, near the center of the island, was home to the wealthiest of the wealthy because that was where the royal family lived.

The cab driver gave Mark a long funny look. Mark wished he'd shaved on the plane; he figured he probably smelled too. The dress shirt he was wearing still had food stains on it from the day before, when he'd helped with Daria's stew.

Mark pulled open the rear door to the cab and slid inside. When the cabbie didn't start driving, Mark said in English, "Sorry, my Arabic stinks. Riffa? Mosque?"

"I'm Pakistani. I don't speak Arabic."

"Good."

"Many police are around Riffa."

"OK."

"The police are at checkpoints."

"Is that going to be a problem?"

The cabbie looked Mark over again. His expression made it clear that he didn't like what he saw. "Why do you want to go to this mosque?"

Mark pulled a wad of Bahraini dinars out of his front pocket—he'd exchanged five thousand dollars at the airport—and offered forty dinars, about a hundred dollars, to the cabbie.

"Perhaps we can say we are just driving through," the cabbie allowed.

Once they were out of downtown Manama and speeding south toward Riffa, the hatred many Shias harbored for the royal family was plain to see. Newly built apartment buildings and run-down shops were scarred with graffiti at ground level. Most of the graffiti was in Arabic, but some of it was in English: *Down with the King, Terrorism is a British Industry, US get out!* Bahraini security forces had tried to cross out the slogans with spray paint of their own, resulting in a nightmarish mess that conveyed little but mutual anger.

That anger was also evident in all the brick-paver sidewalks that had been ripped up—to be thrown at the police, the cabbie explained. Streets were charred with black marks where fires had been burning, further evidence of nightly conflicts, and blackened tires had been pushed to the sides of the road. Men in *thawbs*, the white robes that were common to the region, stood on rooftops, surrounded by rusted satellite dishes as they stared down with hostile expressions at the passing traffic. The remains of battered effigies, presumably representing the king, hung from a few lamp posts.

Mark began to feel the desert in a way he hadn't in Manama. The sun was intense and the land flat. Many of the cinderblock and stucco buildings were the color of sand. On the side roads leading off the main highway, he could see patches of barren desert.

Just past a tall clock tower on the outskirts of Riffa, red signs appeared that said REDUCE SPEED NOW and CHECKPOINT, STOP FOR INSPECTION in both Arabic and English. Beyond the signs, thick concrete barriers painted yellow with black arrows directed traffic into a single lane.

A Bahraini soldier greeted them. The cabbie produced his license and said he was just using the highway to take Mark to the oilfields south of Riffa.

The soldier looked Mark over for a moment, inspected his British passport, then waved them through.

On the other side of the checkpoint, a different world greeted them.

Blocky art-deco street lamps lined the right-hand side of the road, many of which were adorned with an image of the king near their base. Palm trees abounded, and unlike those Mark had seen outside Riffa—where many appeared to be struggling for lack of water—these were all healthy and green, as were the clusters of purple-flowered hedge bushes beneath them. The vibrant green of the neatly mowed grass between the hedges stood in striking contrast to the dusty sidewalks and sandy rubble-strewn lots he'd seen outside of Riffa.

High walls rose beyond the palm trees, on the other side of which the tops of stately villas were visible.

No way was this going to last forever, was all Mark could think. The royals might be able to hold off the hordes for a few more years, or maybe even a few more centuries, but eventually the barricades would fall. At which point, new wealthy and poor classes would emerge. And they'd be similar to the old classes, but at least they wouldn't be defined by religious affiliation.

The ivory-colored Sheikh Isa Mosque soon appeared on the left. Minarets topped by Islamic crescents rose high into the sky. It was big enough to accommodate thousands, but Mark had a feeling it rarely did. It was too uncluttered, too clean. His cabbie pulled into the parking lot.

"OK?"

"OK," said Mark. He slipped the guy another five dinars and stepped out of the cab.

30

Kyrgyzstan

The last time Decker had been to the Lake Issyk Kul resort town of Cholpon-Ata was in August.

His mind flashed to the lake scene back then: women in string bikinis, guys in board shorts, fat elderly Russian men lounging around in Speedos, jet skis, beer on the beach, concerts at night, ice cream vendors, and a big catamaran that he'd paid to take him and the woman he'd been with at the time out for an hour-long ride on the lake . . .

All that was over now; what remained was a long stretch of beach littered with bits of half-buried garbage.

The morning sand was cold and gravelly beneath his bare feet. Last night, via a brief e-mail communication with Mark, he'd learned Muhammad's name. Then they'd all stayed up too late—a result of the child's long afternoon nap—and slept in. Now Muhammad was running around on the beach.

"Hey, careful there, bud." Decker jogged over to an orange-and-yellow paddleboat that had been pulled up onto the sand; Muhammad was climbing on as if it were a jungle gym, jumping up and down on the seat and occasionally pulling at the wheel and pretending to drive as he sucked on his pacifier.

Although Decker was afraid the kid was going hurt himself, Muhammad looked like he was having fun and Decker didn't want to be a buzzkill.

The hotel had sold them a bag of beach toys—a little plastic bucket and shovel and a few sand molds in the shape of trucks—but Muhammad had rejected them.

"Hey, you want to dig a hole?" Decker picked up the plastic shovel and started digging in the sand. "Hey, Muhammad, check it out. Let's dig a huge hole."

Muhammad kept bouncing on the seat until he fell off, banged his head, and started to cry.

"See, buddy, that's what I'm talking about."

Decker picked Muhammad up and started bouncing him on his hip. The pacifier had fallen into the sand, so Decker scooped it up and did the suck-it-clean thing again. Once he had his pacifier back, Muhammad started squirming to be let down.

Decker put him on the sand next to the plastic shovel, but Muhammad headed for the paddleboat and started climbing on it again.

"You're a persistent little bugger, Muhammad, you know that?"

As Muhammad climbed on the paddleboat, Decker wondered how much longer all this was going to last. All Mark had said in their e-mail exchange last night was that he was working 24-7 trying to figure out what to do with the boy, and to hang tough.

Decker was worried about his dad, but didn't want to call home again until he could say he was on his way back to New Hampshire.

He sighed. Turning away from Muhammad for a moment, he looked back toward the hotel, wondering where Jessica was.

And that's when he saw Holtz.

31
Bahrain

Minutes after Mark arrived at the Sheikh Isa Mosque, a long white Cadillac Escalade pulled into the parking lot and came to a gentle stop a few feet in front of him. The driver got out and opened the back door. Mark climbed in.

The well-manicured greenery lining the side streets he was driven down suggested a peaceful, almost idyllic existence for the residents of Riffa. Mark remembered hearing that many considered Bahrain to be the original site of the garden of Eden; looking at the well-watered plants all around him—an oasis in the middle of a desert island—he could almost believe it.

They eventually turned into a wide driveway and pulled to a stop in front of a solid metal gate; the gate had been painted white and was the only break in a white wall that appeared to encircle an estate.

The driver of the Cadillac spoke into his cell phone and the gate swung open. Two soldiers, dressed in camouflage uniforms and carrying M16 assault rifles, waved the car through.

The two-story house in the center of the estate was large—maybe ten thousand square feet or so, Mark guessed—but not overly ostentatious. It was coral colored and stuccoed like most of the rest of the residential buildings in Bahrain. A wind tower rose up on the left-hand side, though Mark guessed it was more for ornament than function. The original wind towers, found throughout the Middle East, had been constructed to capture the wind that blew above the trees and channel it down into the living quarters below. But that had been in the days before air-conditioning.

Mark was pretty sure that the people who lived here had all the air-conditioning they needed.

32

Kyrgyzstan

Decker figured he could have tried to run when he saw Holtz—he'd spotted his boss from a couple hundred feet away, across the beach—but what was the point? If Holtz had been able to find him here, he'd be able to find him again no matter where he ran.

"What the hell do you think you're doing, Deck?" Holtz was staring right at Muhammad.

"What do you mean, buddy?"

"Don't 'buddy' me." Holtz walked right up to Decker. They were both big men, roughly the same height and weight, though much of the weight that Holtz—a former linebacker—carried was around his waist. "You know what I'm talking about. I came to see you in Bishkek and you ran out on me. And slashed my tire. What the hell was that all about?"

"I don't know what you're talking about."

"Yes, you do."

"I haven't been back to my house since before I went climbing."

"Bullshit." Holtz poked his finger into Decker's chest.

Decker just looked at his chest, and then at Holtz.

"I'm taking the kid," said Holtz.

"No can do, Bruce."

"This is way over your pay grade, Deck. I know Mark must have asked you to do him a favor, and I can appreciate that you guys are friends and that you owe him for what went down in Iran, but you have to back off on this one. And slashing my tire, man. That was bush league."

Decker deliberated for a moment and concluded there was no point in continuing to lie.

"How'd you find me? I ditched the car and my phone."

Holtz smiled. "You kept the key to the Explorer, though."

Decker's hand went to his front right pants pocket.

"I had a GPS transmitter wired to it," said Holtz. "Runs off the same battery that unlocks the car."

Decker smiled. "Bastard."

"Hey, I was doing it for your own protection. Now move. You've abducted a child that isn't yours and I'm taking him back."

"He's an orphan. He came from Daria's orphanage. Mark asked me to take care of him."

"I've been hired by our government—*our* government, Deck, the United States of America—to do a job. And I intend to do that job."

Holtz took a step toward Muhammad, who was oblivious to the discussion that had been going on. Decker put up his arm, blocking Holtz.

"No," said Decker. "I promised Mark."

"Take your hand off me now, Deck, or you're out of a job. Plus I'll blacklist you with DoD and the Agency."

Decker kept his hand in place. "You didn't bring any backup, did you?"

He and Holtz had gotten along pretty well over the time they'd known each other. They'd talked a lot of football, had played poker over beers . . . It occurred to Decker that this superficial familiarity had led Holtz to misjudge the situation.

"You don't scare me, Deck."

"It was a mistake not to have brought backup."

"I said, take your hand off me."

"Or?"

"Or nothing. But I'm still taking the kid."

Holtz pushed forward, prompting Decker to throw a fake punch with his left hand to Holtz's head. When Holtz ducked and blocked the blow with his right forearm, Decker threw all his weight and strength into a massive uppercut to Holtz's solar plexus. His fist connected with a thud and Holtz was thrown back a few feet, dazed but still standing.

Decker followed up with a chokehold that lifted Holtz off the ground and a leg sweep that sent him tumbling into the sand. He straddled Holtz on the ground, threw a handful of sand into his face, and then fired off two lightning punches to the gut, knocking the wind out of Holtz for a second time.

Muhammad noticed what was going on and started crying.

"Sorry, guy," Decker said to the boy as he flipped Holtz onto his belly.

Using the rough, frayed rope attached to the end of the paddleboat, Decker hog-tied Holtz as fast as he could. That done, he stood, pulled out the key to his Explorer, threw it down in the sand next to Holtz, and said, "I parked in Tokmok, at the gas station that's right off Route 365. You can catch a cab there for fifty bucks. In the meantime, I'll be taking your Jag."

So much for ever working for CAIN again, he thought.

Decker stuck his hands into Holtz's pocket and pulled out a set of keys. There was probably a tracking device on the Jag too, but he'd use the car to put some distance between him and Holtz in the next hour and then figure something else out.

"Hey, Muhammad! My man! We're going on another adventure, how about that?"

Muhammad looked apprehensive, but he didn't resist when Decker picked him up and began to jog toward the hotel. When Decker got to their room, he yanked open the door.

"Jess! We gotta blow."

At that point, Decker got a whiff of something that stank. His first thought was that maybe Jessica had done something she wanted to fess up to, but then he saw that the yellow polypropylene climbing shirt he was wearing was stained with something that looked—and smelled—like shit.

"Oh no, don't tell me," he said. He lifted Muhammad up off his hip at the same time Muhammad started to cry.

"What's going on?"

"We've got a problem."

"Ah . . . that really sucks," she said.

"It's not funny."

"I know." Jessica started laughing. Decker couldn't help but smile too.

"OK, it's a little funny."

Everything was so chaotic and awful—the crying, the shit, Holtz, Mark, and all this on top of his father, God he hoped his father was going to be OK—that it had swung around to being funny. The chaos of war he could handle, but when it came to a two-year-old and ailing father, he was out of his depth.

"Listen," said Decker. "Grab the pull-ups, we'll change him in the car. We gotta go."

33

Bahrain

A frail man with thin gray hair and a thick gray mustache sat at a table in the shade of a date palm tree, in a garden courtyard that abutted the side of the house with the wind tower. He wore dress slacks and a starched white shirt that was open at the neck. His brow was creased, his cheeks and the skin under his eyes drooped, and his ears and nose were old-man large. In front of him sat a glass of ice water that was wet on the outside from condensation. Behind him, louvered shutters had been closed over tall windows, leaving only the stained-glass fanlights above the windows exposed. A carved wooden door framed by intricate plaster molding opened from the house onto the garden.

"You may leave us," said the old man, without looking up.

The driver who'd picked Mark up gave a slight bow of his head and walked away.

The old man glanced briefly at Mark. "Please, have a seat." He spoke English with a British accent. "You may call me Abdullah. I am a cousin to the king and an uncle to the boy of whom we will speak. And you are?"

"Stephen McDougall," said Mark, giving the name that was on his British passport.

Abdullah's expression didn't change. He took a sip of his water.

Mark added, "Thank you for agreeing to meet with me."

"From what I have been told, I am the one who should be thanking you."

He looked more weary than thankful, thought Mark. And although his words suggested gratitude, his tone didn't. "And what is it you have been told?"

"That you have in your custody a relation of mine. A boy named Muhammad. And that you wish to right a grievous wrong that has been done to the boy and to my family. I am Muhammad's uncle. You may release him to me."

"What happened to Muhammad's parents?"

"They died in a car accident two months ago—an accident precipitated by a mob of Shia beasts throwing firebombs. Muhammad was in the car at the time."

"I'm so sorry."

"He has been raised here, by my family, ever since."

Mark looked around. The grounds were impeccable. Armed guards stood at different points along the perimeter fence. There was no sign of children's toys, or jungle gyms, or anything that might suggest a child lived here.

"And you wish to care for Muhammad now?"

Abdullah's gaze intensified but he didn't answer immediately. Mark got the impression that he was angry, and trying to hold himself back.

"What I wish to do, or not wish to do, is irrelevant." Abdullah raised his voice ever so slightly. "What is relevant is that you are in possession of a child who doesn't belong to you."

"I'm just trying to help."

"Bah." Abdullah dismissed Mark's claim with a wave of his hand.

"What's that supposed to mean?"

"It means, Mr. McDougall, that for as long as I have been alive my family has been friends with the Americans. And in our hour of need, this is how we are repaid?" Abdullah spoke with derision. "Yes, I know your American CIA friends tried to make an agreement with the Shias and it didn't work. And that now they lie. After Mubarak in Egypt I should not be surprised, but still, the depth of the betrayal is hard to fathom."

Choosing his words carefully, Mark said, "My government does not always send as clear a signal as perhaps it should. I understand your frustration."

"Do you? Do you know that the vast majority of Bahrainis, even the Shias, still support the king? Because he brings stability to the island?"

Abdullah's hands were trembling. Mark had the strange sense that the old man was now on the verge of tears.

"I'm sure he does," said Mark diplomatically.

"The people who protest like hooligans in the street, they are a small minority. Yet you Americans would hand Bahrain over to these ruffians?"

The passion with which Abdullah spoke unsettled Mark.

"I don't know anything about that. The only reason I'm here is to help reunite a boy with his family."

"Then I encourage you to do so. Now."

"I was told you would provide some documentation?"

Abdullah looked as though Mark had just insulted him, but then he glanced over his shoulder and nodded—at whom, Mark couldn't see. Moments later, a younger man with short-cropped black hair and eyes so dark they looked black appeared. He was dressed in a *thawb* robe and carried a leather-bound folder.

Abdullah spoke quickly in Arabic, prompting the younger man to produce a number of documents marked with official-looking stamps and flowing signatures.

"Muhammad's birth certificate." Abdullah slapped the piece of paper in front of Mark, followed by two more. "His mother's death certificate, and his father's death certificate. You will note that the names of the parents on the birth certificate are clear, as are the names on the death certificates. And that his surname clearly marks him as a member of the royal family."

Mark examined the documents. Though they were written in both Arabic and English and the information on the certificates corresponded to what Abdullah was telling him, Mark had no idea whether the documents were legit or not.

"What about photos of Muhammad with your family?"

Abdullah said something in Arabic to his helper, who promptly walked away. A minute later, a woman with long dark uncovered hair emerged from the house. She wore a stylish white ankle-length skirt, a matching long-sleeved blouse, and tasteful makeup. But she looked haggard, as though she'd been up all night on a bender and was now trying to pretend she wasn't painfully hungover. In her hand she held a small point-and-shoot digital camera.

Mark pegged her to be at least thirty years younger than Abdullah.

"This is my wife. She has been helping to care for Muhammad."

Abdullah's wife turned on her camera, clicked through a few photos, and then handed the camera to Abdullah. Abdullah, in turn, handed the camera to Mark.

"Here is my wife with Muhammad. This photo was taken just five days ago."

Mark examined the image. The boy in the photo did appear to be Muhammad. And the woman standing next to Muhammad in the photo was the same woman standing before Mark now. It was just the two of them in the photo, sitting next to each other on a couch. Mark took the liberty of clicking through a few more of the photos. Though he didn't recognize any of the people in them, they all appeared to have been taken at a recent party. Time stamps indicated the photos had indeed been taken just five days earlier.

It wasn't definitive evidence, Mark thought—images could be doctored. And it bothered him a bit that the photo of Muhammad and Abdullah's wife had been taken at a group event, when people who didn't know each other all that well might encounter each other, rather than just around the house. But big events tended to be when people took pictures.

Mark, thinking it was time to end this, handed back the camera and said, "OK, thank you for sharing that. Last thing—Muhammad keeps talking about a woman I believe is named Anna. Do you know who she is? Does Muhammad have a nanny?"

Abdullah's smile tightened and his Adam's apple bobbed as he swallowed. Speaking slowly, he said, "I think you misunderstand your role. You are not here to question. You are here to tell me how and when the boy will be delivered to his family. I have given you clear evidence that he belongs here." Abdullah stared Mark down. But after a long silence, he sighed, then said, "Yes, Muhammad has a nanny. But her name is not Anna."

Mark studied Abdullah. He noted how tightly the old man was clasping the glass of water, and observed the hint of tension in his jaw. The strain in Abdullah's voice had also been unmistakable. Mark sensed that he was a man under enormous pressure.

"What is her name?"

"Hasini Ahmed. She is his cousin. Recently she had a case of appendicitis, so for the past week she has been in a hospital in Manama recovering from her operation."

Over the years, Mark had grown increasingly confident of his ability to detect when someone was lying to him. Sometimes the signs were obvious—forced smiles, inability to make eye contact, a statement followed by a cough or some other covering gesture—but sometimes they weren't, and then he just had to rely on his gut. Other than exhibiting tension, Abdullah wasn't showing any obvious signs that he was lying.

But the old man was lying now. Of that Mark was certain.

Dammit, he thought. Why would Abdullah lie about something as basic as who the kid's nanny was?

The answer was obvious, of course—because divulging the identity of the real nanny would jeopardize the transfer of the child to Abdullah. Otherwise, there would be no reason to lie.

Dammit.

When it came to royal families, Mark figured Muhammad could do a lot worse than the one that ruled Bahrain. They were known, for the most part, for being reasonably enlightened, at least when compared to the other rulers in the region. Not so enlightened that they wouldn't torture political prisoners—they did—or censor the press and the Internet—they did that too—but they did allow people to vote for members of parliament, they didn't kill or imprison gays, women were permitted to drive, and people were generally free to practice whatever religion they choose—especially if you weren't a Shia.

So he wasn't opposed to handing Muhammad over to the royals. But he was opposed to being lied to.

Mark said, "This nanny. May I speak with her?"

"Unfortunately, no. There were complications with her operation."

"And you don't know anyone named Anna?"

"No. If you don't speak Arabic, perhaps you misunderstood what the boy was trying to say."

"I don't think so."

"Then he may have been trying to say something to you in English. He is being taught English at our local school. He goes every Sunday."

Mark got the idea that Abdullah was offering that bit of information as further evidence of his relationship to the child.

"Isn't he a little young for school?"

"Not too young to learn a language. At his age, the mind is like a sponge. This is the kind of opportunity we provide for the boy. Now speak to me of Muhammad and how you intend to return him to his family."

Mark considered his options. And what Daria would do in this situation. After a moment, he asked, "Can you make arrangements to fly Muhammad from Bishkek back to Bahrain?"

"Of course."

“Then I’ll have the boy transferred to your representative first thing tomorrow morning.”

“Why not now?”

“He’s not in Bishkek now.”

“Where is he?”

“With people I trust somewhere in the countryside, a good distance from the city, in hiding. I don’t even know myself exactly where. The reason for this is the boy’s own security, of course.”

“Of course.”

“It won’t take much time for me to reach my people and for them to bring the boy to the city, but it will take some. The roads are awful, and the country is large. I’ll have him brought to the lobby of the Hyatt Regency hotel in Bishkek at six tomorrow morning.” Mark checked his iPod. It was nine forty-five in the morning. “Will that give you enough time?”

“More than enough.”

“Bishkek is three hours ahead of Bahrain.”

“It will not be a problem.”

“The boy has no passport or documentation. I’d recommend a private plane.”

“I understand. And your arrangements. Would you care to make them from here?”

“I would not.”

34

Delhi, India

Rad Saveljic groaned as he clutched his stomach. Maybe it was cancer, he thought. Because he couldn't imagine how spicy food and a bad salad could make him feel this awful.

After breakfast at the Connaught, he'd caught a rickshaw to thc vacant Dclhi lot where the new BP office building would be located. Within minutes, he'd thrown up right in front of his boss. Then he'd thrown up again in the rickshaw he'd hired to take him back to his apartment. Then he'd dry heaved over the toilet for twenty minutes before stripping off his clothes and collapsing on the bed in his boxer shorts and undershirt.

Now, after trying to fall asleep for the better part of an hour as his stomach writhed, he threw the single cotton sheet off his body, stood up, and put his hand up to the wall-mounted air conditioner gurgling above his bed. He knew it. The air coming out of it wasn't cold, not cold at all!

The building superintendent had come over the day before and supposedly fixed the thing. For a while Rad had thought he'd detected slightly cooler air coming out of it, but now the air conditioner was functioning more like a heater—and a loud one at that.

It was early afternoon and it seemed hotter than it had been in days past. Ninety degrees at least, and this in November for crying out loud. The pollution seemed thicker, too. And even though it was the middle of the day, it was hotter inside than out. He felt as though he were in a steam room.

Rad was half-tempted to take a rickshaw right back to the Connaught Hotel and check himself in for the night. But that would cost him a hundred and seventy bucks. He'd already been spending too much on food at the Connaught.

Better to just crack a window, see if he could get a bit of a breeze going.

But then he'd have to worry about the monkeys.

They were all over the city, begging and stealing food, terrorizing little kids. The day he'd moved in, a gang of them had clustered in his backyard. At first, he'd thought they were cute. He'd even taken a picture of one of them and texted it to his fiancée. How cool is this! Monkeys! Then he'd tried to feed one of them half of an apple he'd been eating. The little bastard had snapped at his finger and seconds later a half a dozen other monkeys had gathered around him, screeching.

He'd been driven back inside his apartment. Shaking. They'd scratched at the rear door and windows. Ever since, he'd kept out of the back garden and made sure to keep all his windows and doors shut tight.

But it was so hot in here. Surely everyone in Delhi didn't keep their windows shut twenty-four hours a day. He'd overreacted. Reassuring himself that the monkeys weren't going to climb through his window, Rad slid off the bed, walked to a nearby double-hung window, unlocked it, and slipped the top part down. A puff of air—not a cool one, but cooler than the stale air in his bedroom at least—wafted across his face. He stood there for a minute, enjoying the light breeze and listening for monkeys.

He heard nothing.

Another open window would make the air flow even better, he thought—get a cross draft going. He walked into his living room, but none of the windows there would open. They'd either been painted shut or become swollen shut from the humidity. So he cracked the door that led out to the back garden—just a few inches—and made sure the screen door was locked.

Then he went back to bed. This time, he was able to fall into an uneasy sleep.

35

Bahrain

As a young operative, Mark had never felt much sympathy for those in the CIA old guard who'd sat behind their desks at Langley, mourning the end of the Cold War. At least with the communists, there had been a defined enemy—the Soviet Union—and an ideology—communism—to fight. Now there wasn't, which made things more complicated, so . . .

So adapt, Mark had thought. Yes, the world's morphed into a big chaotic cesspool of sectarian violence and intolerance. Deal with it or retire.

As he'd gotten older, though, he found himself sympathizing with the old guard more and more. Because the cesspool was starting to drive him crazy.

He rubbed his temples, his head spinning as he thought of the Sunnis and Shias and the royal family of Bahrain. The boy, though, what to do with the boy?

One option was to stop trying to figure it all out, declare victory, and hand Muhammad over the next morning as he'd already promised to do. The only problem with that plan was Daria. And what remained of his own conscience.

That old man had been lying.

Dammit.

"Where shall I drop you?" asked the Bahraini taxi driver who was bringing Mark back to Manama.

Mark considered his next move. It was only eleven in the morning; he had the whole day ahead of him. "What's the nearest big hotel?"

Mark checked into the Sheraton in downtown Manama, taking a room with a king bed on the fifteenth floor. It was a business-class hotel near the diplomatic section of the city. The Bahrain World Trade Center—two gleaming wedge-shaped skyscrapers joined by slender sky bridges—was just a short walk away, as was the Central Bank of Bahrain.

He found a men's shop on the first floor and bought a maroon oxford shirt, dark gray slacks, underwear, black socks, black wing-tip shoes, and a soft leather briefcase equipped with a shoulder strap. After completing his purchases, he showered, shaved, dressed in his new clothes, and then picked up his iPod.

A wall of disinformation had been thrown up in front of him. His job was to find a weakness in that wall and exploit it.

After connecting to the Sheraton's Wi-Fi, he googled *royal family Bahrain schools* and learned that most of the extended royal family had been educated, at least at the elementary school level, at an exclusive bilingual English-Arabic private school on the west side of Riffa. He went to the school's website, and saw that regular classes began in kindergarten, for which a child needed to be five years old.

But he also found a weekly child-parent class that was offered on Sundays, which was described as a way for parents to introduce their preschool-age children to the English language. It was restricted to parents whose children had already been accepted as future students at the school and was intended to complement the kindergarten curriculum the children eventually would encounter.

Hoping that Abdullah hadn't been lying when he'd mentioned that Muhammad had been taking English lessons, Mark clicked on the Staff icon at the top of the school's website. It was a small, prohibitively expensive school; there appeared to be only one teacher per grade. The kindergarten teacher, who also taught preschool English, was a woman named Jean Harman.

Today was a Saturday, the last day of the Muslim weekend, so Mark knew it was a near certainty that the school would be closed. He'd have to track Jean Harman down elsewhere.

He googled *Bahrain phonebook* and wound up on the website for Batelco, the main telecommunications company in Bahrain. Typing in the name *Jean Harman* brought up a listing for *Jean and Victor Harman*, beneath which was an address.

36

Bahrain

The bathroom in Rear Admiral Jeffrey Garver's spacious three-bedroom apartment was large enough to accommodate a wide double sink, above which hung an equally wide mirror. Both Garver and his wife Miriam were standing in front of this mirror, staring at their respective reflections.

Garver—who was the director of intelligence for US Naval Forces Central Command in Bahrain—was partially dressed in white boxer shorts and a white undershirt; he had only just gotten around to shaving because he'd spent a sleepless night and then morning videoconferencing with Central Command headquarters in Tampa, Florida. His wife, wearing a pea-green ankle-length skirt and long-sleeve yellow blouse, was applying her makeup, getting ready for an afternoon meeting of the Bahrain Officer Spouses' Club. Their apartment was on the sixth floor of a high-rise located on the west side of Manama, less than a quarter mile away from the US naval base.

Through the bathroom window, Garver could just see the building where he worked, and a green baseball field. Past the base, in Manama Bay, he could make out two guided missile destroyers.

God willing, he thought, pulling his razor carefully down his cheek, this view wasn't going to change much in the years to come. The Fifth Fleet was responsible for patrolling the Persian Gulf, that narrow body of water through which twenty percent of the world's oil passed. Saudi Arabia, Kuwait, Iraq, Iran, Qatar, and the United Arab Emirates all touched its waters. Take away the fleet, and all hell might break loose.

"I spoke with Jason last night," said Miriam, referring to their youngest son. "He sends his best."

Garver forced himself to smile. "Decent of him."

"He seemed busy. Fitting in all right, I guess."

"Who?"

"Your son, are you even listening to me?"

The Garvers' youngest son had just joined their oldest at the US Naval Academy, which was also Jeffrey Garver's alma mater.

"I'm sure he doesn't miss us a bit," said Garver. He ran his razor under hot water, rinsing off the shaving gel and stubble, then brought the blade to the underside of his chin.

Three more had died today.

It amazed him that his wife could be so oblivious—indeed that so many Bahrainis could still be so oblivious—to what was happening. People really did live in a fantasy world. Not for long, though. If the news didn't break today, it would tomorrow.

Moments later, as she applied eyeliner, Miriam said, "Reema came yesterday."

A fifty-eight-year-old Bahraini mother of four, Reema came twice a week to clean, do the laundry, and occasionally buy groceries.

"I saw."

"She was on time, I'll give her that."

Garver cleaned his razor off again, leaned in closer to the mirror, and began carefully shaving under his nose.

"She asked," added Miriam, "whether instead of taking off the first week of December, she might take off the second. Something about the date of her nephew's wedding getting changed due to—"

"Miri—" That was Garver's nickname for his wife. "You know I don't want to hear it."

He spoke sharply.

"I know, dear. I know."

"These people always have reasons a mile long, and it always has something to do with their damn second cousin, younger brother, aunt, or whatever. At some point, you have to decide between trying to please every last person in your family and doing your job. I know that sounds harsh, but . . ."

"Don't be mean, dear."

"Fair is not mean. What did you tell her?"

"That I would ask you, but that you were a navy man, and that navy men didn't like changing the schedule after it was set."

Garver shook his head. With everything else that was crashing down around him, this was the last thing he needed to deal with.

"She should know that by now. How many times do I have to tell these—"

"Now, Admiral, you know I don't like to hear those words."

Heeding his wife's warning, Garver stopped himself from saying what he'd been thinking. But he'd be damned if he was going to let the housekeeper walk all over him.

"No. No, she can't change the date. She made a commitment and I expect her to honor it. We don't do ourselves or her any good by tolerating bad behavior."

No doubt, thought Garver, that ruling would earn him a few nasty looks the next time he saw the housekeeper. She'd fault him, try to make him out to be the bad guy, just because she, like so many other Arabs, refused to plan her own life properly. That was the problem with this whole region.

For the hundredth time, Garver thought of the catastrophe that had hit the island, and of the boy and the failed mission to retrieve him, and of what he'd been forced to do as a result of that failure—at great risk to his career and his family. If only Miri knew . . .

The Bahrainis had failed to protect the boy, and the Saudis had failed to retrieve him. Damn incompetents. Garver was sick to hell of it.

37

The town of Al Jasra, where Muhammad's schoolteacher lived, lay ten miles west of Manama.

Though the houses there were much smaller than those in Riffa, many still sat behind high walls, some of which had been topped with shards of glass. The schoolteacher's home was encircled by such a wall, but the front gate had been left open, and two boys were playing soccer in the driveway.

Behind the boys, a small, white stucco house lay nestled amid acacia trees and pomegranate bushes. It was eleven thirty in the morning.

"Hey there!" Mark called, as he stepped through the gate. His new leather briefcase hung from his shoulder.

The boys stopped their game and turned to him, suspicious. Mark was glad he'd shaved and showered. In the friendliest voice he could muster, he said, "Sorry to interrupt your game, guys, but I'm looking for Mrs. Jean Harman?" He smiled as best he could. "I don't suppose she would be the mother of one of you boys?"

The taller of the two eyed Mark for another moment, then turned toward the house and yelled in a British accent, "Mum, someone here for you!"

Mark gave a little wave of his hand. "Hey, thanks so much."

No one appeared though. After a minute of just standing there, the boy yelled again, this time as loud as he could. When that didn't produce a response, he finally trudged up to the front door, opened it, and yelled some more.

This time, a woman around Mark's own age, with dirty-blond hair and bangs, did appear. She wore a yellow sundress that came down to her shins.

Mark smiled meekly and walked up the driveway toward her.

It wasn't a nice thing he intended to do, but then, many of the things he'd done over the course of his long career as a spy hadn't been nice. The reason he'd done them was that he'd believed the alternatives to be worse.

"I'm sorry to disturb you, ma'am. I'm looking for a Mrs. Jean Harman?"

She flashed him a wary but not unwelcoming smile. "You've found her."

"I'm with the American embassy in Manama."

Mark produced his old embassy ID back from when he used to be the CIA's station chief in Baku, introducing himself as Mark Sava as he handed it to her. She took the ID reluctantly and examined it.

"Counselor for political affairs," she read. And then, "But this is for an embassy in Azerbaijan."

"It is. I was just transferred." He added, "Because of the troubles."

"Oh, I see." She handed back the ID card.

"I'm here at the request of the Bahraini government. Now, I understand you teach at the elementary school in Riffa?"

"I do."

Mark reached into his briefcase and searched through some of the manila folders and legal pads he'd purchased on the drive out from Manama.

He pulled out one of the pads and dragged his finger across a list of names he'd written down. "And a young royal, a two-year-old boy named Muhammad, is one of your preschool English students?" Mark studied his legal pad. "He attends your Sunday class, if I'm not mistaken?"

"I'm sorry, but were you going to tell me what this is about?"

When training to be a CIA officer, Mark had read of a study where someone had sent hundreds of Christmas cards to random people in the phone book; many had sent Christmas cards back, just out of a sense of obligation—you get a card, you give a card. The need to reciprocate was a common human impulse.

It was also an impulse that any good spy, or con artist, knew how to exploit. Which is why, before Mark tried to pry information out of someone, he often tried to give them something first. It didn't matter if they didn't want what they'd been given. Most people would still feel the need to give something in return anyway.

With that in mind, he said, "I'm here, Ms. Harman, because I've been told there's a custody battle going on at the moment, one that involves your student, Muhammad. Now, I don't mean to alarm you, but as the child's teacher, you have a relationship with Muhammad that I'm told some of the royals who want custody of him may seek to . . ." Mark paused, as if choosing his words carefully. ". . . to abuse."

Jean Harman brought her hand up to her mouth. "But I hardly know the boy."

"Be that as it may, I've been authorized to offer you the assistance of the US government should you ever feel you need it. If you should ever feel any undue pressure, by all means—"

"Pressure? Why would anyone want to pressure me?"

"If you were called to testify, I assume."

"Testify about what?"

"The boy's well-being, I suppose."

"I would hardly know about that, would I?"

"Maybe not. But if you should feel pressure from either side at any point, please don't hesitate to call either of the two numbers I'm going to leave with you. The first is my direct number, the second is for the department at the US embassy that's handling this matter."

Mark wrote down two phone numbers. He ripped the sheet of paper off his legal pad and handed it to Jean Harman.

"Thank you, thank you so much," she said, looking confused. "I'm still not sure—" She paused, sounding hesitant. "I guess I still don't understand why the US embassy is involved in this?"

"All I know is that we received a request from the Bahraini interior minister and we decided to honor it. I suspect they don't trust their own people in this matter."

"Good lord."

"Now, there are a few things you might be able to help with. There's some concern that Muhammad's caretaker, a woman named"—Mark read from his legal pad—"Anna . . . I'm sorry, I'm transliterating from the Arabic, and that's not my specialty, am I getting that right?"

"No, I don't think you are. The woman who always brought Muhammad to class was named Kalila."

"Hmm . . ." Mark scanned his paper.

"Kalila Safi."

"OK, I have her. There's some concern regarding her whereabouts. She's disappeared, and the concern is she's taken Muhammad with her."

Jean Harman gave him an odd look. "Well, why wouldn't she?"

"I don't know. It's clear I don't know as much about the situation as you do. What's Kalila's relationship to the royal family?"

Jean Harman looked uncomfortable with the question. "Really, if you don't know already . . ."

"Maybe I'm focused on the wrong person. I've also been told about another one of Muhammad's caretakers named Hasini Ahmed. Is there anything you can tell me about her?"

"I've never heard the name."

Mark observed the awkward expression on Jean Harman's face. He sensed she didn't want to tell him to bug off, but that she would if he pushed her any further.

"Well, Ms. Harman, I think that's all. Thank you for your time. Have a wonderful day."

She studied him for a moment, with a confused expression on her face. “And you, Mr. Sava.” She held up the paper he’d given her. “And thank you for this.”

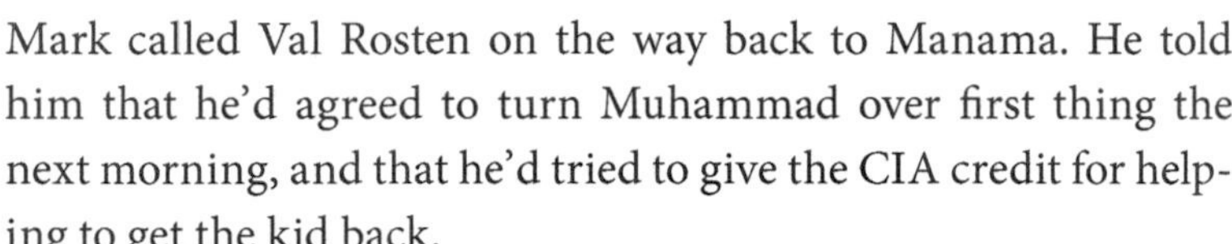

Mark called Val Rosten on the way back to Manama. He told him that he’d agreed to turn Muhammad over first thing the next morning, and that he’d tried to give the CIA credit for helping to get the kid back.

So things were on track. No worries.

Rosten didn’t thank Mark, but he didn’t seem displeased either. More than anything, he seemed distracted.

“There’s just one other thing,” said Mark.

“Yeah, what’s that?”

“I got a name I was hoping you could have the Bahrain station run.”

“Ah, and what name would that be?”

Mark told Rosten what he’d learned about Kalila Safi.

“What’s the end game here, Sava? The kid’s a royal, he belongs with the royal family. So what if they’re lying about some nanny? That’s their business. Tell me you’re not thinking of holding up the transfer.”

“No.” Mark wasn’t about to tell Rosten the truth. “I just sense a potential leverage point. Might not be leverage we want to use now, but if it’s worth it to the Bahrainis to lie to us about this nanny, it’s worth it to us to figure out why they’d want to lie. I’m throwing you a bone here, Val.”

Rosten took a moment to respond. “I’ll make a few inquiries.”

38

Mina Salman, a huge seaport on the eastern edge of Manama, was owned and operated by the Bahrainis, but the US Navy leased a large portion of it and had recently signed a deal to lease a larger portion still; as a result, Rear Admiral Jeffrey Garver spent a lot of time shuttling back and forth between the port and the landlocked US naval base nearby.

At present, Garver was in uniform— his service dress blues— driving down the main half-mile-long pier, en route to meet the DEPCOMNAVCENT, the deputy commander, US Naval Forces Central Command. They had been scheduled to inspect the nearly completed personnel barracks and then review progress on a bridge that was being built to connect the port of Mina Salman with the US naval base; instead they were going to meet aboard a guided missile destroyer that was moored in Manama Bay, for the purpose of discussing what to do when and if Bahrain descended into chaos.

Garver had just passed a sign that read *RESTRICTED AREA* when his cell phone rang. It was Val Rosten, the deputy director of the CIA's Near East Division. Garver knew him well; as the head of naval intelligence in Bahrain, he often coordinated with the CIA.

Rosten explained that he needed information about a woman named Kalila Safi; she either worked for, or was a member of, the royal family. "You work with more of the royals than I do. Any chance you can ask around about her without making waves? She might be employed as a nanny."

"Does this have anything to do with—"

"It might."

"I'll see what I can come up with."

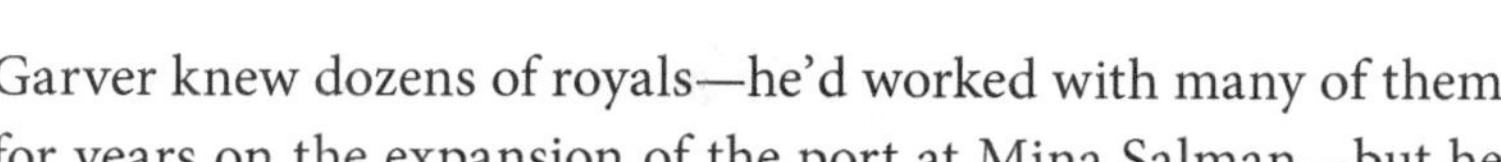

Garver knew dozens of royals—he'd worked with many of them for years on the expansion of the port at Mina Salman—but he didn't bother trying to call any.

Instead he called Saeed al Yami, a high-ranking officer in the Saudi General Intelligence Presidency, the Saudi equivalent of the CIA. As a function of his job as director of naval intelligence, Garver had been working with Saeed and Saudi intelligence for the better part of five years now—although never as much as over the past four days.

When Saeed picked up, Garver explained what Rosten wanted.

"Do you know this Kalila Safi?" asked Garver.

"I do," said Saeed.

"Who is she?"

"No one you need to worry about."

"Does this have anything to do with the boy?"

"It does."

"Should I be worried?"

"No. The information you provided us with yesterday has allowed us to develop a contingency plan to ensure the delivery of the child. I'm ordering that contingency plan activated as of now."

"Don't screw this up, Saeed."

39

Delhi, India

Monkeys!

Rad opened his eyes and knew instantly that that was what had woken him up. He looked at the digital clock on the end table next to the bed. It read two thirty p.m. He'd only been asleep for an hour.

He could hear those dirty cocksuckers in the back garden, chattering, screeching, scurrying up walls like demonic rats, racing after each other across electrical wires . . .

The back door. He had to close it.

Rad sprang out bed and walked quickly to the door. Before closing it, he listened for a moment, surprised by the silence that had suddenly descended. Just as he was wondering where the monkeys had gone, a black figure crashed through the screen door and plowed into him, knocking him to the floor.

At first Rad thought it was a crazed monkey. He began to fight it off with his hands, kicking and punching blindly. However, when he tried to scream, a human hand closed over his mouth. He bit the hand, but then felt a stab of pain that felt as though someone had stuck a needle into his thigh. Twisting as hard as he could, he tried to shake his leg free.

A boot came down on his shinbone, and he heard a loud crack. Seconds later, a woozy feeling washed over him and he passed out.

40

Bahrain

Mark was in a taxi, speeding into Manama on King Faisal Highway when Rosten called.

"I got some intel on the nanny."

"I'm listening," said Mark.

"She's fifty-six years old. We tapped her credit card history. Lots of purchases in Riffa. Then three days ago we have one purchase at an airport coffee shop in Dubai. Two days ago, a purchase at a clothing store in Dubai. After that, nothing."

"Can you call Dubai station, ask them to track her down?"

"This was a highly compartmentalized op. Dubai station isn't in the loop."

"You can't ask them just to track a name?"

"Not without getting permission from the DNCS, and I doubt he'd give it." The DNCS was the director of the National Clandestine Service, which was the division of the CIA that did the actual spying.

"What else?"

"Nothing for now. I have a call in to naval intelligence here in Bahrain, though. They've been in on this from the beginning—"

"Oh, great."

As chief of station/Azerbaijan, Mark had sometimes worked with military intelligence officers. To a man, they'd been decent and earnest. But often it was just a case of too many cooks in the kitchen.

"Frankly," said Rosten, "with all the construction jobs the navy's been bidding out to the Bahrainis, naval intelligence has got far better contacts with the royals than we do. I'll let you know when and if I hear anything more. Have you moved your people in place to transfer the kid?"

"I'm working on it."

"Don't screw me on this, Sava."

Mark clicked off his prepaid phone. *Can't even run the name of Kalila Safi by Dubai station. We'll see about that.*

Mark was fast approaching the skyscrapers of downtown Manama. To his right, a road construction project was underway on what used to be the site of a three-hundred-foot monument that paid homage to Bahrain's ancient pearl-fishing industry—a monument the government tore down after it became a rallying point for Shia protests. To his left lay the Persian Gulf.

As traffic slowed where an onramp joined the highway, a dark blue Chevy tried to cut in front of them. Shaking his fist, the taxi driver muttered some curse in Arabic and wouldn't give way.

Mark pulled out his iPod and searched his Contacts folder for the name of someone he used to work with at the CIA—Larry Bowlan. Bowlan, he recalled, worked at the consulate in Dubai. He might be able to track down Kalila Safi.

Suddenly a red Ford Taurus cut in front of him. Glancing at the Taurus's rearview mirror, Mark locked eyes with the driver for a brief moment and realized he had a problem. Because he was ninety percent sure that the guy behind the wheel of the Taurus was the older of the two Saudis who'd tried to kidnap Muhammad back in Kyrgyzstan.

Mark had assumed the Bahrainis had been tracking him ever since his visit to Riffa. But unless he backed out of delivering Muhammad the next day, he'd figured they wouldn't bother him. He doubted, though, that he'd get the same hands-off treatment from the Saudi in the Taurus.

He looked behind him. The Chevy sedan that had tried to cut him off was now tailgating.

Mark pocketed his iPod. They were approaching an exit off to the right. When they'd almost passed it, he leaned over and yanked hard on the steering wheel, sending the taxi screeching off the highway onto the exit ramp.

The driver fought for control of the steering wheel, which Mark released as soon as they were on the exit ramp.

Yelling at him in Arabic, the cabbie pulled to a stop.

Mark pointed behind him. "Problem!" he said, speaking English.

The guy in the Chevy sedan behind them hadn't been able to react fast enough to make the exit ramp, but he was now backing up on the shoulder of the highway.

Mark fished a twenty-dinar note out of his front pocket. "Go," he said, handing the money over. "Government Avenue."

The cabbie looked at the money, and then at Mark. Government Avenue was a busy thoroughfare that cut through the old part of Manama.

"*Min fadlak*," Mark added. *Please.*

The cabbie pocketed the money and started driving, though not as fast as Mark would have liked. They passed a big open parking lot and a Papa John's, then cruised through an intersection, but before merging onto Government Avenue, heavy traffic forced them to stop behind a pink, blue, and white conversion van emblazoned with the words *ICE CREAM FRUITY.*

Mark jumped out. Fifty feet or so behind him, a man wearing sandals, jeans, and a white shirt burst out of the front passenger door of the Chevy.

Mark ran across Government Avenue, then turned down a narrow street. He was in a pedestrian-only district packed with little shops, an old part of Manama. One of the store owners had wheeled a rack of *thawb* robes out into the street for display. Without breaking stride, Mark pulled two twenty-dinar bills out of his pocket, handed the money—as though it were a relay baton—to a surprised-looking merchant, and grabbed one of the robes off the rack. Still walking quickly, he slipped it over his head and buttoned it up tight, right up to the priest-like collar.

From behind him came the sound of several men running on pavement. Mark turned left down another alley-like street, speed-purchased a Yasser Arafat–style kaffiyeh headdress from a street merchant who'd spread his wares all over a carpet, and arranged the kaffiyeh on his head as he walked.

In front of him, a man in dark slacks and sandals scanned the crowd. Though it wasn't the same guy who'd jumped out of the Chevy, or the Saudi Mark had recognized, he didn't look as though he was there to shop.

Mark spied a no-frills restaurant on his right; old men and young couples were sitting outside on chairs constructed of rough wood planks that had been painted bright blue. Mark slid into an open seat, positioned himself so that he was facing away from the street, and got the attention of a bored-looking teenage waiter. When the kid approached, Mark pointed to a Coca-Cola bottle on an adjacent table and held up one finger.

The kid brought the Coke, which came in a thick recyclable bottle that looked as if it had been in use since the 1950s. Mark took a sip, then a few deep breaths, listening more than looking. He didn't hear footsteps running in the streets. The conversation behind him sounded normal.

The damn Saudis. What had they been up to? Why try to take him now? Had his visit to the teacher rattled them?

It must have.

A few older men sat smoking nearby, their elbows resting on plastic sheeting that had been stretched tight over the tabletops and stapled to the undersides. They wore *thawbs* like Mark's, only theirs were unbuttoned at the neck, revealing T-shirts underneath.

Mark looked at the creases on the men's faces. He imagined their families. Bahrain was their home, not his. *They* should be dealing with Muhammad.

A big part of him wanted to go back to the Sheraton, e-mail Decker with instructions on how to hand Muhammad over to the Bahrainis, take a long hot shower, and then settle in for the evening at the bar.

He took a sip of his Coke, and thought of Daria. No, he'd see this through to the end. He'd figure out what was up with this damn nanny, then make a decision about the best course of action.

Mark pulled out one of his prepaid phones. It was time to call Larry Bowlan.

41

While Ted Kaufman had been Mark's last boss at the CIA, Larry Bowlan had been his first.

They'd met in Tbilisi, Georgia, just before the fall of the Soviet Union. Mark had been studying abroad on a Fulbright scholarship, having a blast living with his Russian girlfriend. Bowlan had been a middle-aged, Yale-educated CIA operations officer looking to expose a mole that had infiltrated an anti-Soviet student group. Mark's decision to help Bowlan had led to his being kidnapped, interrogated, and tortured by the KGB. It had been a brutal introduction to the intelligence game.

Mark considered that history for a moment, then called the main number for the US consulate in Dubai and asked for the visa processing department.

His call was transferred and a woman picked up. Mark told her who he was trying to reach, adding, "He's old. And cranky. White hair."

"Yeah, I know him. And who are you?"

"Just tell him it's an old friend from Tbilisi. He'll know who it is."

An exasperated sigh, then, "Hold on."

A minute later, Mark heard whispers:

Who is it?

He wouldn't say.

Jesus, I don't have time for this crap.

Quiet, he's on the line.

Someone grabbed the phone. A couple of buttons beeped, as if someone had pushed them by mistake.

"Who is this?"

The voice on the phone was gravelly and rough, the result of too many cigarettes over too many years. Mark could picture his former boss—the big Adam's apple, the wrinkled cheeks, the thin red booze lines clustered around his nose . . .

"Hey, Larry."

A pause, then, "Oh, Christ."

"I need a favor."

"Of course you do, why else would you call?"

"I'm close by, in Bahrain."

"On a job?"

"Of sorts."

Bowlan sighed. It sounded to Mark like a sigh of envy.

His old boss had retired at the age of sixty-five—Mark had sent him a bottle of Johnny Walker Blue as a send-off—then rejoined the Agency at the age of sixty-six, having failed miserably at being a retiree. And when he'd been hired back, it hadn't been at his high-ranking GS-14 civil service pay level—Larry liked his drink too much for that—but instead as a GS-9 who took orders from a CIA pencil-pusher half his age.

Mark said, "I'm looking for a fifty-six-year-old woman who flew into Dubai three days ago. Can you search the visa records?"

Last Mark had heard, one of Bowlan's jobs at the consulate was to help the CIA help the United Arab Emirates vet suspicious visa applications.

"Is she a Bahraini?"

"I don't know."

"Well, if she's Bahraini or from one of the other Gulf states, she wouldn't need a visa so there won't be visa records."

"Would you have access to general entry records?"

"Yes, but the searches are tracked. If I do an unauthorized search and it's questioned—which it will be—I'll lose my job. You ever hear of privacy regulations, Sava?"

"This is important. And we have history."

"Yeah, I know. That's what you said last time you called. And I delivered for you because of that history. I figure now we're even."

"Larry."

"I could lose my job, Mark. Granted, it's a crap job, but it's the only one I've got."

Behind him, Mark heard the sound of a pot clanging as it hit the floor. A second later, a bearded twentysomething guy with a cell phone pushed past a waiter who'd been heading toward the kitchen to investigate the sound.

The bearded guy eyed Mark, then spoke into his cell phone.

"Damn, Larry, I gotta blow. I'll call you right back. Stay at this number."

Mark hung up on Bowlan and stood up, prepared to run, but the bearded guy pocketed his cell phone with one hand and pulled out a gun with the other.

"Stop!"

The bearded guy pulled a badge out of his back pocket and held it up not only for Mark to see, but for the surrounding spectators as well. The badge identified him as a member of the Bahraini National Security Agency. Mark knew them as the *mukhabarat*, or secret police. "You're coming with us."

Us? thought Mark. He glanced behind him. Two more guys had just run up.

The Saudi who'd tried to abduct Muhammad in Kyrgyzstan had a pistol drawn. Mark stared at him.

As if reading Mark's mind, the Saudi said in Turkish, "Down here, we Bahrainis and Saudis all work together."

Mark raised his hands in the air. "All right then. Let's get this done."

42

Mark was marched out through the Bab al-Bahrain, an old arched gateway that led from the shopping district to Government Avenue. Five armed men encircled him, one of whom held his elbow.

The blue Chevy was parked in a nearby roundabout behind a line of taxis. Mark was stuffed into the back seat, next to another armed man.

They drove west out of the city along King Faisal Highway, then south through a chaos of broken roads and graffiti-scarred buildings, then through Riffa. Mark thought maybe he was going to be taken back to the house of the old man who'd claimed to be Muhammad's great uncle, but when the turnoff came they kept driving.

Riffa was on a bit of a plateau—fifty feet or so above sea level—which was high ground for Bahrain. So when they exited the city, Mark could see the bleak southern desert sprawled out below them in the hazy distance.

He could also see, right on the edge of the desert, what looked like a golf club.

The Royal Golf Club wasn't actually limited to royalty.

Mark discovered that upon entering the place and observing all the well-dressed pasty-white Westerners milling around. Nor, however, was it open to the public—that much was also clear.

There was too much marble and reflective glass, too many leather couches, pleasant vistas, and objets d'art for that. A private country club, he concluded—with membership fees set high enough to keep the undesirables at bay.

He was led by one of his abductors into a nearly empty dining area that looked out over the golf course. The contrast between the edge of the southern desert—where little grew other than occasional patches of sad scrub brush—and the brilliant green fairways was striking. All the more so because a breeze was blowing, lifting up sand from the desert and swirling it around in a haze that reminded Mark of 1930s dust-bowl photos.

Seated at a table near a window was a man Mark guessed to be in his early sixties. He wore a dark gray suit with a forest-green tie, though he'd removed his suit jacket. His skin was olive toned and his dark hair was flecked with gray, as was his goatee. He had a cup of coffee and an unopened menu in front of him.

He gestured to the chair opposite his own with an open palm. "Please."

Mark took a seat.

The man took a sip of his coffee, used the napkin on his lap to wipe his mouth, then said, "You may call me Saeed."

Mark didn't respond.

Saeed continued, "And you, I believe, are Mark Sava." He spoke English, but with a heavy Arab accent. His voice was deep, his tone serious.

"What do you want?"

"I'm with Saudi intelligence." Saeed spoke flatly. "What I want is for you to do what you have already promised to do. To hand over the child."

At first, because Saeed was seated, Mark hadn't noticed what a big man he was. But he did now. Saeed's arms were remarkably long, his shoulders unusually wide. Not in a muscular way, or Mark would have noticed right away; it was simply as though a normal deskbound person had been enlarged by fifty percent.

Saeed added, "We're working with the Bahrainis on this."

"I've already arranged to hand over the child tomorrow. First thing in the morning. My men are retrieving him and bringing him to Bishkek as we speak."

"So I've heard. And I have also heard that you have promised as much to your friends at the CIA. But I'm not convinced you intend to meet your obligation."

"Now why would you think that?"

"Because I have observed that you have been going to places you shouldn't be going, and asking questions you shouldn't be asking, rather than making plans for this transfer in Bishkek."

They stared at each other for a long moment. Mark turned his gaze to the row of windows that looked out over a nearby fairway. A man in Bermuda shorts was swinging a driver as his golf partner and a caddie waited behind him. It made Mark think of the band that kept playing while the *Titanic* was sinking.

This place, he thought.

Saeed said, "I brought you here to give you an opportunity."

"An opportunity."

"To expedite the return of the child." Saeed gestured to a menu that lay on the table. "You make whatever calls you need to make, we eat a civilized meal while waiting for the transfer to occur between our respective associates. After it does, you leave to live your life as you wish."

Choosing his words carefully, Mark said, "While I thank you for that opportunity, as I said, I have already given the authorization for the child to be brought to Bishkek. At this point, the process cannot be expedited."

Saeed folded his hands carefully in his lap and leaned forward in his chair. He did so in a way that said, *I'm going to pretend to be pleasant to you now, little man, but we both know I could crush you like a bug and I will do so if I need to.*

"Let me explain something about the Middle East to you, Mr. Sava. It's not like in the United States. Here, allegiance is not to country. It is to family and tribe."

Mark had read enough briefings on the Middle East over the years to know that Saeed was grossly oversimplifying the matter. Iranians and Egyptians were plenty patriotic. And the urban young in the Middle East seemed to care a great deal more about getting a decent job than they did about upholding ancient notions of tribal fidelity.

But it was true enough that the ruling families of many Persian Gulf states were still influenced by tribal values that prized familial bonds above many Western notions of right and wrong. Nepotism here wasn't a sign of corruption—it was a sign of commitment to family.

Saeed continued, "I don't think you understand that. I don't think you understand how arrogant you appear when you meet with this boy's uncle, and you listen to him state that he has been responsible for the care of the boy and that he wishes to continue to care for the boy, and instead of making arrangements to give the boy to him, you question his sincerity. It is not your place to question."

"I didn't question his sincerity."

Saeed clicked his tongue as he shook his head. "Then what were you doing in Al Jasra earlier today?" When Mark didn't answer, Saeed said, "This need to meddle, this lack of respect, is the same kind of thinking that leads America to think it can force democracy on people who want nothing to do with it. If you truly understood Bahrain, you would not think you had any right to decide what is best for a child like Muhammad. You would understand that this is a matter for the boy's family and his tribe to decide. Not you."

"He's got a pretty big family as I understand it."

"Any member of which is far more entitled than you are to decide what to do with him."

"See, the problem here—"

Raising his voice, Saeed broke in, "The problem is that you continue to put what *you* think is right for the boy above what I am telling you is right."

"Here's the thing, Saeed. When your men showed up at that orphanage in Kyrgyzstan, they didn't come with a nice explanation like the one you've offered to me. Instead they lied, and then tried to take Muhammad by force. My girlfriend helps run that orphanage. And when your men crossed her, they crossed *my* tribe."

"A girlfriend is not a tribe, Mr. Sava."

"It's a small tribe, I'll give you that."

Daria and Decker, thought Mark. That was pretty much the extent of it. And though the CIA's Central Eurasia Division was a tribe of its own, they were definitely an ally he'd at least consider fighting for.

"Americans don't have tribes. They have America."

Not so, thought Mark. "I don't need a lecture, Saeed. I just need the truth."

"Mr. Sava, I'm not a man who takes pleasure in threatening a fellow intelligence officer."

"Then by all means, don't."

"But you leave me no choice—I warn you, the consequences of your intransigence will be grave. And I strongly urge you to consider the fact that this is not your battle to fight."

"Who is Kalila Safi? And why have people been lying to me about her?"

"Is that your answer?"

Saeed leaned back. His big knees stuck out on either side of his chair.

"I suppose it is."

"You disappoint me."

"I disappoint a lot of people."

Saeed sighed, then glanced behind him and nodded. Three men appeared from opposite corners of the restaurant. One of the men was the older Saudi Mark had clashed with in Kyrgyzstan. He smiled at Mark and opened his sport coat just enough to reveal a shoulder-holstered 9mm Heckler and Koch P7.

"You will go with these men," said Saeed. "If you resist you will be shot. They will show you something. When they do, remember that I warned you, Marko. I warned you."

"*What* did you call me?"

43

Mark was loaded back into the blue Chevy, which looked out of place next to all the Lexus and BMW 7 Series sedans also parked in front of the golf club entrance.

So this is where it starts, he thought. The blackmail, the manipulation, the coercion. Mark didn't blame Saeed for playing it that way. He blamed himself for not having seen it coming. For letting himself be blindsided like this.

Marko.

The use of his birth name meant they'd broken his cover, the identity he'd painstakingly crafted, had meticulously backstopped bit by bit over the past twenty years.

But how?

The answer, once he thought about it, was obvious—his personnel file had been violated. There was no other way.

And who might have violated his personnel file?

Rosten.

The call about Kalila Safi must have spooked him. So he'd cut a deal with the Saudis, figured he'd get them to do his dirty work. Well, if Rosten thought he could violate highly classified records with impunity, he was in for a rude awakening, thought Mark. No matter what happened with Muhammad, Rosten had crossed a line that *should not have been crossed.*

As they drove south, deeper into the desert, the older Saudi sat next to Mark in the back seat, pistol drawn. The car smelled like man sweat.

The sky was a hazy gray and the land a dull brown. In the vast flatlands that extended out from either side of the road, enormous excavators were loading sand into dump trucks; other trucks sent trails of dust in the air as they transported the sand to an industrial complex.

He saw an exit sign for Isa Air Base— home of the Bahraini Air Force—and wondered if that was where they were taking him. But they passed the exit without turning off.

Oil fields appeared. Chain-link fences encircled nodding-donkey pumps that were connected to each other by tangles of pipeline. Flare stacks—tall chimneys that burned wasted natural gas—dotted the landscape. The fires at the tops of the towers shimmered in the midday sun. Random pieces of discarded industrial equipment lay baking in the sand.

They pulled off on a little dirt road and drove for maybe a mile, until they came to a crater-like depression in the sand. It looked to Mark like an abandoned excavation site.

"Get out," said one of the Saudis.

Mark did what he was told.

"Walk down."

Mark did so. They're not going to shoot you, he told himself. Not while you still have Muhammad. But do you? Had they found Decker? Saeed had said there was someone he needed to meet. Was that someone Decker? By now it had to be around one in the afternoon, which would make it four in the afternoon Kyrgyzstan time. He tried to imagine what Decker and Daria and Muhammad were doing but drew a blank.

"Sit."

Mark sat down on the warm sand in the center of the crater. The men guarding him took turns rotating in and out of their air-conditioned car, listening to bad Arabic pop music, drinking cans of some local soda, and telling jokes. Occasionally, one of them would piss near the lip of the depression.

Mark spent most of the time with his head down, facing away from the sun. It was hot, but not oppressively so. Though he speculated about what they planned to do to him, he primarily thought about what he planned to do to Rosten. He considered trying to escape but ruled it out—both because he doubted he could pull it off and because he was curious about how they intended to try to manipulate him.

Marko.

That had been a warning.

For a while, he thought about the Chinese restaurant in Bishkek and his narde buddies. He wished he was back there with them now, tucked away in a dark corner of the restaurant, drinking beer and listening to the narde pieces smacking against the wood playing board. Once or twice he even drifted off to sleep; when he did, he dreamed of Daria.

But always when he woke, he came back to that name. *Marko.* And to the reason he no longer used it.

Elizabeth, New Jersey, 1985

At three thirty in the afternoon, on the fourteenth of April, the bell announcing the end of the school day rang at Elizabeth High. Knowing he had only ten minutes before he needed to begin work at his father's gas station, Marko Saveljic darted through the crush of students, hurrying to exit the building. His diligence paid off; just five minutes later, he'd reached his home on Coventry Avenue, which left him plenty of time to change into his work clothes and walk down to the gas station.

Marko pushed open the gate in the chain-link fence that stood outside his home and climbed the pitted concrete steps to the front door. A blue Maxwell coffee can, nearly full of cigarette butts, sat to the left of the door. Mounted at chest height above the coffee can, was a rusted black mailbox. His mother, he noticed, had neglected to retrieve the mail.

That was his first clue that something was wrong. The second was the silence.

Marko had two younger brothers, one of whom was five, the other three. They should have been home from preschool by now, he knew. But when the boys were home, they made noise, and lots of it; noise that was easy to hear, even from the street, because the Saveljics' narrow row house had thin walls and drafty windows. Marko looked all the way down Coventry Avenue, to the gas station on the corner. He could just make out his dad, fueling up a Plymouth Volaré station wagon at one of the pumps.

That much, at least, was normal.

Maybe the mail had just come late today, he thought, as he pulled a Sears catalogue and an electric bill out of the mailbox. But when he looked at the neighbors' mailboxes—all the way down the row of connected houses, he saw that the mail had already been taken in. So it couldn't have come that late.

Marko opened the front door and stepped into the cramped living room.

"Hello?"

No one answered. As he studied the room, he didn't like what he saw.

On a mahogany table to his left was the phone. An answering machine connected to the phone was blinking rapidly, indicating that several messages were waiting to be listened to.

The door to the basement was open. At that moment, he knew.

"Hello?" called Marko. "Mom?"

The house sounded empty. It felt empty. He wanted to be wrong.

He looked at the basement door again, then turned away.

The long lace curtains in the living room were drawn. The dark maroon walls had been rendered darker still by a sickly film of cigarette smoke residue. A staircase with chunky oak balusters led to the second floor. Pictures of Marko, his younger brothers, and his older sister lined the wall that led to the second floor. There were school photos, baptism photos, a few from the Jersey shore . . . Marko recalled that his mother had personally framed and hung every one of them.

No, he thought. He had to be wrong. But he couldn't block out the memory of the fighting from the night before. His mother in tears, accusing his father.

Opposite the staircase, on the other side of the living room, his father's prized icons—Eastern Orthodox religious paintings—decorated the walls. Two-dimensional and stiff, they made Marko think of the Dark Ages. Jesus with his halo, John the Baptist holding a tri-bar cross . . . His father's parents had brought the paintings with them when they had emigrated from Serbia. The paintings had been passed on to Marko's father when they'd died.

The open door to the basement beckoned him. He took a step toward it. The light in the basement was on.

"Mom!"

The steps creaked as Marko descended them.

Laundry lines, sagging with the weight of wet clothes, criss-crossed the basement, and Marko detected the pleasant smell of detergent and bleach. Recognizing many of his own clothes, he wondered whether that had been intentional—whether she'd made a point of doing one last thing for him.

She'd hung the jury-rigged noose from a floor joist right in front of the staircase. The chair she'd stood on lay kicked to the side. Her bare feet dangled inches from the floor, her tongue was—

Marko turned away.

What she hadn't intended was that he would be the one to find her. Of that he was certain. His father was supposed to have been the one to walk down these steps. On his lunch break.

He considered cutting her down and calling for an ambulance. Maybe she wasn't really dead yet.

He forced himself to take another look. No, she was long past saving.

Unable to think, speak, or cry, he fell back onto the steps. All he wanted to do was run. But he couldn't even force himself to do that. Eventually his thoughts turned to his brothers. And that's when he understood what the blinking light on the answering machine was all about.

He stood, walked back up the stairs, and pushed play on the machine. As he expected, it was the secretary from the local preschool. No one had come to pick up his brothers. The boys were at the office, but the office would be closing soon. Someone needed to come get them.

Marko considered picking up his brothers himself. But would the school even release them to him? He was only seventeen, a brother not a parent . . . and if they did, where would he bring them? Not here, that much was certain.

He should call the cops.

No. His father could deal with that.

He felt for his wallet in his back pocket. It was still there. Inside was his brand-new driver's license and twelve dollars. That would have to do.

The walk down to his father's gas station on the corner only took a couple of minutes. It was a dismal place. The neon sign on the corner said SAVE-A-LOT, *only the* L *was dark. The pumps were all at least twenty years old. His dad still owed the previous owner lots of money, which meant money was tight in the Saveljic household. Too tight. That had been part of the problem.*

As Marko approached, he saw that his father was cleaning the windshield of an orange Dodge Duster, behind the wheel of which sat an old biddy of a woman. A clock on top of one of the pumps read 3:44. Marko was supposed to have shown up for work four minutes ago. For years now, pumping gas at his father's station had been his sole after-school activity.

"You're late." His father had broad shoulders, deep-set eyes, a hard jaw, and hair that was cut tight to his scalp. His voice was menacing and accusing. Tiny holes riddled his grease-stained work pants, a result of battery acid splatter.

"Why didn't you go home for lunch today?" Marko asked.

Marko's father finished cleaning the windshield and put his squeegee back into a bucket next to the gas pump. "How do you know I didn't?"

"I just know."

Marko's father looked puzzled. "One of the pumps broke. Had to wait for a part from Romano's. Why don't you have your coveralls on? You show up late and you're not even dressed for work?"

He positioned himself so that the old lady in the Duster couldn't see him and gave Marko an unfriendly push on the shoulder.

He'd smothered her, thought Marko. He'd kept her in that dark cave of a home and had done little over the years but criticize the few friends she'd dared to make, criticize her hair, her weight, her mothering abilities, what he perceived to be her lack of faith . . .

Marko's mother had come to the United States from Soviet Georgia when she was five. English had been her second language, and her timidity with the new tongue had spilled over into the rest of her life. His father had taken advantage of that timidity. He'd taken a gentle, kind, beautiful woman and turned her into a lost soul, starved for love.

And then he'd cheated on her. Marko had gleaned that much from their argument the night before. It seemed that his father had been having an affair with a woman from the Orthodox church, a young widow he'd supposedly been counseling.

"Mom's waiting for you back at the house."

"Eh?"

"She's in the basement. She has something she wants to tell you."

"Now?"

"Yeah, now."

"Dammit, Marko! We've got work to do."

"I'm quitting."

A moment passed. Marko sensed a blow might be coming, but he just stared at his father, not backing down. Though they were about the same height, Marko didn't yet possess his father's strength.

"I don't have time for this, Marko."

"By the way, don't forget about the boys. Someone needs to pick them up from school."

"No one's picked them up?"

"No. Mom can explain it. Like I said, she's got something to tell you."

Marko turned and began to walk away.

"Marko! Get back here! You gotta watch the pumps while I talk to your mom!"

Marko broke into a run. His father, he decided, was as dead to him as his mother was. From this day forward, as far as he was concerned, he was an orphan.

"Hey!"

Mark heard the voice, but was too absorbed in his thoughts at first to respond.

"Hey! Get up here. We're leaving."

Mark opened his eyes. He looked at the sun, and guessed it was around five in the afternoon, which would mean he'd been in the desert for four hours. He stood up slowly and stiffly, then walked back up the embankment to his abductors.

They returned to the main road they'd been on earlier and continued south. But they hadn't been going long before they turned down a dirt road and pulled up to a little maintenance shack that sat near a cluster of oil pumps.

"Get out," the driver ordered in English.

In case Mark hadn't gotten the message, the older Saudi gestured to the door with his gun. Mark stepped out of the car.

44

Rad Saveljic was hungry, thirsty, panicked, lonely, lightheaded, and deeply depressed. On top of all that, his right leg was killing him. He couldn't put any weight on it; hell, he couldn't even touch it without flinching. It throbbed like a second heart down by his shinbone.

What had happened? And why had it happened to him? Where was he? How much time had passed? Was it about a ransom? Had someone contacted his boss, or his dad back in New Jersey, asking for money?

But these guys hadn't said anything about money. They hadn't said anything about anything. They'd just blindfolded him, stuffed him into a car, bundled him onto a plane, and then brought him to . . . Rad didn't even know where he was.

Someone removed his blindfold.

He appeared to be in a shack of sorts. The floor was sandy and the air smelled of diesel fuel. It was hot. A few bags of dry concrete lay in a corner. He was seated on the floor, still wearing only his underpants and undershirt. From somewhere outside the shack, he could hear a rhythmic creaking, as though a baby were being rocked in a cradle. He wondered whether he was still in India.

Ten feet in front of him, a single guard, dressed in civilian clothes and armed with a large pistol, sat on a wooden packing crate. He didn't look Indian.

Rad's hands were cuffed behind his back with plastic ties that cut into his wrists. His stomach was still a hard knot, but at least he no longer felt like vomiting; the pain in his leg had cured that. He asked the guard what was going on, and where he was, and for something to drink.

The guard ignored him.

Rad heard voices outside, then what sounded like men walking across gravel. He fixated on the nimbus of weak sunlight leaking in from around the perimeter of a metal door. Strange, he thought, that it was still daytime; it should have been past dark in Delhi by now. Maybe he'd lost track of the time, and hadn't been traveling for as long as he'd thought. He heard footsteps outside. As the door handle rotated, and then the door opened, his stomach did a little flip.

Light spilled in. Squinting, the guard stood up and aimed his pistol at Rad's head.

"Don't!" Rad put his hands up to shield his head. "Please, don't do it!"

Before Rad turned his eyes from the bright low sun, he caught a glimpse of a bleak desert landscape and a line of telephone poles that seemed to extend out into infinity.

The guard lowered his pistol, aimed it at Rad's chest, and squeezed the trigger. The shot was so loud Rad felt as if he'd gone deaf. At least he didn't really shoot me, Rad thought, confusing—for a brief moment—the pain in his shoulder, and the fact that he'd been thrown back against the wall, with a bad dream. This whole thing was a bad dream.

Damn, his shoulder hurt. The ringing in his ears subsided a bit, and he blinked his eyes. He could see now.

He *had* been shot. He was bleeding, and his chest was wet. *Oh God*, he thought. *Oh God.*

Rad couldn't move his left hand, so he put his right hand up to his chest, thinking he'd try to stop the bleeding. It wasn't his chest though, it was his shoulder. He squeezed where he thought he'd been shot and then screamed as the pain rocketed up into his brain.

A man of average height with unkempt hair appeared in the doorway to the shed. Rad couldn't see the man's face all that well because it was backlit by the sun.

"Who is this?" Rad heard the man say in English, in a voice that was hard and mean, but somehow strangely familiar. And then, "Why did you shoot him?"

Someone shoved the man into the shed. Then the door slammed closed.

Rad tried to see through the darkness but by now his eyes had partially adjusted to the bright light outside so he still couldn't see the man's features.

"I've been shot," said Rad.

"Yeah, I'm aware of that."

"Who are you?"

The man didn't answer. Instead, he quickly knelt down. His hand darted out, snakelike, toward Rad's shoulder.

Rad screamed in pain again, and tried to pull back, thinking that maybe this guy had been sent into the shed to torture him.

"Listen," said the man, "I'm going to try to help you, but I need you to calm the fuck down."

45

Mark grabbed the man's good hand. "If you don't want me touching your shoulder, then you'll have to do it yourself. Stick your hand up there and apply some pressure, for Christ's sake."

He didn't know who had just been shot, or why, but working on the assumption that the enemy of my enemy is my friend, he figured he'd try to patch the guy up before he bled out.

Mark leaned in and used his teeth to start a rip in the guy's wife-beater undershirt.

"What are you doing?"

The voice was panicked.

"Trying to help you, like I said." Mark ripped the undershirt into strips to use as bandages, then turned his two front pockets inside out and ripped them out of his pants. "Stay still." He slid a strip of the undershirt beneath the man's armpit, quarter-folded his ripped pockets, placed one over the entry wound and the other over the exit wound, and began to wrap the shoulder. "I said stay still!"

"It hurts!"

"I don't care."

Labored breathing, then, "Am I going to die?"

"I don't know. Probably yes, if you don't shut up and let me work." Mark quickly applied a serviceable field dressing, making it as tight as he could. But the wound was still bleeding a bit. "I've gotta put my hands on your shoulder. I'm going to have to hold them there for a while. It's going to hurt—a lot—but it will help stop the bleeding. You ready?"

A long pause. "OK."

Mark placed one palm on either side of the man's shoulder and pressed them together hard. As he held them there, the wounded man sat with his back to the wall, eyes closed, teeth clenched.

Mark didn't think the wound was life threatening, provided it was treated at a decent hospital soon, before any infection had a chance to set in. The lack of spurting blood told him the bullet hadn't hit an artery. So the real question was, why shoot the guy in the first place? Had they meant to kill him? And if not, why?

After maybe five minutes, Mark released his hands. "Let's see how that goes." He walked to the door and tried the handle. It was locked. Before turning around, he considered that something about the wounded man's voice was bugging him—he had a sense that he'd heard it before.

"What's your name?" Mark asked.

For a few moments, there was just the squeaking of the nodding-donkey oil pumps going up and down, and the man's heavy, labored breathing.

Then, "Rad."

Mark stiffened. In his head, he replayed the voice he'd just heard. "Rad, what?"

"Rad . . . Saveljic."

Mark slumped back into the dirt.

He was stunned, though he told himself that he shouldn't be. Not after the Marko business with Saeed. But Mark hadn't anticipated that the Saudis would be able to get to an actual family member so quickly. The United States was a long way away.

"*Radovan* Saveljic?"

Mark spoke the name as a question, but now that he looked at Rad, there was no question about it. His brother was older, and much heavier, and he had a thick cheesy mustache. But the low forehead, the high cheekbones, the big ears . . . the way his brother cocked his head and said his name, the Jersey accent—it was definitely Rad.

"Yeah. How do you know?" The question came out as an accusation.

Mark's eyes were still adjusting to the light. The last time he'd seen his brother had been fifteen years ago, in New York City. Mark had been Stateside for a month, working to help train intelligence analysts at Langley. He'd come up to New York for the day to have lunch with his three siblings. Rad, then an eighteen-year-old freshman at Union County College and full of big ideas, had arranged it all—it had been an earnest, if ill-fated, attempt on Rad's part to try to bring the four Saveljic siblings closer together. They'd eaten at a bar and grill in the Village. His older sister, who was mildly autistic and had already left home by the time of the suicide, had driven over from central Jersey where she'd been working as a lab technician for a big pharmaceutical company. The conversation had been awkward. They'd talked a lot about his sister's cats. Rad had chimed in with the latest news about the Giants. Mark couldn't remember his younger brother, then sixteen and still living at home, saying anything at all. The last time he'd seen either of his brothers prior to that lunch had been seven years earlier; he hadn't seen his sister for twelve.

"Because we know each other," said Mark.

"How do we know each other?"

Mark considered that Saeed's men were almost certainly listening. He'd have to be careful not to tell Rad anything the Saudis didn't already know. "It's me, Rad. Marko. Your brother."

Rad's head jerked back. He sucked in a quick breath, then opened his eyes wide, as though struggling to see through the darkness. "Marko?"

"Yeah." Mark hadn't gone by that name in over twenty years.

Rad's breathing grew more labored, and Mark worried his brother was going into shock. At least it was warm in the shed. That would help.

Mark added, "I know. It's been a while."

A brain aneurism. That was what Mark's father had told everyone had been the cause of death. Back then, suicide wasn't talked about, and the cops and funeral director could be counted on to maintain the fiction. Mark had declined to tell his brothers and sister the truth. It would have accomplished nothing except to make a bad situation worse for them. Better that his siblings think that they had an enigmatic asshole brother than that they learn that their mother had been driven to suicide by their father's infidelity.

"What the hell is going on? Why am I here?"

Rad sounded as though he was wavering somewhere between desperation and anger.

"Some people who are upset with me are trying to get to me through you."

"What people?"

He'd told Rad that he worked for the State Department, and Mark assumed that's what Rad still believed.

"Mostly Saudis."

"Saudis? What in God's name are you involved in, Marko?"

"Where were you when you were taken?"

"India. Delhi. They broke my leg."

Mark glanced down. Near his shin, Rad's right leg was swollen tight and had an unnatural bump a few inches below the knee; it did look broken.

"What were you doing in India? And calm down, you're breathing too fast. Don't panic."

Rad said nothing for a minute, then answered, "I'm a project manager. For BP. The oil company. I was on a job."

"That explains it."

"No, that explains shit, Marko!" Rad's voice quivered. "That explains shit!"

"What I mean is that you were a target of opportunity. India's just a three-, four-hour flight from here. And it's a hell of a lot easier to smuggle someone out of India than it is out of the US."

Now Mark understood why he'd been kept waiting in the desert; his captors had been waiting for Rad to arrive.

"What happens now?" Rad groaned and clutched at his shoulder, then asked, "What are we gonna do?"

Mark was still taken aback at seeing his little brother like this. The Rad he really remembered was still a little boy, running around the house, getting in trouble for writing on the walls or throwing rocks at the neighbor's car. He'd been a funny kid, a friendly kid, and they'd gotten along well enough before the suicide; with a twelve-year age difference between them, they hadn't had anything to fight about.

Mark didn't think most people changed that much over the course of their lives—at least not as much as they liked to think they did—but realistically, that little boy was long gone. The fact was that Mark hardly knew the grown man who was lying in the dirt in front of him.

But he's your brother.

Mark said, "I'm gonna find a way to get you out of here."

Three deep breaths, then, "How?"

"The point was for me to see them hurt you."

"Freakin' insane."

"I know."

"You were lying. About working for the State Department." A grimace. "Weren't you?"

Mark considered that the Saudis already knew he worked for the CIA. "Yes."

"I fuckin' knew it. Where are we?"

"Bahrain."

"Where the hell is Bahrain?"

"The Persian Gulf. It's an island north of Saudi Arabia. Some people I'm pissing off here thought they could get to me by getting to you."

"But we hardly know each other."

"Guess they didn't know that. Or if they did, they didn't care."

"Who are you, Marko?"

Mark turned to look at Rad. "I'm an intelligence operative." Taking in Rad's blank look, Mark added, "Sometimes in this business, you have to divide your life up, throw some of your real life away, make other parts up. Compartmentalize your life . . . you know what I'm saying?"

"Yeah. You bullshit people. Like you're bullshitting me now."

"After college, I got involved with a whole other world. The kind of world where, once you're in it, you tend to stay in it. And it's important to keep that world separate from your family. Even your brother. For their own good."

"You're a spy."

"I prefer intelligence operative."

"For the United States?"

"It's complicated. It's one of those 'the more you know, the more you're at risk' deals."

Rad was quiet for a while. Mark listened to the voices outside. There were still at least three men.

"What's going to happen to me, Marko? Are they going to let me die?"

"*I'm* not going to let you die." Mark wasn't sure that was true, but he'd try his best to make it true. "I'm sorry about this."

"I'm supposed to be getting married."

"Congratulations."

"I can't die, Marko. I've got too much going on."

"I said I'd handle it."

Mark sat cross-legged in the dirt for a while, thinking about what to do next.

"Give me your wrist." Mark felt for a pulse. It was high, around 140. "Listen," he said. "You're going into shock, which is normal after what you've been through. I'd say lie down, but right now we want to keep your shoulder high. So just sit back, get as comfortable as you can, and try to relax. Focus on your breathing. Keep it slow and steady. Don't panic. Try to meditate or something."

"You gotta be kidding me."

"Then pray, think of your favorite movie, whatever. The point is—get to a calm place in your head. And don't lose hope. You're not going to bleed out now. We can set your leg later. You're hurt, but believe me, you can survive for a long, long time like this."

No one spoke for a minute. Then Rad said, "You got any water?"

"No." Eating or drinking a lot when you were going into shock wasn't a good idea, Mark knew, but a little water wouldn't hurt.

He stood up and tried the door, but it wouldn't open, so he banged on it for a while.

"A little water in here!" he yelled.

He banged on the door some more. When no one came to open it, he sat back in the dirt next to Rad.

Moments later, the door opened. A Saudi used his pistol to gesture to Mark. "You. Get out."

"Give him some water first."

"No."

"I'm not leaving, which means I'm not handing over the kid until he gets some water. All he needs is a little. Too much will make him sick."

The Saudi muttered a few words in Arabic and two more men appeared. They grabbed Mark, hauled him out of the shed, then threw him into the back of the blue Chevy.

46

Mark was driven to the little town of Awali, which lay on the southern edge of the desert, not far from the golf course. They stopped near the center of town, in front of an apartment complex spray-painted with depictions of Shias who had been killed by the government. Before they shoved him out of the car, the driver handed Mark a phone. It was on. Mark raised it to his ear.

"Bring the boy *immediately* to the Hyatt Regency hotel in Bishkek. A plane will leave Manama shortly. It should touch down in Bishkek in five hours."

Mark gripped the phone hard in his hand. He pictured Saeed slicing into a steak at the golf course, watching the sun slowly set. Or driving around in a fancy car with leather seats, the air-conditioning humming as he crossed the causeway that connected Bahrain to Saudi Arabia. Then he pictured Rad bleeding in the dirt.

"I wasn't lying about needing time to get the boy to Bishkek. He's in a remote region in Kyrgyzstan. The roads are awful. I'll get him there as soon as I can," Mark said.

"The sooner you get the boy to the hotel, the sooner your brother will be released."

"Five in the morning, Bishkek time. That's two in the morning Bahrain time, a little more than eight hours from now."

"My men will be there."

"Treat my brother well."

"We're not animals here. He will be treated as a guest. But if the transfer of the boy doesn't take place as planned, you can bring a body bag when you come to pick up your brother. Consider yourself warned."

"If I need to reach you before the transfer, how do I contact you?"

"You don't. You just deliver the child. I sense you're a man who likes to bargain, Marko. But there will be no more bargaining because I won't be there for you to bargain with. In a moment, you will be released to make whatever arrangements you need to make, and I will disappear. The only thing that will save your brother is if you deliver the child. If you do so, I will have him transferred to the Royal Bahrain Hospital in Manama. If you don't . . . well, I think we have an understanding now, no?"

"Oh, yes," said Mark. "We definitely have an understanding."

What Mark understood was that he'd have to be an idiot to trust Saeed to hand over his brother once Muhammad had been delivered. What incentive would Saeed have to do so? What could he possibly stand to gain?

Rad now knew his captors were Saudis. He'd be able to recognize many of them. If the Saudis were to release Rad, he might make a stink with the US embassy in Manama. He might go to the press. His employer, BP, might get involved. The only reason to release Rad would be to placate Mark.

And Mark wasn't convinced that was enough of an incentive. He thought it just as likely that the Saudis—once they had Muhammad—would try to kill both Saveljic brothers and be done with the whole mess.

Mark had been playing this game for far too long to walk like a lamb to that slaughter. No, the best way to secure Rad's safety—and to do right by Muhammad—was to insure that Saeed was properly motivated to do the right thing.

Money was an option. Mark had over a half million dollars he could wire to Saeed overnight. Though that might do the trick, Mark doubted it would. Saeed was just a representative of the Saudi intelligence apparatus, and to Saudi intelligence, a half million dollars was pocket change. Other common tools—appealing to a person's ego or conscience, or offering them an opportunity to exact revenge upon an enemy—were also almost certain to fail in this case.

Dredging up compromising information about Saeed was definitely on the table. Maybe Saeed was an adulterer, or had tried to embezzle money, or was gay—a potentially capital offense in Saudi Arabia. But those were leverage points that—if they even existed—would take time to uncover.

Extortion through other means was possible, though. Especially if it were combined with some of the cruder tools of his trade. A plan began to form in Mark's mind.

PART III

47

Mark caught a cab back to the Manama Sheraton. By now it was a little after six. The sun was beginning to wane.

He connected to the hotel's Wi-Fi and used his iPod to call Kaufman. When he got sent into Kaufman's voicemail, he hung up and called again. And then hung up and called a third time. This time Kaufman answered on the fourth ring.

"I can't talk to you, Sava. You're radioactive on the seventh floor."

The offices on the seventh floor of CIA headquarters in Langley, Virginia, were occupied by the men and women at the very top of the Agency's bureaucracy.

"Someone on the inside shared my personnel file with the Saudis, Ted. I think it was Rosten."

"He wouldn't. Not the file of a former operative." Kaufman, however, sounded less convinced than his words implied.

Mark explained all that had happened since he'd taken Muhammad from the Saudis, concluding, "I don't know what deal Rosten tried to cut with the Shias, but whatever it was, it didn't work. So now he's going to throw the Shias under the bus and back the royals. But for that to happen, he needs for me to deliver the kid. He was worried I wouldn't, so he shared my personnel file with the Saudis so they could put the squeeze on me."

"I'm sorry about your brother, but maybe you *should* just deliver the kid. Did that ever occur to you?"

"My personnel file is chock full of intel from my time with Central Eurasia. Your division. This isn't just a shot fired at me, it's a shot fired at the whole division. If Rosten did this, you need to sound the alarm. Or, if it turns out management approved this, at least have the decency to tell me so I know what I'm dealing with."

"Mark—" Kaufman sighed.

It was a weary, maybe even frustrated sigh, but Mark was guessing that in the end Kaufman would help. His old boss was like that—always complaining, never eager—but when it came to defending Central Eurasia's turf, he was a seasoned infighter who looked out for his own.

"This isn't just about me, Ted. Something big is going on down here. I don't know what it is, but—am I telling you something you already know? Do you already know what the hell is going on here in Bahrain?"

"Unfortunately, no. All I know is that yesterday the deputy director personally ordered me to order you to show up at the embassy in Bishkek, and that once you got there you were supposed to do whatever Rosten told you to. Beyond that I'm in the dark."

"You know as well as I do that there should be a record of whoever accessed my file. There's only a handful of people with that clearance."

"I'll pull your file and find out who else has accessed it. But if it turns out it's Rosten, or someone even higher up, things are going to get sticky."

Mark called Larry Bowlan. "So, how'd you like a job?"

A pause, then, "Have you been drinking, Sava?"

"I mean it."

"No, 'Hello Larry, how've you been since the last time we talked'? No, 'Sorry for hanging up on you but thanks for hanging around the office for an extra hour, after everyone else has gone home'? Just insults?"

"I'm not insulting you."

"I have a job."

"I mean a real job. Hundred and fifty thousand a year base salary for intel work, with an opportunity for bonuses depending on risk factors."

"You pulling my leg?"

"No, Larry. This is the real deal. A real offer. You'd be working for me. I've been doing some private contract work—"

"I know what you've been doing. You've been working for that clown Bruce Holtz. Honestly, I thought a guy like Holtz was a little beneath—"

"I'm going out on my own."

"As of when?"

"As of now."

"You're not inspiring confidence."

"I can guarantee your salary for a year."

Bowlan didn't answer right away. "I'd be more comfortable with a year and a half."

"You're seventy-one years old, Larry. And you haven't exactly led what I'd call a healthy life. You could be dead in six months. Take a chance."

"I quit smoking. Doing the patches."

"Good for you."

"Year and a half."

"Fine." Mark knew Bowlan would have taken a year contract—would have taken six months for that matter—but he didn't want to haggle too much with his old boss. He needed Bowlan motivated.

"And I want a contract."

"I'll have one drawn up within the week."

"Really?" Bowlan sounded surprised, in the way someone who's just been told they've won the lottery might sound surprised.

"Yeah."

"When do I start?"

"Well, see, that's the thing."

"Here it comes, the catch."

"You start now. That's why I called."

"I thought the contract wouldn't be ready for a week?"

"Maybe sooner. Hell, I'll fill out a contract on a napkin and fax it to you now if you want. But I'm juggling a few things at the moment, and I can't be dealing with lawyers. If you really want the job, you're going to have to work on faith for a few days."

"When's my first paycheck?"

"Whenever I get around to paying you," Mark snapped. Then, thinking better of it, he added, "Whenever, Larry. Tomorrow if you need it."

Bowlan took a moment to answer, but Mark was certain it was just for show. He'd known Bowlan would be an easy recruit, and not just because of the money. Bowlan wanted to be back in the game.

"OK. You got yourself a deal, Sava. But I would advise you not to try to take advantage of the elderly. I may be a few years past my prime, but I'm a vindictive son of a bitch and I don't have a lot to lose, so keep that in mind."

"Welcome aboard, Larry. You're officially the first employee of Global Intelligence Solutions."

Mark had signed a non-compete agreement with Holtz, but he figured that wasn't going to be an issue for much longer. The Central Eurasia Division would almost certainly put out a burn notice—whether formally or informally—on Holtz. CAIN's business in Central Asia was about to dry up, at least as long as Holtz was running the show.

"Did you just make that name up?"

“This is the deal . . .”

Mark brought Larry up to date, including about what had happened to his brother.

Instead of expressing sympathy or alarm, Bowlan said, “So you’re telling me this isn’t a private intelligence op that you’re undertaking on behalf of a paying client. This is just a bail-out-you-and-your-brother op.”

“The first thing I need you to do is track down a few Saudi princes for me. I’m sure you get a steady stream of them coming into Dubai.”

“We do. . .” Bowlan sounded wary.

Laws in Saudi Arabia allowing polygamy, combined with astounding wealth, meant that there were thousands of members of the Saudi royal family. Many had business interests in places like Dubai and Bahrain, destinations that were popular not only for their pro-business tax and regulatory policies, but also because of the availability of alcohol and prostitutes—two attractions that were in short supply in Saudi Arabia.

“I need you to find me a few that have recently left Dubai for Bahrain. Is that something you can handle?”

“I can tap into the Emirates database, but when I do, I’ll leave a trail. It’ll be questioned, and if I don’t have good answers, which I won’t, I could be—”

“Fired, I know. That’s not relevant now.”

“And prosecuted. The same way whoever broke your cover can be prosecuted.”

“That’s the job, Larry. Take it or leave it. I didn’t promise a risk-free working environment.”

“Understood. But keep in mind, my data tap might be questioned in two days or two minutes. Point is, if you were counting on my having access to the consulate resources in the days and weeks to come, don’t.”

Mark continued as if Bowlan hadn’t spoken, “At the same time, I need you to search arrival records for a woman named

Kalila Safi. She would have flown in from Bahrain around three days ago. Fifty-six years old. Find out everything you can about her. How's your Arabic?"

"I'm still as sharp as ever."

Mark recalled that Bowlan, thanks to a few courses at Yale fifty years earlier, was able to speak a formal form of Arabic. It was a variation of the language that virtually no one spoke in real life, except maybe when giving a dry academic dissertation, but Larry was at least able to make himself understood—albeit barely.

"Glad to hear it. Track her down and talk to her. Tell her about Muhammad. Get her take on what's going on."

"Hang on. I'll call you back."

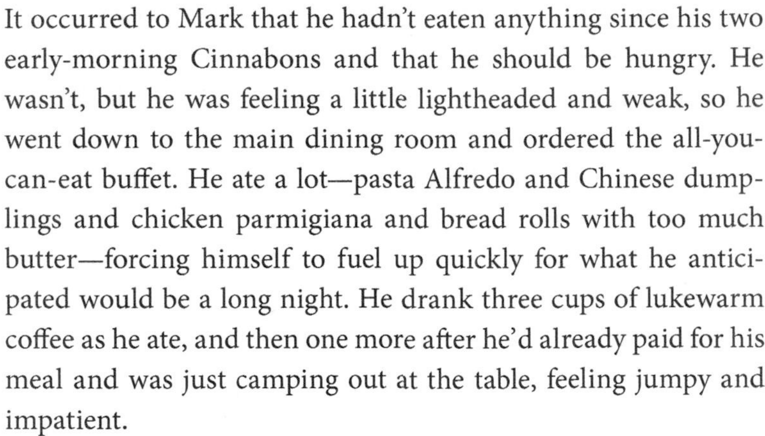

It occurred to Mark that he hadn't eaten anything since his two early-morning Cinnabons and that he should be hungry. He wasn't, but he was feeling a little lightheaded and weak, so he went down to the main dining room and ordered the all-you-can-eat buffet. He ate a lot—pasta Alfredo and Chinese dumplings and chicken parmigiana and bread rolls with too much butter—forcing himself to fuel up quickly for what he anticipated would be a long night. He drank three cups of lukewarm coffee as he ate, and then one more after he'd already paid for his meal and was just camping out at the table, feeling jumpy and impatient.

He didn't like the fact that he had to rely so much on Bowlan.

Come on, Larry. Enough already.

He thought about Rad, and then forced himself not to. He thought about Daria, and hoped she was safe. He wanted to call or e-mail her, but didn't want to have to explain his plans. She wouldn't approve—of that he was certain—though she'd approve of the result if he managed to pull it off.

Finally, fifty-two minutes after they'd last spoken, Bowlan called back.

"OK, you ready?"

Mark was relieved to hear the old man's voice again. "Shoot."

"Kalila Safi did pass through customs three days ago. And if she's the Kalila Safi I think she is, she's the sister of a wealthy developer here in Dubai. I left a few messages at residential and business numbers I was able to dredge up for the developer, but no one's called back."

"Great. Keep pushing until you talk to Kalila herself."

"Yeah, I got it the first time. As for the Saudi princes, I got two live ones. First is Bandar bin Fahd. He works for a private equity firm in Manama and is the son of a provincial Saudi governor. It's a pretty good bet that what he really does is just invest all the money his dad makes by bilking the government. He left Dubai for Bahrain yesterday. Then we've got Abdulaziz bin Salman, son of the deputy minister of agriculture, lists his job as civil engineer. He left Dubai for Bahrain two days ago."

"Spell the names."

Bowlan did.

Mark googled them with his iPod, then said, "Nothing on Abdulaziz. With Bandar, I'm looking at a bunch of hits related to his private equity work . . . and, hold on . . . and a press report that says he was caught with three prostitutes at the Four Seasons in London, bit of a minor scandal." Mark took thirty seconds to skim the rest of the article. "He's also a grandson of the king, but he isn't anywhere close to being in line for the throne. Does he travel a lot to Bahrain?"

Mark heard Bowlan pecking slowly at a keyboard. "Pretty regularly, looks like once or twice a month."

"You wouldn't happen to know where he stays while he's there?"

"Ah . . ." After a minute, Bowlan said, "No. Those records would be with customs in Bahrain. But he lists the Hilton here in

Dubai under his contact info. I'm looking at two years of data here, multiple entries each month, and he always stays at the Hilton. I'd bet he does the same thing at one of the higher-end hotels in Manama. Probably keeps a suite there like an apartment. The Saudis with money to burn do that. They like the room service."

"Is there a Hilton in Bahrain?"

"I don't know."

Mark googled it. There wasn't. Nor were there any Hilton affiliates. "Is he married?"

"Yes."

"Does he travel with his wife? Or a bodyguard?"

"I doubt he'd travel with his wife. One, it would cramp his style. Two, Saudi women don't travel much. However, he does list one travel companion on all his applications. Could be his driver, bodyguard, lover, all of the above, whatever."

"OK—e-mail me Bandar's photo." Mark gave Bowlan an e-mail address.

"You got it. That's it?"

"Get in touch with Kalila Safi."

"Yeah, I know. I meant besides that."

"What's your cell number?"

Bowlan read it off.

"I'll be calling you soon," said Mark. "Be ready to move."

48

Mark agreed with Bowlan's assessment that Prince Bandar bin Fahd of Saudi Arabia probably stayed at one of the upscale hotels in or around Manama, but that didn't help much. Bahrain was a wealthy nation. There were lots of upscale hotels. And it was a near certainty that every one of them would have a strict confidentiality policy that would prevent them from revealing whether Bandar was a guest. So he figured he'd work the prostitution angle instead.

He caught a cab, got dropped off in the busy Awadhiya section of Manama, spent fifteen minutes ducking in the front doors and out the back doors of various shops until he was certain he'd gotten rid of anyone who might have been tailing him, then caught another cab—this time to the Juffair district of Manama, not far from the US naval base.

Mark didn't know anything about prostitution in Bahrain. But he was betting the area around the navy base wouldn't be a bad place to start learning about it.

Al Shabab Avenue was the main drag of Juffair, a long Americanized strip of road lined with a Chili's, Baskin-Robbins, Dairy Queen, McDonald's, and dozens of other Western chains. Given its proximity to the naval base, Mark was also counting on finding what he saw next—a sign advertising a GENT'S SALOON. Next to the saloon was a Chinese massage parlor.

He put his eyes up to the tinted window of the saloon and saw that it wasn't a saloon at all—it was actually a barbershop whose owner had added an extra letter *o* to the word *salon*.

But the Chinese massage parlor looked like the real deal. The doorframe around the front entrance was grimy, the red-and-white neon sign above the door, garish. When Mark stepped inside, he noted the red carpet was in need of a good steam cleaning.

A slender Asian woman who looked to be about sixty greeted him. She sat in a dim front parlor, at a desk trimmed with what looked like Christmas icicle lights. Behind her hung a poster depicting a buxom, dark-haired woman riding a Chinese dragon. The place smelled like licorice-infused incense and cigarettes.

Mark told her that he'd come for a massage, asked what her prices were, and listened as she told him.

The businesslike way she spoke, the assurance with which she carried herself, the way she looked at Mark as she might an article of clothing she was considering purchasing—all these signals made Mark reluctant to try to tap her for information. He assumed that she'd sell him information for the right price, but he feared she'd tell him anything she thought he wanted to hear, true or not.

"The regular fifteen-dinar massage will be fine," he said.

The woman frowned. "The special massage is much better."

"With someone who speaks English?"

"Yes, yes, of course."

"OK, I'll take the half-hour special massage."

"One hour is the best price."

"I only have a half hour."

The woman frowned again.

"Take it or leave it," said Mark.

He paid in advance and tipped the woman five dinars. She led him down a narrow hall. Red lightbulbs set in cheap brass wall sconces had been fitted with tiny white lampshades. The eerie light cast distorted shadows onto the walls.

The woman opened a door at the end of the hall. Inside was more red light.

He walked into the room and closed the door behind him. It was a small space, no more than eight by ten feet. Just enough room for a massage table and a small end table, on which sat an incense burner, some sticks of incense, and a big bottle of citrus-scented oil.

He ran his hand over the massage table, confirmed there weren't any residual body fluids on it, and then hoisted himself onto it.

"Lie down please. Clothes off."

The masseuse picked up the bottle of citrus-scented oil. Her arms were slender, and her small breasts were partially visible through her negligee. About thirty years old, Mark guessed, although maybe that was the light—she could have been older. He caught a whiff of perfume.

"I prefer to talk first," said Mark.

The woman had been about to unscrew the cap on the bottle of oil, but she stopped. "You paid for a massage."

"Do you ever have any Saudi clients?"

Her eyes darted to his face. She looked confused, and suspicious.

Mark said, "Hold on." He pulled a twenty-dinar note out of his front pants pocket, and placed it on the end table, next to the burning incense. "A tip. I'm searching for someone. Any help you can give me would be appreciated."

"No Saudis, mostly Americans. Soldiers. Sailors."

"Saudis *never* come here?"

"Not usually. Only with Americans, not alone."

"Ever hear of a guy named Bandar bin Salman?"

A long pause, then, "No."

"If I were from Saudi Arabia, where would I go for an *extra*-special massage? The kind where I could get anything I wanted?"

The masseuse waited a second, then said, "Hoora. But this is not a nice place."

"Where in Hoora?"

"It is better to get an extra-special massage here."

Mark pulled another twenty-dinar note out of his wallet. "Where in Hoora. Please, I'm searching for someone. Someone I want to help."

"Exhibitions Avenue," she said. "All the Saudis go here. For drink." She paused. "For special massages."

"Where on Exhibitions Avenue?"

"All over."

"Where would you go?"

"I don't go."

"If you were from Saudi Arabia and wanted a special massage?" When she didn't answer, Mark said, "Please. Your best guess."

"Maybe Victory Towers. I hear many Saudis go there."

"Is it a hotel?"

"Apartments. But you can rent them for one day. You rent them, someone gives you a phone number, then you can call someone for your extra-special massage."

"Thank you." He slid off the table and headed for the door.

"But you already paid," said the masseuse.

"Your lucky day," said Mark. "I forgot, I have to be somewhere sooner than I thought."

49

Bahrain might have been on the verge of revolution, with nightly street battles being fought in the poor suburbs, but little of the tension that was gripping the country was visible on Exhibitions Avenue in downtown Manama. The sidewalks teemed with people who had come to patronize all the electronics shops, nightclubs, and bars. Police patrolled the traffic-clogged streets in SUVs with windows protected by metal grates. Young men, some wearing white robes, roamed the streets looking and sounding a little boozed up as they chattered away on their cell phones, occasionally laughing a bit too loud. When Mark passed a woman loitering on a street corner, decked out in a short skirt, sky-high heels, and a spangly top, he knew he must be getting close.

Victory Towers, a complex of relatively new seven-story sand-colored buildings, was located not far off the main strip. Mark entered the front lobby of the building nearest the street and was greeted by a pasty-faced receptionist with a pencil-thin mustache, pencil-thin sideburns, and slicked-back hair. He stood behind a granite-topped counter, in a clean and freshly painted—but unusually spare—lobby. No pictures hung on the beige walls. There was nowhere to sit.

When Mark said he wanted to rent a one-bedroom apartment for the night, the receptionist, smiling with an unctuous false deference and speaking with a Russian accent, indicated that the cost would be eighty dinars.

Probably Russian mafia, Mark guessed. He knew they controlled many of the prostitution rings in Dubai and guessed the same was true in Bahrain.

"Does that price include companionship?"

"No. You want escort, this cost you negotiate with escort service."

"And you can provide me with the names of some suitable escort services?"

"Yes, of course."

Mark paid cash and was given a form to fill out that asked for his name and address and passport number. He made everything up, figuring he could get away with it in a place like this—and he was right. The receptionist didn't ask for any identification.

His room was on the fifth floor, and looked down on a busy roundabout below. There was a single bedroom, with a bed that had been made up with clean sheets. Across from the bed was a flat-screen TV and media center. A reasonably new-looking blue couch was the only object in the main room. Nothing else.

He pulled out the business card that the receptionist had given him. It read EXOTIC ENCOUNTERS and listed a phone number, which he called.

Another Russian answered. Mark explained that he needed a woman who was used to catering to Saudi tastes, but who spoke Russian or Turkish or English. He was alone, but some Saudi friends might be joining him soon. The woman had to be comfortable with that.

Not a problem, he was assured.

"Tonight I'm at the Victory Towers, but tomorrow I'll be at the Sheraton Hotel. If I like her, would it be a problem for her to come there?"

That too was not a problem. Exotic Encounters serviced all of Manama.

When the woman knocked, Mark opened the door and gestured she should sit down on the couch. She did so without making eye contact with him. He'd left a hundred dinars—the agreed-upon price—on the center cushion. She picked up the money, rolled it up, and put it in a pocket inside her short skirt.

She was depressingly young. Around sixteen, Mark guessed. Her bare arms and legs were too thin, her cheekbones too pronounced. Because she was so young, she was still beautiful, but it was the fragile, waifish beauty of an anorexic, or an AIDS victim.

"What is your name?" he asked in English.

Mark didn't have any problem with prostitution, at least not in theory, when both parties entered into the negotiation willingly, when both parties were adults and the woman—or man—was adequately compensated. The problem was that that was rarely the case.

She didn't answer him, so he tried Russian. "What country do you come from?"

Hesitation, then in barely audible Russian, "Bulgaria."

"What is your name?"

"Ivana."

"Thank you for coming, Ivana."

She still hadn't looked him in the eye.

Mark said, "I want you to look at a picture." But the moment he said it, her head dipped lower, and he knew he'd erred. "Not a bad kind of picture. Just a picture of a man's face. I'm searching for someone. That's why I'm here." Just in case she didn't get it, he added, "I'm not here for sex. You're a beautiful girl, it's just that I'm trying to help someone I care a lot about, and this man . . ."

Mark took out his iPod and pulled up the photo that Bowlan had sent him. "His name is Bandar bin Salman. He's a Saudi."

Ivana took the iPod reluctantly when Mark offered it to her. She glanced at it, then shook her head.

"He comes to Bahrain often. Maybe some of your . . . friends, maybe they would know where he stays, where I might find him. He might have come to a place like this, or he might have had a woman come to him."

Ivana just shrugged. And then put the iPod down on the couch.

"It's worth a lot to me. A lot of money. I'd be happy to share that money with you. And your friends."

She didn't seem enthused by the prospect. Mark wondered whether she'd even be able to keep extra money if he gave it to her. Or whether she was searched after each assignation.

"I have to ask my boss," she said. "Maybe he can ask the other girls."

"OK."

"So you want me to go now?"

"Will you bring your boss?"

She shrugged.

"Yes. Please. See if anyone is interested in making money. One thousand dinars to the person who can tell me where to find this Saudi man."

Ivana stood up. As she was leaving, Mark said, "Are you OK? Do you need help?"

She just walked out the door.

His question had been stupid, Mark thought, as he waited in the empty room. Of course she wasn't OK, of course she needed help. The problem was, the kind of help she needed wasn't the kind of help he was prepared to give. Or maybe even could give.

He imagined she'd been lured away from a bleak life in a small village with the promise of adventure and money—waiting tables in some fancy restaurant halfway across the world—only to discover, once she got there, that the people who'd promised her the world had been lying.

Mark considered just handing Muhammad over to the Saudis and instead trying to do something to help Ivana.

It was a silly idea, he knew. The world was drowning in pain, more than any individual, or even any single nation, could deal with. Whether it was kids losing their mothers, or girls being sold as sex slaves, or the millions that died of hunger every year, it was futile to react to every suffering individual just because you happened to witness their pain. If he knew about the widespread existence of a particular atrocity and had done nothing to help stop it before, then why should seeing a real-life example of such depravity make any difference to him?

It shouldn't.

Dammit, thought Mark. He closed his eyes and rubbed his temples, trying to refocus his thoughts. You've got your brother and Muhammad to deal with. And you've got very little time. Put this awful place out of your mind and concentrate.

But concentrating on his brother and Muhammad didn't do him any good either; until he got intel on the Saudi, he was stuck.

Five minutes later, the door opened and a tall blond man with a crooked nose entered the room. He wore black jeans and a silk short-sleeved collared shirt that he'd left open at the neck, exposing a gold necklace. Behind him stood a tank of a man who wore a sport coat that did a poor job of hiding the bulge of a pistol holstered under his left arm.

Typical, thought Mark. These Russian mafia guys were caricatures of themselves. He'd dealt with them in Azerbaijan, in Georgia, in Kyrgyzstan. No matter what country they turned up in, the front men were always the same. Young and aggressive, with just enough life experience to be good at being an asshole, but not enough experience, or education, to be good at much else. He studied the guy with the gold necklace. He had small eyes and teeth that—while not rotten—could have benefited from some orthodontia. As a pimply fifteen-year-old kid growing up in the slums of Moscow, he would have been pitiful. As a guy in his mid-twenties, pimping in Manama, he was easy to detest.

Mark stood up.

"Sit down," the pimp ordered in Russian.

Mark remained standing. "Did Ivana tell you what I need?"

"I said sit down."

"Thanks, but I'd rather stand."

The pimp glanced behind him and nodded. The bodyguard was older than the pimp, and looked meaner. Mark detected a spider tattoo on the man's neck, possibly indicating that he was, or had been, a thief. There were also tattoos on the guy's hands and fingers.

The bodyguard closed the distance between himself and Mark in a few swift strides.

Mark saw the punch coming but didn't counter it; he wasn't there to get in a fight. He did turn, so that the blow grazed the top of his head instead of hitting him right in the nose, but the guy was strong and the punch still did real damage.

Mark blacked out for a second as he fell back into the couch. The pimp walked over and slapped him hard in the face.

"When I say sit, I mean sit."

Mark hated having his head hit like that. He'd already taken a lot of physical abuse over the years. He didn't want to wind up like one of those punch-drunk boxers who've taken too many hits and wind up losing their minds at fifty. On top of all that he was tired, pissed to hell at the Saudis for what they'd done to Rad, and bitter about not having helped Ivana or anyone else escape from this loathsome place.

He rubbed his head. "You didn't need to do that. All I need is a little bit of information. And I'm willing to pay a lot for it. I'm asking to do business with you. You're a businessman, aren't you?" He tried to affect a submissive attitude, but he was too pissed off to pull it off.

"You come here," said the pimp. "You buy a beautiful girl. One of my best. And then you reject her. You are a fucking faggot?"

Mark pulled out his iPod. "I'm just looking for information about this man."

He extended the device to the pimp, who smacked it out of Mark's hand.

"Dude. I'm not here to fight." Mark's voice had an edge to it now. "I'm here to make a deal."

"Are you police?"

"No."

"Good." The pimp slapped Mark hard again on the face. Then he turned to his bodyguard. "Beat up this piece of shit, take his wallet, take all his money, find out who he is, and then throw him in the trash." The pimp turned back to Mark. "If I ever see you here again, I'll kill you. I don't care who you work for or why you are here. We don't give out information about other clients. Understand?"

"Yeah, but you don't have to—" Mark stood up again as the bodyguard approached. He put his hands up as he backed away. "Hey, hey, hey! I'll just leave! You don't have to—"

Mark wasn't a big guy, but he'd always been fast, and willing to fight dirty.

He started backing up into a corner, as though scared, but as soon as the big Russian's hand came up, Mark jabbed his own fist right into the bodyguard's throat, aiming for the windpipe in the hopes of collapsing it. A half second later he kicked the guy in the balls, jabbed a thumb in his eye, reached for his shoulder-holstered pistol, saw in that split second that the safety was off, and pulled the trigger.

The bullet traveled up into the bottom of the bodyguard's head and out through the back of it, splattering blood, bone, and brain onto the carpet and the wall directly behind them.

Without pausing for even a second, Mark raised the pistol—a Makarov, he noted—aimed for the pimp's head, and said, "*Nyet.*"

The pimp froze, but Mark had seen his eyes dart toward the door.

"You go for that door, you're dead," Mark warned. He spoke with authority. The pretense of fear was gone.

Mark could hear the pimp's breathing. It had turned loud, as though he'd just finished sprinting down the street and was trying to catch his breath. He was staring intently at Mark.

Mark was breathing heavily himself. His gun hand was rock steady, but his mind wasn't.

He'd acted out of instinct. His fight-or-flight reaction had kicked in and the verdict had been fight. But had he really needed to kill the guy? There had been other options. What the hell was wrong with him?

Get off the shrink couch, he warned himself. You're in a dangerous place. Just act.

"We have no problem," said the pimp. "You can just go."

"I'm not going anywhere. This is what we're gonna do."

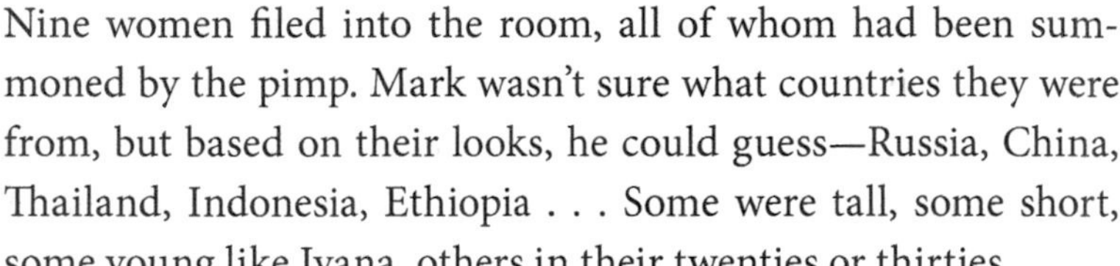

Nine women filed into the room, all of whom had been summoned by the pimp. Mark wasn't sure what countries they were from, but based on their looks, he could guess—Russia, China, Thailand, Indonesia, Ethiopia . . . Some were tall, some short, some young like Ivana, others in their twenties or thirties.

Mark sat on the couch as they lined up in front of him. The pistol he'd stolen from the bodyguard was hidden under his left thigh. He'd had the pimp drag the bodyguard into the bedroom and then clean up in the front room as best he could, using a towel from the bathroom and bed sheets. Even so, there were stains on the carpet that just wouldn't come out.

The women didn't seem to notice the stains, but they certainly suspected something was wrong, that much was obvious. They kept their heads down, and no one smiled. Mark supposed that anything out of the ordinary was cause for concern, but a mass summons from their boss—a summons that wasn't clearly sexual in nature—was cause for real fear.

The pimp stood near the door to the bathroom, holding Mark's iPod. His temples glistened with sweat.

"Start," Mark said to the pimp.

The pimp lifted up the iPod. "I want each of you to look at this man, and tell me if he has ever been one of your clients. His name is Bandar bin Salman, but he might have used an alias." When none of the women responded, the pimp thrust the iPod at the girl on the far left. "Do it. Translate what I said for the rest of the girls."

The pimp's hand trembled as the girl took the iPod. The girl looked at the image of Bandar, claimed not to recognize him, then translated the pimp's directive into English and Arabic as she handed the iPod to the next girl.

She didn't recognize Bandar either, but the sixth in line, an older woman with black hair and almond-shaped eyes, did. She only spoke Thai, though, so another Thai woman had to translate what she said into English.

"Maybe three months ago she meets this man. One night only."

"Does she know where?" demanded the pimp.

"The Golden Tulip," she replied.

The pimp breathed an audible sigh of relief. "The Golden Tulip," he repeated to Mark.

"Yeah, you know, I heard. Give me your phone."

The pimp handed Mark his smartphone, which Mark used to google *Golden Tulip Bahrain*. After finding the hotel website, he clicked on the Accommodations button.

"How many beds were in the room?" he asked.

The question was translated. The answer came back as one.

"A big bed? The biggest size?"

The girl confirmed that yes, the bed was huge.

Mark opened up three different tabs on the Internet browser. On each tab, he followed links to a different sample photo of the available room options. The first was of a standard room with a king bed, the second of a deluxe room with a king bed, and the third was of an executive suite with a king bed. The carpet, bed-covers, headboard, and furniture were the same in the standard and deluxe rooms, but different in the executive suite.

The girl only needed a moment to confirm that she was certain she'd met Bandar in the executive suite. She recognized the distinctive metal scrollwork on the headboard.

"Which room?" asked Mark.

She didn't remember the room number, but she said she thought it had been one of the corner suites.

50

As Mark fled the Victory Towers complex via a fire exit stairwell, he wondered whether he'd been caught on any closed-circuit surveillance video. The likelihood that there'd been a camera in the lobby, or outside, was high. It was even possible that a camera had been hidden in the room itself, though he doubted it; he'd questioned the pimp at gunpoint, and the guy had insisted the room was clean. In the end, he decided that trying to track down and remove all evidence of his presence at the Towers would take too long and potentially just result in more violence.

Mark hadn't gone into the complex intending to kill anyone—he'd done far too much of that already over his long career—and, in retrospect, he shouldn't have, even considering the circumstances. He'd already disabled the bodyguard with the punch to the throat. The shot to the head had been gratuitous, a product of anger, or rather disgust, at a moment when he should have been focusing on the larger problem.

He also knew he shouldn't have crossed the Russian mafia. They had long memories, and a well-deserved reputation for exacting revenge. If the killing had helped even one of those women escape from that life—he thought of the young Ivana—he wouldn't have had any regrets. But he was certain it hadn't.

He hoped that he'd get lucky on this one and that he hadn't compromised the larger mission. Hoping to get lucky was a lousy way to pursue intelligence, though. He was too old to be making mistakes like that, too old to be acting out of anger.

File it in a dark corner of your mind and forget about it, he told himself. Compartmentalize it. It's done.

He pulled out a prepaid cell phone as he ducked down a side road off Exhibitions Avenue. It was a little after nine, just over three hours since he'd last spoken with Saeed. He was past due to check in with Kaufman.

"You were right. There was a breech," said Kaufman.

"No kidding. It was Rosten, wasn't it?"

"Nope. Guy named Gregory Larkin. He's been with us for nine years. I've worked with him, I thought he was solid."

"Is he one of Rosten's men?"

"No. He's Africa Division. But he had the clearances he needed to pull your file."

"Africa Division?"

"You ever hear of a guy named Rear Admiral Jeffrey Garver?"

"No."

"He's the director of naval intelligence in Bahrain. Turns out Gregory Larkin used to work in naval intelligence, got his start working under Garver. Anyway, I just got done talking to Larkin—he claims Garver called him yesterday all in a panic. Something about an imminent attack in Bahrain about to go down, bombs going off within the hour. Larkin claims that Garver said it was imperative that he be able to see your file, that you had intel that could stop the attack but there wasn't enough time to make the request through normal channels."

"That's a load of BS. There's something big going down here, but if I had intel that could stop some imminent attack, you or Rosten could have just asked me."

"Larkin seems to think he was just doing what any patriot would, bending the rules in a time of crisis because he had to. He trusted Garver, they were friends."

"How do you know that?"

"I told you, I just got off the phone with Larkin. He admitted it to me as soon as I confronted him. Honestly, I think he was shitting bricks about what he'd done. He said he never heard back from Garver after he transferred the file."

"Garver handed parts or all of my file to the Saudis, and the Saudis are now using it as leverage against me. That guy Larkin *better* be shitting bricks."

"But why?" asked Kaufman. "What would Garver stand to gain? Or, if he's doing this on behalf of the navy, what would the navy stand to gain?"

"Who else knows about this?"

"No one yet. I figured I'd talk to you first. But I can't let this breech stand. Larkin will be fired and Garver will likely be court-martialed."

"Give me a day before you sound the alarms."

"Why?" When Mark didn't answer, Kaufman said, "Oh, I get it. You're going to lean on Garver."

"Hard to bargain with someone who's being dragged off to the brig. I don't suppose you could dredge up Garver's contact info for me?"

51

Mark caught a cab to a shopping mall in downtown Manama where he bought a small suitcase and supplies he might need for the evening. Then he took a cab to the Golden Tulip.

The hotel sat just across from the Sheraton, offering easy access to the newer diplomatic area of Manama. A large hotel that catered to business travelers, its interior was marked by the same white-marble sterility of the Royal Golf Club. A woman with long dark hair only partially covered by a black headscarf trimmed in gold stood behind the reception desk. A small ceiling-mounted security camera was pointed at them.

As he pulled out his wallet, Mark told her he wanted one of the executive suites. He was informed that the whole fifth floor was a first-class section of sorts and that all the executive suites were located there.

"I need one with a king bed. Which rooms are available?"

"Ah . . ." The woman consulted the laptop computer on the desk. "Well, everything except 508, 516, and 517."

Mark had suspected that, with the protests on the island heating up, the hotel would have a lot of vacancies.

"One of the corner suites."

"Well, I can offer you 502, 511, or 523. Five seventeen is a corner suite, but as I said, that's taken."

"Five twenty-three will be fine."

"I take it you've stayed with us before?"

Mark ignored her question. Instead, he slid his British passport and accompanying credit card across the reception table. "One night, please."

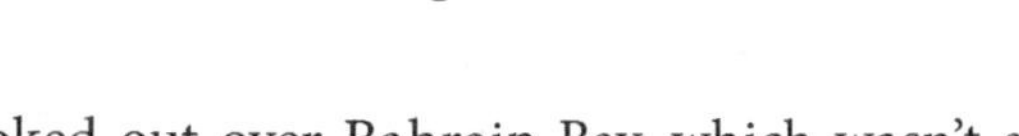

Room 523 looked out over Bahrain Bay, which wasn't a bay at all but a massive patch of reclaimed land that used to be a bay and which, if the country didn't fall to pieces, the bellhop said, would soon be the site of a Four Seasons Hotel and a big investment bank.

After explaining about the bay, the bellhop tried to show Mark around, pointing out as he did so that a dedicated executive-floor attendant was available, and an exclusive executive-floor lounge, and—

Mark cut the guy off with a thank-you and a tip, then strolled down to room 517— the only other occupied corner suite on the executive floor—wheeling the small suitcase he'd bought behind him. He looked for security cameras in the hall but saw none.

The gun he'd taken from the pimp's bodyguard was wedged between his gut and his belt. There were seven rounds left in the magazine.

He stood outside the door for a minute. Hearing nothing, he knocked.

Come on, he thought, feeling the butt of the Makarov pistol through his shirt. He'd run through several different scenarios in his head. A direct confrontation was the riskiest, but also the fastest.

He knocked again. No one answered, so he walked back to his room, lay down on the big king bed, propped a few pillows under his head, and pulled out his iPod. After connecting to the hotel's Wi-Fi, he checked the schedule of commercial flights from Dubai to Bahrain. There were typically fifteen or so; the first left before dawn, the last, well after midnight. It was just an hour-and-fifteen-minute flight, so Bowlan could get here quickly if need be.

Mark closed his eyes for a moment. He was so tired he felt he could fall asleep if he wasn't careful. Visions of Rad, and Muhammad, and the fallen bodyguard kept looping through his mind.

He placed a call to the front desk. The bathroom in his room was dirty, he explained.

"Dirty, sir?"

"The bathroom. I'm afraid it hasn't been cleaned."

"The entire room was cleaned this afternoon, I don't—"

"Well, the bathroom wasn't. I'm going out for an hour or so. If the issue could be resolved by the time I return, that would be wonderful."

After hanging up, Mark walked to the bathroom, lifted the toilet seat up, and then sprinkled some water around the bowl and the floor. He unwrapped the hand soap by the sink, and then did the same with the little bottles of shampoo and conditioner. He dribbled some shampoo into the sink, smeared it around before replacing the cap, then wadded up a few pieces of toilet paper and tossed them into the waste bin.

Mark watched, his eye at the peephole in the door, as a young man with a cleaning cart approached.

The cleaner knocked twice, loudly, on the door. When no one answered, he reached into his right front pants pocket and pulled out an electronic key.

Mark stepped back from the door, lay down on his bed, and put one of his cell phones to his ear.

He heard the sound of a key card being inserted into and then removed from the electronic lock, then heard the click as the lock disengaged. The door opened. The cleaner slipped the electronic key in his hand into his left front pants pocket and wheeled his cart into the room.

The cleaner's key, Mark noted, looked exactly the same as the room-specific keys issued to guests.

"Listen, I'll call you back later tonight." Mark said into his phone, as though there were someone else on the other end of the line. Turning to the cleaner, he said, "It's the bathroom."

"So sorry to disturb you, sir. I was told you were out. Is now a bad time?"

Mark noted the cleaner was slender, and his black pants were baggy, as though a size too big.

"No, now's fine."

"I'll just be a moment."

As the cleaner tended to the bathroom, Mark rehearsed in his mind exactly what he planned to do. He thought of the gypsy children in Baku who had such nimble hands. He looked at his own hands. They weren't large, but they weren't exactly small either. As he stood listening to the cleaner pad around the bathroom, he practiced slipping his key in and out of his front pocket, using his index and middle finger as pincers.

He considered that some aspects of tradecraft were like riding a bike, in that one never really forgot how to do them. But physical tricks were more difficult—they required regular practice. Though Mark had successfully pickpocketed before, the last time he'd done so had been over ten years ago, when he'd still been in the field. Now, he was rusty. And this would be a dicey operation, because he'd need to both pick and plant at the same time.

He sat down at the foot of the king bed. The TV remote lay on the bed to his left. He'd palmed his room key in his right hand. When he heard the cleaner emerge from the bathroom, he bent down, his back to the cleaner, as if tying his shoe. The television was positioned opposite the bed.

He listened to the nearly silent footsteps traversing the padded carpet. When he sensed the cleaner was right behind him, he grabbed the TV remote, stood up, turned on the television, and took a quick step into the cleaner. Their bodies collided, though with a little more force than Mark had intended.

Mark cried out as his fingers dipped into the cleaner's front pants pocket. The television was shockingly loud and set to a music video station that was playing Arabic music.

"Whoa!" Mark cried, putting his left hand, which was still clutching the remote, on the cleaner's right shoulder. The cleaner had dropped his bucket. Mark stepped away from him. "Who listens to television that loud!"

"I'm so sorry, I'm so sorry."

Mark stepped back, pointed the remote at the television, and turned it off. "Good Lord, whoever was watching that last must have been deaf." Turning to the cleaner, he said, "Are you OK?"

"I'm fine, sir. So sorry."

"No, I'm sorry. I didn't know you were there."

"No doubt, sir."

Mark helped the cleaner load his bucket back up, then slipped him a ten-dinar note on the way out.

"No sir, that's not necessary."

"Actually, it is," said Mark.

Two minutes after the cleaner left, Mark knocked on the door across the hall, waited a minute, then knocked again. When no one answered the second time, he dipped the cleaner's key into the electronic lock.

The lock beeped, and the LED light flickered from red to green. He had one of the hotel's master keys.

52

Mark walked back to room 517 and knocked.

As before, no one answered. So he inserted the master key into the lock and let himself in, wheeling his suitcase behind him.

It was a suite like his own, spacious and with a view that overlooked both Bahrain Bay and the diplomatic zone. But this suite looked more lived in, more like an apartment than a hotel room. A large office desk cluttered with papers and pens and a Dell laptop sat in one corner. The dresser was filled with clothes, the armoire stocked with custom-made suits and Kiton ties and *thawbs* that smelled freshly laundered. Mark inspected the *thawbs*. They were made of cotton, but with such fine thread that they felt like silk. The cuffs and collars were starched.

A bottle of Laphroaig single-malt scotch sat on a table next to the entertainment center. Mark was tempted to take a plug.

There were no suitcases, indeed no luggage at all save for a small carry-on made of soft black leather. Though the carry-on piece was empty, a tag designed to accommodate a business card was attached to it.

Mark opened the leather flap that covered the tag. On a card embossed with gold script were a series of characters in Arabic that Mark couldn't read. The English translation underneath the Arabic was perfectly legible, however—it read *Bandar bin Fahd*.

Mark sighed. All right then, he thought. This just might work.

He called Bowlan, told him to catch the next plane to Bahrain, and ran through a detailed list of tasks that he needed performed. Then he called Garver.

53

Rear Admiral Jeffrey Garver settled back in an easy chair, swirled the ice around in the tumbler of Maker's Mark bourbon—Garver's favorite after-dinner drink—that Captain Hugh Jackson had handed him, and sighed.

"I tell you, Hugh, it's been a *hell* of a day."

Jackson, a black, six-foot-two, gray-templed fellow Tennessean and the commander of Naval Support Activity Bahrain, said, "Well, I certainly wouldn't want your job. Not right now at least."

Over dinner, with their wives in attendance, they hadn't really been able to talk about all the wartime-like preparations that were going on at the naval base. Of course, their wives knew something was up, but not the extent of it.

"Anybody want coffee?" called Jackson's wife from the kitchen, where she and Garver's wife were packing up leftovers from the Romano's Macaroni Grill takeout meal they'd just eaten. "I can make decaf."

Jackson eyed Garver, who shook his head no and lifted his tumbler of Maker's Mark, indicating he already had his drink of choice.

"No thanks, dear. We're all set out here."

Although both Tennesseans, Garver and Jackson had grown up in different worlds; Jackson in Memphis, Garver in the wealthy suburbs of Nashville. As kids, neither would have been a likely friend for the other. But they were friends now—bound by the traditions of the navy, by their mutual love of the University of Tennessee football program, by Maker's Mark, and by the fact that their wives liked each other. Garver had come to realize that, once you got to a certain age, you really couldn't be friends with a man if your wives didn't get along.

His cell phone rang. "That damn thing's been going all day. I'll just let this one go."

He didn't care if it was Saeed or the commander of CENTCOM. Or the president himself for that matter. If it was important, whoever it was would leave a message and he'd check it then.

He leaned toward the coffee table, picked up a Ritz cracker, and loaded it up with cheese spread. His phone stopped ringing.

"So'd I tell you I'm two guys down on the Force Protection Unit?" asked Jackson.

"That so?"

"Brass *suggested* I beef up Emergency Management with a couple of officers who'd been cross-trained. As if Force Protection isn't going to be front and center if things go to hell around here."

"I don't see—"

Garver's phone rang again. He didn't recognize the number, but someone was obviously trying to get through to him. With all that was going on . . . "I'm sorry, Hugh."

"Don't worry about it, take the call."

Garver put down his drink, stood, and walked over to a window in the living room that looked out onto the Jacksons' small garden. "This is Admiral Garver."

Garver's stomach did a little flip when the man on the other end of the line gave his name. For a moment, he was speechless. Then, "Who gave you this number?"

"We need to meet."

Garver's mind raced through the reasons Mark Sava might be calling him directly. "I'm not sure that's a good idea."

"Tonight."

"Mr. Sava—"

"I'm going to give you one chance to make this right. One chance to avoid being court-martialed for exposing the identity of a former CIA operative to a foreign intelligence agency."

Garver's heart started racing. He felt as though the floor had fallen out beneath him. "I have no idea what you're talking about."

"Drive to the Manama fish market. Park in the main lot and wait for me to arrive. I might get there in an hour, or it might be a lot longer than that. If you value your career, you'll be there when I arrive. Tell no one—including your Saudi buddies—about our meeting."

54

Kyrgyzstan

John Decker woke up to the sound of a fifty-year-old Kyrgyz man shoveling dried cow dung into a little pot-bellied stove. He and Jessica lay on the ground; Muhammad lay between them, swaddled in heavy felt blankets; there was a raised platform next to the stove, which was where the man-and-wife Kyrgyz owners of the yurt slept.

After the confrontation with Holtz, Jessica and Decker had fled to the mountains north of Lake Issyk Kul, a part of the country Jessica had trekked through when she'd first come to Kyrgyzstan two months ago. The yurts that had been there in September to accommodate tourist trekkers had long since been taken down for the winter. But those belonging to the local sheepherders remained.

The inside of this one smelled like a sheep, Decker noted. Which didn't surprise him, given that the felt blankets that had been stretched over wooden trellises to form the walls of the yurt had been made from sheep's wool, as had the blankets that lay over the roof ribs. On top of that, the exterior-facing side of the blankets had been waterproofed with sheep's fat. Decker still hadn't gotten used to the pungent, musky smell.

He turned over onto his side. The glow of the cow-dung embers in the open stove was just bright enough to illuminate Muhammad and Jessica.

He thought back to earlier in the day, when he and Jess had taken Muhammad on a pony ride. Although the terrain up here was barren and cold, the boy hadn't cared—he'd loved the little horse, had buried his hands in the pony's mane, squealing and bouncing with delight. Decker had to admit, the kid was growing on him. He wondered whether Muhammad would remember any of this when he was older. Did two-year-olds make permanent memories? Decker didn't think so; he couldn't remember anything from when he was that age. Just as well. Decker had little doubt that a couple of pony rides weren't going to outweigh all the awful things that had happened to Muhammad in the last few days. Better not to remember any of it.

Trying to recall some of his own memories from when he'd been a two-year-old made Decker think of his dad again. The guy hated hospitals and couldn't stand being cooped up. Being bedridden must be killing him.

Decker exhaled, then twisted around looking for Jessica's phone, which she'd placed by her head next to a bottle of water. He navigated to the e-mail account he and Mark were using to communicate. Since they were high above the cell towers near the lake, the reception here was decent.

During the day, he'd checked that e-mail account at least once an hour. But it had been nearly two hours now since he'd last looked. His hopes weren't high. He'd resigned himself to having to call his family again the next morning and make another excuse for his absence. By tomorrow night, though, he'd be making his excuses to Mark.

To his surprise, there was a message.

Take package immediately to Bishkek. Further instructions regarding delivery of package to follow shortly.

"Jess, Jess, wake up," said Decker, gently shaking her shoulder. "We're outta here."

55

Bahrain

Bandar bin Fahd returned to his suite at around eleven that evening. Hidden under the bed, Mark heard him pour himself a glass of what he imagined was Laphroaig. A thirty-minute conversation in English followed—with, Mark gathered, a London-based employee of Fahd's private equity firm.

Fahd began with an update on a 180-key hotel in London he was considering purchasing, then went on to talk about what the turmoil in Bahrain might mean for one of his firm's current investments—a water park south of Manama. He sounded nothing like the whoring, drunk idiot Mark had hoped he'd be. After Fahd showered and listened to the BBC world news for ten minutes, the lights went out. Mark swept his finger over his iPod. It was nearly midnight.

He started thinking about Rad.

He'd seen his brother all of three times since his mother's suicide. The first time had been just two days after it had happened. He'd come back home, not because he was tired of being homeless—he wasn't—or wanted to reconcile with his father—he hadn't, but because he'd been concerned about Rad and his youngest brother.

But he needn't have been.

The woman his father had been "counseling" down at the Eastern Orthodox church was caring for his brothers—the same woman his father married six months later.

The second time Mark had seen Rad was a full seven years after the suicide. Mark had just received his first paycheck from the CIA. He'd come back to New Jersey to check on his brothers, to see if they needed anything now that he had something to give. One of the priests who'd remembered Marko had arranged for him to meet them at church after Sunday school. Mark had asked Rad and his younger brother whether they were doing OK. They were. He'd asked whether they needed anything. They didn't. Not from Mark, at least—indeed, they'd hardly remembered him.

And then there had been that lunch in New York City fifteen years ago. After that, there'd been a couple of phone calls, and Mark had sent some money when Rad had graduated from college. But they'd never seen each other again in person.

So why are you doing this?

Because he's your brother.

A few shared genes, that's all that was, thought Mark. What mattered was the relationship between two people, not the fact that they were related. Human beings and mice shared a lot of genes but nobody—or almost nobody—went around thinking they owed anything to mice. Why should it be any different with humans you shared a few genes with?

Intellectually, Mark couldn't think of a good reason why it should be different. But it was. He wondered where Rad was, whether he was still thirsty, still panicking. Probably.

Hang in there, brother.

At one in the morning, Mark received a text message from Larry Bowlan:

Ready.

He inched his way out from underneath the bed. Fahd's breathing was steady, and he snored lightly.

Experience had taught Mark that it was almost always better to proceed slowly and deliberately in an operation like this—and to shut down the natural impulse to get it over with quickly just because you felt exposed. So he timed his micro-movements to Fahd's breathing, moving slightly each time the Saudi exhaled.

It took him five minutes to make his way out from under the bed, and another two before he was standing next to Fahd. By now not just his movements, but his own breathing was tied to Fahd's.

Though all the curtains in the room had been pulled shut, just enough dim light from the street seeped through so that Mark, his eyes now fully adjusted, could see through the gloom. Fahd had a dark neatly trimmed mustache. He wore a white sleeping robe and had pulled a single sheet up to his chest, having cast the heavier blankets to the side. His hands were folded on his stomach.

This was a disciplined man, Mark thought. Odd that he would use prostitutes as much as he did, but then people *were* odd. And the Saudis sure did have some screwed-up ideas when it came to women.

Mark positioned one hand just above Fahd's throat, and the other above Fahd's head, inches from the pillow. He waited for the Saudi to start his exhalation—better to attack when the lungs were empty—and then struck with precision and speed.

The palm of his right hand came down on Fahd's throat as his thumb and fingers pressed down on Fahd's carotid arteries. At the same time, he used his left hand to rip the pillow out from under Fahd's head and press it down over Fahd's nose and mouth.

Mark leaned down, exerting just as much pressure as was needed but no more. The Saudi fought for maybe thirty seconds or so, then went limp—knocked out, but not dead.

Mark immediately released his hands from Fahd's neck, reached beneath the bed, and pulled out a roll of duct tape from his suitcase.

He used a bed sheet to wrap the Saudi up, as if swaddling a baby, and then bound him with the tape. Just as he was finishing, Fahd began to regain consciousness. Mark slipped a pillowcase over Fahd's head, pulled out the Makarov he'd taken from the dead bodyguard, racked the slide quickly and loudly, and said, "I need you to be quiet and compliant. Nod if you understand."

Fahd stopped struggling. Moments later, he nodded.

"I'm going to continue to bind you. If you fight me, I'm going to knock you out again. If you yell, I'll have to silence you quickly. You understand what that means?"

Fahd nodded again.

"But if you handle this like a professional, I will too, and I promise you'll be free within the next twelve hours. It's all up to you. Do we have an understanding?"

Fahd nodded, and didn't put up a fight as Mark finished binding him.

"Stand up."

Fahd tried to.

As he did, Mark said, "I'm going to pick you up." He crouched down, placed his shoulder at Fahd's midsection, and struggled to hoist the Saudi up onto his shoulder in a rough approximation of a fireman's carry.

Mark made his way slowly to the door, which he opened with one hand while steadying the Saudi on his shoulder with the other. Along the way, he grabbed the bottle of scotch.

Before exiting the room, Mark listened for footsteps in the hall. Hearing nothing, he stepped into the hall, cast a wary eye at room 516, where he suspected Fahd's bodyguard was sleeping, and turned right. He walked fifty feet before stopping at a utility closet, which he unlocked with the master key. Inside was a large laundry cart with canvas sides.

"You're going to feel . . ." Mark took a few deep breaths. " . . . a bump." He tried to lower Fahd gently into the cart.

It was more than a bump—more like a big bag-of-concrete-hitting-the-ground flop—because Mark lost control at the end, but he managed to get Fahd into the cart and cover him up with several clean towels that had been folded and stacked on a nearby linen shelf.

Mark rolled the cart down the hall toward the elevators. No one was in the elevator, nor in the main fourth-floor hallway. Directly across from the bank of elevators was a large framed photograph of the king of Bahrain. Mark pushed the cart over to it, slipped his hand behind the frame, and felt along the bottom edge. Near the left-hand corner, an electronic key card had been taped to the frame.

Bowlan had come through for him.

Relieved, Mark pulled off the key card. Written on the tape that was affixed to it was the number 432. He wheeled the cart to that room and inserted the key. The lock opened. Though he could have used his master key, that might have left an electronic record.

Bowlan's standard room was far more cramped than the luxurious corner-room executive suites on the fifth floor. Two small chairs were arranged in a corner around a low circular table. Two twin beds took up most of the remaining floor space; between them was an enormous red suitcase.

Mark stripped the sheets from one of the beds, draped the fitted bottom sheet over one of the chairs, moved the chair so that it stood in front of the one window in the room, then hung the top sheet over the heavy curtains that covered the window.

"I'm going to move you," he warned Fahd. He slowly tipped the linen cart over, dragged Fahd out of it, and pulled him up onto the chair.

A reading light was mounted on the wall between the beds; Mark turned it on, pulled out his iPod, set it to camera mode, and stood behind Fahd. "Now I'm going to remove the pillowcase from your head. Look directly in front of you. Don't turn around."

Mark was careful to stand directly behind Fahd.

After removing the pillowcase, Mark extended his iPod in front of Fahd's face, and snapped a quick picture.

"Who are you?" whispered Fahd. "Why is this happening?"

Mark inspected the image. As he'd hoped, the white sheets had masked any distinguishing features of the hotel room.

Fahd added, "I can pay you myself. I am a wealthy man."

"It's not about money and it's not about anything you did or didn't do. The only reason you're here is because of your connection to the Saudi royal family. But again, if you do as I say, you'll be released unharmed tomorrow. If you don't, then you'll have problems."

Mark set the iPod to video mode. Without warning, he reached his right arm around Fahd's face and dug his fingers deep into the soft spot between the Saudi's skull and neck, just below the ear, where there was a sensitive cluster of nerves.

Fahd let out an involuntary yelp accompanied by a spasmed tilt of the head. Mark whipped his right hand away and, with his left hand, recorded a two second clip of Fahd writhing.

Then he put a hand over Fahd's mouth and spoke in his ear.

"Easy there. I had to hit you with that. No one's going to take this kidnapping seriously if they think that you're living it up, getting room service, and being treated like royalty. If you cooperate from here on out, though, I promise that will be the end of the pain. Be thankful I didn't shoot you in the leg, or the shoulder, and record that. Because sometimes, that's how it's done. And no more talking. No more crying out. Just face forward, and listen."

Mark stepped back, grabbed a glass from the table behind him, and pulled a small plastic bag out of his pocket. The bag was filled with a white powder—eight 50mg Benadryl tablets that he'd bought and crushed up on the way from Exhibitions Avenue to the Golden Tulip, because sleeping pills weren't sold over the counter in Bahrain. He dumped the powder into the glass, opened the bottle of scotch, poured out a healthy amount onto the powder, and mixed everything up.

Fahd was hyperventilating.

"Now's the fun part." Mark gently swirled the alcohol in the glass as he spoke. "It'll be better for both of us if you're relaxed. So I want you to drink some scotch. Enough to help you forget what a lousy time you're having tonight. I'm going to put a glass to your mouth, and I want you to take a big drink. We're going to do this once a minute until I think you've had enough."

Mark first showed Fahd the bottle of Laphroaig, then put the glass up to Fahd's lips. The Saudi smelled it, then took a big thirsty slug of it, almost too much.

"Easy there. Don't have so much that you throw up."

After Mark had fed Fahd what he gauged was the equivalent of around eight shots, he put the bottle down.

"That's enough. From here on out, I expect total silence and minimal movement. Don't panic and everything will be OK. I'll be here throughout the night and tomorrow, keeping an eye on you. Try to sleep."

He left Fahd gagged, blindfolded, and strapped to a chair in the bathroom. Taking the giant red suitcase that Bowlan had placed between the beds, he stuffed it full of blankets and sheets and pillows so that it was bulging. Then he closed the door to the bathroom and turned on the television set in the main room—not so loud that it might trigger complaints, but loud enough to drown out minor noise.

On the elevator ride down to the lobby, he uploaded the two-second video of Fahd to YouTube, using one of his Gmail accounts to do so. He saved the web address in his Contacts folder.

From the moment he exited the elevator, he walked slowly, as though the suitcase he was wheeling behind him was extremely heavy and he was struggling with the load.

He passed the receptionist in the main lobby. A uniformed doorman opened the glass exit door for him.

"Do you need help with your bag, sir? Or a taxi?"

"No, thank you."

Idling in the circular drop-off area in front of the hotel was a burgundy Lincoln sedan. A tall, white-haired man wearing a blue blazer, a white oxford shirt, and thick black-rimmed glasses that might have been considered fashionable in 1962, stepped out of the car. He had big ears, and his face was creased with smoker's wrinkles, making him look older than his seventy-one years. But he moved quickly and surprisingly fluidly as he exited the car and popped open the trunk.

"Good to see you, Larry."

"Sava."

They shook hands. Bowlan's grip was firm.

"Give me a hand getting this suitcase into the trunk. It's supposed to be heavy, so act as if it is. You're on stage. You grab one end, I'll grab the other."

"How heavy?"

"About the weight of an average-sized Saudi."

Together they made a show of bending down, lifting with their legs, and muscling the suitcase into the trunk. After it was in, Larry made a show of breathing heavily, hands on his hips.

"Don't overdo it," said Mark.

The air had cooled, and there was a slight breeze. The city was quiet all around them. Bowlan slipped into the driver's seat, and Mark got in beside him.

"Where to?" asked Bowlan. He was glancing in his rearview and sideview mirrors in a way that might have appeared normal to a casual observer, but Mark could tell Bowlan was in that hyperalert zone. Mark was there himself.

"Manama fish market."

"I know it."

When considering the best place to meet Admiral Garver, Mark had remembered reading once that the fish market in Manama was a huge daily affair, renowned throughout the region. He figured people would be there even in the middle of the night, getting ready for the market to open before dawn. It was neutral territory, and only a short drive away.

As they were pulling away from the Golden Tulip, Mark asked, "So'd you talk to Kalila Safi?"

"No, but I talked to her brother just before I got on the plane . . ."

56

Rad woke up thinking about the drive from the oil fields. Sometime after dark, they'd pulled him from the shack and dumped him in the back of a pickup truck. Though he hadn't been able to see over the walls of the bed of the truck, he'd been able to glimpse the bright flames atop the tall flare stacks.

The truck had driven through the desert over dirt roads, and all the bouncing around had been excruciating. But he'd tried to remember Mark's advice—to stay alert and calm to fight off shock. He recalled passing a gate in a chain-link fence, and a building that had looked like military barracks. And then he'd blacked out. Or had he been drugged? He vaguely remembered a hand coming down over his mouth, but maybe he'd dreamed it?

He certainly felt groggy now. His shoulder still ached, but not as much as before.

Where was he? He raised his head from the table he lay on. Though he was now shirtless, he was still wearing the same boxer shorts that he'd had on when he'd been abducted in India. Bright lights shone down from above, making it hard for him to see. To his left, he thought he could make out what looked like the steel walls of a warehouse. To his right, arranged on a small metal tray, was a collection of scalpels.

Rad stared at the scalpels.

He wasn't in an operating room. So what the hell were the scalpels doing there?

He heard voices conversing in a language he didn't understand. He wondered what Marko would do. Rad knew next to nothing about his brother, but he felt certain that the battle-hardened man who had come to see him in the shack in the desert—the man who'd snapped at him to shut up—would fight back.

A black man in a white coat appeared above him.

Rad took a few deep breaths. He'd been drugged, he knew that now, and he wasn't thinking clearly. But he was thinking clearly enough. With his good hand, he reached out, grabbed one of the scalpels, and stabbed the leg of the man in the white coat as hard as he could.

The man screamed.

Rad sat up and pushed himself off the table. He was dizzy as his feet hit the ground. He tried to run, but fell on his face. That's when he remembered his shinbone was broken.

A foot appeared in front of him and he stabbed it with the scalpel. Then he felt a hand press a rag over his mouth. He breathed in something sweet, and blacked out.

57

Mark hopped out quickly, before the car had even come to a full stop, as Bowlan pulled up to the fish market warehouses. It was one forty in the morning. Muhammad was supposed to be transferred to the Saudis in the lobby of the Hyatt Regency hotel in Bishkek in twenty minutes.

The whole area reeked of a heady mix of saltwater and fish guts, the odor pungent even though the new day's catch had yet to arrive. As the warm stench rose up in Mark's nose, it made him feel more alert, as though he'd just inhaled smelling salts.

As he jogged toward the market, he considered what Bowlan had just told him about Kalila Safi. Assuming Bowlan hadn't been lied to, then it was just as Mark had suspected—the Saudis weren't looking out for Muhammad's best interests any more than the royals here in Bahrain were.

At the market, men were setting up chopping tables and unloading ice in open, brightly lit warehouses. Mark imagined that the fish would begin to arrive in a few hours—freshly caught grouper, tuna, parrot fish, and shark—hauled in from the shallow waters of the Persian Gulf. They'd be sliced up with razor-sharp fillet knives and weighed on the old cast-iron scales Mark saw out on the chopping tables before being sold to Bahraini housewives or luxury restaurants in Manama.

The parking lot lay just beyond the warehouses. A refrigerator truck and an old pickup that had a big wooden table lashed to its bed pulled in just as Mark got there; they parked next to several other vehicles that were clustered in an area close to the market.

One car in the vast lot sat apart from the rest—a silver Buick, in the far southeastern corner. The interior lights were off, but Mark saw the silhouette of a man sitting behind the steering wheel.

He began to walk toward the Buick.

When he got close, the driver's side window opened, revealing a man with a square jaw and high forehead. He wore a white, neatly pressed, short-sleeved civilian shirt and dark blue slacks that looked to Mark like the bottom half of the navy's blue service uniform. His graying hair had been cut high and tight.

"Admiral Garver?"

"Yes."

Mark walked around to the other side of the car and slid into the passenger-side seat. Garver offered his hand. It was a stiff, formal gesture.

Mark glanced at Garver's hand, shook it, and said, "So why'd you do it?"

"Mr. Sava. My team and I work closely with your friends at the CIA. That's why I'm here tonight—because I know you're involved in a sensitive Agency operation that I also happen to have been briefed on." Garver spoke with clipped precision, like the high-ranking military officer he was. "So I'll hear what you have to say. But let's dispense with the accusations, shall we?"

"Your friend Gregory Larkin's already talked, Admiral. There'll be corroborating phone records. Even if I can't prove that you shared my personnel file with the Saudis, which I know damn well you did, asking Larkin to illegally violate my file is enough in itself to end your career and then some."

Garver was silent for half a minute. He'd turned away from Mark and was staring blankly out the side window. His chin was thrust forward, his lips pursed tightly together.

"Who else?"

"Who else, what?"

"Knows."

Mark said, "I need you to tell me what's going down on this island, Admiral, and then I need you to contact Saeed for me. The only other person who knows is the head of the CIA's Central Eurasia Division. He's the one who investigated the breach and confronted Larkin."

"Why only him?"

"Because I need you motivated to help me. And I've noticed that people who have already permanently lost everything they love in life are hard to motivate. The division chief of Central Eurasia is a guy named Ted Kaufman. I know him well. I asked that he not turn you in just yet so that if you were to help me, I'd have something to give you in return. Like a chance to avoid prison."

Another long pause.

Mark added, "I'm pissed to hell about what happened with my file, and about what the Saudis have done to my brother—"

"What happened to your brother?"

"But I'm not looking for revenge. I'm looking for results."

"What happened to your brother?"

"I don't want to talk about it." Mark didn't know whether Garver was playing dumb or was genuinely out of the loop; either way, he didn't want to talk about it—at least not with Garver.

"I did what I thought was right," said Garver.

"I don't doubt it."

"Don't patronize me. Is your brother hurt?"

"I've told you what I'm here for, Admiral. Either you're going to give me what I want, or you're going to take it on the chin. What's it going to be?"

"It happened six days ago," said Garver, continuing to stare out the side window.

Mark waited, then said, "*What* happened?"

"The king was turning sixty-two. It was a small party, mostly just family. The next morning, people started vomiting. At first, they thought it was food poisoning. But the sick just kept getting sicker. Are you familiar with ricin?"

"Oh, Christ."

Ricin was a powerful poison, one that was widely available and relatively easy to produce since it came from castor beans. Mark recalled that the KGB used it during the Cold War. Saddam Hussein had produced a bunch of it. Various terrorists had tried to use it.

"Yeah, that was my reaction. A purified powder was dissolved and injected into the wine. Many of those who got sick have already died. The king is in a coma and on kidney dialysis. Given the damage to his liver and heart, it's thought that he'll die soon. Two of his adult sons died in the last couple of days, and another will likely die within hours if he hasn't already. The people don't know the extent of what's happened, but rumors are flying on the street. The king's uncle, the prime minister, was one of the few who didn't drink at the party. He's been doing everything he can to prevent the papers from reporting on the absence of the royal family, hoping the king will get better and take control, but he won't be able to do that much longer—it's unlikely the king will get better, and they won't be able to hold off on the burials much longer. An announcement is going to be made no later than noon today. This island is a bomb that's waiting to go off."

Mark had known that some trouble was brewing, but this was infinitely worse than he'd imagined. He couldn't help but think that if he'd been on his home turf, in some Turkic-speaking country, he'd have sensed more was wrong.

"Who did it?"

"Sunni extremists who hate the fact that the Sunni royal family drinks alcohol, and turns a blind eye to prostitution, and does business with the US Navy. One of them worked at the palace. He's confessed. The irony is that it's the Shias who will benefit. They'll call for elections. And if that happens . . ." Garver shrugged as he stared out the front windshield. "Well, let's hope it doesn't. A lot will depend on what happens to that boy you have in your possession."

"He's one of the king's grandsons," said Mark. Muhammad's true parentage was one of the many things that Kalila Safi's brother had revealed to Larry Bowlan.

"Yes, he is. And Muhammad's father, the king's second oldest son, died three days ago, as did his mother. Which means if the king dies, the boy is next in line for the throne. He won't actually rule, of course, there would be a regent for that—probably the prime minister, who is next in line for the throne after the boy. But the boy could be the difference between the monarchy surviving and falling. The country wouldn't hesitate to get rid of an old politician like the prime minister. No one likes him. But if the prime minister was just a placeholder for the grandson of the king? That could be another matter entirely.

"Unfortunately, the Shia political leadership in Bahrain also realize the importance of the boy. When Muhammad was brought to the hospital to be monitored for food poisoning, he was placed in the care of a doctor who was secretly a Shia partisan. This doctor knew what was happening to the royal family, and immediately grasped what it meant for the line of succession if the sick began to die. He was the conduit to the Shia leaders who decided to kidnap the child and blame it on the same zealots who had poisoned the royals."

"Only the CIA found out about the plot."

"Yes. They've infiltrated the Shias."

"And instead of forcing the Shias to return the boy, the CIA cut a deal with them. They'd help hide the boy and then support elections in Bahrain, elections the Shias would win, if in return the Shias guaranteed that the Fifth Fleet could stay."

"It was a deal with the *devil*," said Garver, his voice rising. "What kind of human beings help to steal a two-year-old boy from his family? And mark my words—when and if the Shias ever take over this island, the Fifth Fleet's days in Bahrain will be numbered. It won't matter what deal the CIA has cut with them. Those Shia fools aren't ready for democracy. This place will go to hell and then to Iran."

Garver took a moment to collect himself, then continued, "I knew what the CIA was up to, I was kept in the loop. The only way to stop it was to tell the Saudis what was going on. So I did—I told them where to start looking for the boy. Then I told them you had the boy, and shared your file with them. And I'm glad I did. And now you need to let the Saudis bring that boy back to Bahrain and give him back to his family. Surely now you can see it's the right thing to do?"

Mark didn't answer. He doubted Garver knew about Kalila Safi. "I need to talk to Saeed," he said.

"I already told him I was meeting with you. He said he suspected you would try to use me as a conduit to get to him but that he won't talk to you. He just wants you to keep your end of the bargain."

"Text him."

It was five minutes till two. Mark assumed Saeed would be waiting for a confirmation that the boy had been delivered to the hotel.

Garver pulled his phone out of his front pocket, turned it on, and tapped on the touchscreen. "I'll try. What do you want me to say?"

Mark spelled out the name Prince Bandar bin Fahd and then recited the YouTube address for the video clip of Fahd.

"That's it?" asked Garver.

"That's it."

A few seconds later, Garver said, "OK, I sent it. What now?"

"Now we wait."

"What does this Fahd guy have to do with anything?"

"Better you don't know."

"Can you really stop the CIA from investigating me?"

"Probably." Mark would certainly try to hold Kaufman off. Garver's actions had directly led to Rad's being shot, but Mark had done plenty of things himself that had resulted in unintended consequences for innocents. Garver had just been doing what he thought was right—and in Mark's book, that counted for something.

They didn't have to wait long for Saeed's response. Less than a minute after Garver had sent the text, the pickup truck that had pulled into the parking lot while Mark was walking in flipped on its high beams just as another car pulled up beside Garver's car.

"I guess Saeed got the message," said Mark. He stepped out of Garver's car and into the glare of the approaching headlights. Behind him, at the edge of the parking lot, a low embankment rose up. Near the top, amid a cluster of palm trees, a man was standing with what looked to Mark like an M4 rifle.

Mark just stood there, bathed in a cold white light, waiting.

58

Saeed stepped out of the car to Mark's left, exiting from the passenger side. Though he was still wearing the same dark gray suit as earlier, he'd removed his tie and his graying hair looked ruffled.

Guess we're going to bargain after all, thought Mark.

Saeed approached quickly. His exceptional height—around six foot six, Mark guessed—combined with unconcealed anger, made him look dangerous. "Where is the prince?"

He sounded flustered. Mark had hoped Saeed would have some family or tribal relationship to Prince Bandar bin Fahd; almost everyone in a position of power in Saudi Arabia had *some* ties to the royal family. Fifty-fifty, he'd guessed. Now he put the odds at eighty-twenty, in his favor. Either way, Saeed wouldn't be able to just ignore the fact that a Saudi prince had been kidnapped.

"This is the deal," said Mark. "In a few seconds, I'm going to walk away. Your men aren't going to follow me."

"No."

"After I'm gone, you're going to arrange for my brother to be transported, while in the care of a physician, to Dubai International airport. He will be brought to the Executive Flight Services terminal, the one reserved for private flights. I'll be there to collect him, either on the tarmac or just inside the terminal. Only then will I tell you the location of the prince."

Saeed smacked the back of his right hand into his left palm. "No!"

"This transfer will take place at seven in the morning—five hours from now. As for Muhammad, I'll likely give him to Kalila Safi. Assuming her brother hasn't been lying to me, like everyone else has."

"And how would you determine whether he's lying? You know nothing of that family. Nothing."

"I have a few ideas. But when and if I do reunite Muhammad with Kalila Safi, under no circumstances will I disclose how and when this transfer will occur."

Saeed took a step closer to Mark, towering over him. "We will stop it."

"I'm giving you half of what you want here. If it were up to the CIA and the Shias, Muhammad would grow up with some middle-class family in Central Asia, never knowing who he really was. Bahrain would never know what really happened to him. By giving him to Kalila, I'm doing the right thing by the kid, but also giving you and Bahrain's prime minister an opportunity. If you want Muhammad back in Bahrain, you'll have to bargain with Kalila and her family, not with me."

"She comes from a family of Shias, Sava! Do you know this? Kalila Safi became a Sunni when she married, but she comes from a family of Shias. Her brother, who she stays with in Dubai, is a Shia. You are condemning this child to be raised by Shias!"

If there was one thing Mark was sick of hearing about, it was the Sunnis and the Shias.

"Kalila Safi has been caring for that child since he was born and she's legally entitled to care for him now. End of story."

He started walking toward the embankment behind the parking lot.

"My men will shoot you."

"Go for it."

He didn't think the Saudis would really do it. Shooting him wouldn't get them Muhammad, and it might mean the death of a

Saudi prince. But he couldn't be sure. People acted in irrational and self-destructive ways all the time.

Mark heard a few lonely cars speeding along King Faisal Highway. He reached the embankment and began to climb, ignoring the armed man at the top. A suppressed shot spit out and a little bit of dirt kicked up by his left foot. He kept climbing.

"Stop!" The shooter spoke in Arabic-accented English.

Mark didn't stop. He didn't even look up. Two more shots spit out. He didn't notice where they went.

He reached the top of the embankment, crossed a small road, hiked up another embankment, and then stepped over the guardrail that marked the edge of King Faisal Highway. Larry Bowlan was waiting for him on the shoulder of the road, in his rented Lincoln sedan, about a hundred yards down the road.

"Airport," said Mark.

"We going to have problems leaving the country?"

"No. They've already decided to let us go."

59

Dubai, United Arab Emirates

Mark stood on the tarmac just outside the Executive Flight Services terminal at Dubai International Airport and watched as a Gulfstream jet landed on the shortest of the airport's three long runways and then taxied slowly over to the executive flight parking area. The early morning sun was pleasantly warm on his face. A light breeze blew across the runways. The sound of massive jetliners landing and taking off mixed with the rumble of tow tractors hauling trailers packed with luggage.

He and Bowlan had arrived on a commercial flight two hours earlier. They'd been deposited at terminal three, a Quonset-hut-like building whose claim to fame was that it was the largest structure in the world when measured by floor space. After using his British passport to procure an on-arrival visa, he and Bowlan had caught a shuttle to the Executive Flight Services terminal—a section of the airport reserved for private flights. It was tiny in comparison to Terminal 3, except when judged by the volume of wealth and power that regularly flowed through it.

Directed by an aircraft marshaller, the Gulfstream came to a stop about fifty feet in front of the executive flight terminal, between two other private jets. A minute later, the fuselage door of the plane opened.

A man dressed in blue hospital scrubs walked partway down the air steps, reached out his arms to receive one end of a hospital gurney, then helped lift the gurney off the plane, extend its collapsible legs, and set it on the tarmac. Rad squinted in the bright sunlight.

Mark called to his brother. "Over here!"

Rad looked groggy and confused. He slowly lifted his head, glanced around, and finally saw Mark. "Marko?"

A tall black man with a stethoscope draped around his neck, a clipboard in his hand, and a satchel hanging from a strap on his shoulder—Mark assumed he was the doctor he'd insisted accompany his brother—limped off the plane and over to the two men in scrubs.

Right on his heels were three Saudi intelligence officers whom Mark recognized from the shack in the desert where he'd last seen Rad. One of them was the older Saudi he'd first encountered in Kyrgyzstan.

Mark approached the doctor.

"Wait," commanded one of the Saudis. He pushed himself between Mark and the doctor, pulled a cell phone from his pocket, dialed a series of numbers, and then handed the phone to Mark.

Mark put the phone to his ear.

"The prince," said Saeed.

"Go to the Golden Tulip Hotel."

"That's where you kidnapped him."

"And that's where he still is."

"We have videotape of you leaving with—oh, I see. He wasn't in the suitcase."

"Room 432."

"Give me fifteen minutes."

"I'll wait."

The older Saudi remained standing near Rad. The other stood near Mark. Behind them, positioned just outside the executive flight terminal but still well within sight, was Larry Bowlan. Next to Bowlan stood three large Arabs—cab drivers Bowlan had paid an inordinate amount to stand around looking tough.

The real plan, if things turned violent, was for Bowlan to call airport security. Which wasn't much of a backup plan, but was better than nothing.

Ten minutes passed. A cell phone rang. The Saudi standing next to Mark took a step back, as though guarding himself against the possibility of a physical assault. Then he slipped his left hand into his jacket and pulled out the ringing phone. His right hand was up inside his jacket. Gripping a pistol, Mark assumed.

The phone had barely reached the Saudi's ear before he lowered it again and handed it to Mark.

"If you don't deliver that child to Kalila Safi, if you try to cut some side deal with the CIA or the Shias, I'm coming after you."

"Nice doing business with you too, Saeed."

As soon as Mark handed the phone back, the three Saudis started walking toward the plane. After ten steps, one of them called back to the doctor and the two men in hospital scrubs. Although Mark couldn't understand what was said, the man's tone was sharp and insistent.

The two men in hospital scrubs started off toward the Saudis.

"Hey, wait a second," said Mark to the doctor. "What's his condition?"

The doctor gave a theatrical French *bof* and a shrug. In French-accented English, he said, "His condition is he's an asshole who attacks those who try to help him. Beyond that, he suffers a bullet wound to his left shoulder. I have cleaned and dressed this wound. Because the bone was not hit, the main danger of course is infection. I gave him an intramuscular shot of antibiotics last night, and I give him a second dose now along with a booster shot of morphine. After that, he takes these."

The doctor handed Mark two pill bottles. "Percocet for the pain, and Keflex, an antibiotic that will prevent infection."

"What about his leg?"

"It was broken. I set it and immobilized it. He will need a cast in a week when the swelling goes down." The doctor pulled two syringe packs out of his satchel, and then two ampules. He quickly prepared the injections then, without warning, jabbed one needle, then the other, into Rad's thigh.

"Jesus!" said Rad, suddenly opening his eyes.

The doctor finished with the injections and dropped the syringes on the tarmac. "I have to go." He shouldered his satchel, and limped off. Mark walked over to Rad and put his hand on the bed, next to Rad's good arm. "Hey."

Rad's eyes were glazed over, the result of the morphine, Mark figured.

"My arm," said Rad. "I can't feel my arm. It's completely paralyzed." His words came out slurred.

Mark reached down to Rad's bad arm and pinched the forearm skin. Hard. Rad cried out and tried to pull his arm away.

"You still have some feeling in it," Mark observed.

Rad looked as if he was trying to focus on Mark's face.

Mark added, "I'm going to transfer you to another plane. I've got something I have to do, so you'll have to wait for an hour or so, but after that I'm taking you home. You're going to be OK. Everything's going to be OK."

60

Kalila Safi was a petite woman, and she wore a frumpy tent-like black chador over a black headscarf. She had thick dark eyebrows, and an ugly hawk's beak for a nose. Mark knew better than to make her uncomfortable by offering to shake her hand when they met inside the executive flight terminal. She wouldn't even meet his gaze. Her face was lined with worry, her eyes deep-set and dark.

A short bearded man, who claimed to be Kalila's brother and was accompanied by four massive bodyguards, introduced himself. Mark shook his hand, and then an awkward moment of silence passed between them.

Mark had nothing to say to them—he'd know soon enough whether they'd been straight with him—and evidently they had nothing to say to him either.

Larry Bowlan stood off to the side with his three cab-driver bodyguards.

"All right then," said Mark. "Should we wait on the tarmac?"

Ten minutes later, an old Dassault Falcon, with a registration number on the tail that matched the number Decker had told Mark to look out for, touched down.

As it taxied toward the executive flight terminal, Kalila Safi clasped her hands in tight to her chest and began to bounce, with what looked like nervous anticipation, on the balls of her feet.

She mouthed silent words that Mark couldn't understand but guessed were a prayer.

So far, so good, he thought. She didn't look like she was faking it.

The plane, which was owned by a charter company frequently used by CAIN, pulled to a stop about a hundred feet away. The fuselage door opened, and the air stairs were lowered.

Decker appeared in the doorway, squinting in the bright sun. Mark raised his arm and waved—what a relief it was to see his friend—but Decker was looking in the wrong direction. As the big former SEAL stepped off the plane, he tried to lower his head at just the right moment so that he wouldn't bang it on the plane, but he banged it anyway.

Mark saw Decker turn, snarl at the doorframe, and give it a little smack with the palm of his hand. But once Decker reached the tarmac, he turned back to the door, smiled, and extended his long meaty arms out wide.

Muhammad appeared. He was smiling too, holding what looked like a dirty stuffed duck in one hand and a plastic shovel in the other. He took a step toward Decker and then half-fell, half-jumped into Decker's arms.

Decker swirled Muhammad around a few times, placed him on the ground, and then tousled the kid's black hair with his oversized hand.

At that point, Kalila took off at a run. "Muhammad!"

"Deck!" Mark cried out. He made eye contact with his friend. "Like we talked about!"

Kalila didn't bother to hold her chador clasped underneath her chin, so the long swath of fabric slipped to the pavement. Muhammad didn't notice her at first, but when she called his name again, his face brightened and he began to toddle eagerly toward her.

At that moment, Mark knew for certain that he'd made the right choice. Decker, who'd witnessed the same thing, gave Mark a thumbs-up. Kalila had passed the final test, the test the Saudis who'd tried to take Muhammad from the orphanage had failed. If Muhammad hadn't responded to Kalila, Decker would have picked the boy up, reboarded the plane, and taken off.

"*Anna, Anna,*" called Muhammad, which Mark now knew to be the little boy's way of saying *Nana*—a common way of referring to one's grandmother in both Arabic and English.

For Mark was now sure that Kalila's brother had not lied to Larry Bowlan last night—she was indeed Muhammad's maternal grandmother. As such, according to Sharia law, she was entitled to custody of Muhammad now that Muhammad's mother had died. More important from Mark's perspective, she'd been helping to care for Muhammad since he was born. She loved him, and apparently he loved her back.

Kalila picked Muhammad up and began kissing his pudgy cheeks and speaking rapidly to him in Arabic, her face streaked with tears.

Well, good for them, thought Mark. That's one thing that worked out at least. God knows, not much else had gone right for Kalila Safi lately.

According to Kalila's brother, her husband had died three years ago. Then, just before Muhammad had been kidnapped, and as her daughter—the youngest wife of a prince of Bahrain—lay dying, Kalila had been kicked out of Bahrain. The prime minister had worried that she might take custody of Muhammad upon the death of her daughter and bring him to live with her Shia relations in Dubai.

Mark had no idea whether the prime minister's original fear had been justified. But in retrospect, it looked like kicking Kalila *out* of Bahrain as a way to try to keep Muhammad *in* Bahrain had been a stupendously bad call.

Mark made eye contact with Decker, who gave a little lackadaisical salute. Mark nodded and returned the gesture. He wished Daria could have been here to witness the reunion. She'd have been out on the tarmac crying with Kalila and Muhammad, he imagined, arms wrapped around them both. He'd call her soon. At least now he'd be able to tell her he'd done right by the boy.

Kalila was running back toward her brother as fast as she could with Muhammad in her arms. As she passed by, Mark called out an enthusiastic, "Good luck!" prompting Kalila to dip her head and turn from him as if he'd uttered a vulgarity.

At that point, Muhammad noticed him too. Mark forced his mouth to form something approximating a smile. "Hi!" he said brightly, waving to the boy.

Muhammad's eyes widened with recognition. Then he scowled and clung tighter to Kalila as she walked away. After all that had happened, Mark didn't blame the boy.

Mark spoke briefly with Bowlan—they agreed to reunite in Bishkek in one week—then joined Decker in front of the Dassault Falcon and shook his hand.

"How's your dad?" He'd talked with Decker on the phone a few hours earlier.

"Out of the ICU. Looks like this isn't the one. I'm gonna go home for a bit anyway, though."

"I appreciate your being there for me, buddy. If I had known—"

"That's why I didn't tell you, so don't worry about it. Anyway, the kid was pretty cool, and I had some help."

Decker told Mark about Jessica, how she'd helped him and how they'd been climbing in the mountains south of Bishkek when Mark's call had come in.

"By the way, we should go climbing sometime," said Decker.

"I'm forty-five years old."

"I'd take you up the easy routes. It's better than just wasting away in the city."

"I like wasting away in the city."

"Whatever." Decker pulled out a small bottle of Dr. Pepper from a combat chest rig he was wearing under his jacket, chugged it down in three big gulps, then fished a tin of Skoal Straight chewing tobacco out from his front pocket. He held the dip tin between middle finger and thumb and snapped it down rapidly several times, thwacking his index on the top of the tin with each flick of his wrist.

After lifting the top of the tin off, he inspected his work. "A damn nice pack," he determined. Deck reached into the tin with his thumb and index finger and transferred a huge wad of tobacco to his mouth. "You want some?" he asked, speaking through the dip.

"That stuff stinks," said Mark.

"Didn't want to dip around Jessica or the kid. Been jonesing for one, so you gotta suck it up. By the way, Holtz and I had a bit of a falling out. He wasn't too keen on me taking the kid."

"I'm done with Holtz," said Mark. "I'm going out on my own. You can work for me if you like."

"Sure." Decker turned away from Mark and spit a glob of dip juice onto the pavement. "So where's our plane?"

61

New Jersey, USA

Mark didn't have to escort Rad all the way from Dubai to Elizabeth, New Jersey, but he wanted to. It was time to go back.

Elizabeth was an old town. It had been the first capital of New Jersey. George Washington and Alexander Hamilton had walked its streets during the Revolutionary War. But little of that history was evident now. Now, Elizabeth was the kind of place Mark guessed people thought of when they laughed about New Jersey being the armpit of the nation. The city of Newark and its busy airport lay on the town's northern border. The Port Newark-Elizabeth Marine Terminal, a huge shipping port, was to the east. Massive oil refineries, and an industrial wasteland known as the Linden Generating Station, lay just to the south.

Mark could see the power plant now. He and Rad were being driven down the New Jersey Turnpike in a private ambulance. The smell of toxic smokestack emissions and rotting marshland near the plant reminded Mark of some of the old oilfields outside of Baku.

The ambulance turned off on exit thirteen. Minutes later, Mark was staring out the window at the streets of southeast Elizabeth where he'd grown up. His first reaction was that the place didn't appear to have changed much. He even recognized some of the stores—Deanna's Hair Salon, Joey's Italian Sausage, the Cuba Bakery . . . Other shops, he didn't—Payless Liquors,

Gupta Auto Repair, a Portuguese deli, a pharmacy with a neon sign that read TARJETAS TELEFONICAS DE VENTA AQUI—but they weren't so different from what used to be there.

Driving down the same roads he'd walked as a boy made Mark realize that, while he'd never regretted leaving, he liked his hometown.

It was on these streets that he'd first learned to fit in, to go unnoticed, to survive—where he'd learned that, even if a place looked a little rough around the edges, that didn't mean it had nothing to offer. The town had a fast tough rhythm to it that Mark knew was still a part of him.

As he thought yet again of how and why he'd left, all those years ago, he realized he was dead tired. Tired of thinking about the past, but also just physically tired. The plane ride from Dubai had chased the sun, adding nine more hours to an already long day.

For the first part of the trip, he'd hung out with Decker instead of sleeping. When they weren't playing electronic narde on Decker's cell phone, or drinking beer from the minibar, Mark had been on the phone with Kaufman, making sure that the CIA was going to fix it so that Rad would be allowed back into the US without a passport.

After a refueling stop in Paris, Decker had gone to sleep and Rad had woken up. Rad had been more lucid at that point, and had been able to call his fiancée on the plane's satellite phone. He and Mark had talked some—about what had happened in Bahrain, about Mark being a spy, about what Rad had been doing with his life—but Rad had mostly been focused on his pain. And a good hour of the flight had been devoted to figuring out how to get Rad safely to and from the bathroom.

As a result, Mark hadn't gotten any sleep the whole trip.

"Jesus, you guys really fixed up the old station," Mark said when they got to Coventry Avenue. Instead of seeing his dad's old gas station with the lousy four pumps and the neon Save-A-Lot sign, there was a huge BP sign out front. And eight shiny new pumps. And a convenience store.

"Where are we?" Rad tried to look over his shoulder, to catch a glimpse of the gas station. From his prone position, however, Rad couldn't see the street the way Mark could.

"Coventry Ave."

"Oh, the old station. Yeah, we redid that eight years ago. You should check out the one right off the turnpike. That one's got twelve pumps."

Mark hadn't even known that his father had expanded beyond the original station. He and Rad had mostly avoided the subject of their father during the flight.

"And you were the project manager for all this?"

"You bet."

Rad began to talk about how their father had first secured the rights to a BP franchise, how that had led to the purchase of a second station, then a third, and how Rad had helped put together the business plans for the banks, how he'd gotten tight with all the Jersey contractors, how . . .

Mark wasn't really listening. They were pulling up to the old house now. The same chain-link fence stood out front, with several plastic garbage cans lined up just behind it. The aluminum siding looked pretty much the same, just a little more chalky and faded. Up near the roof one of the aluminum soffit panels had fallen away, revealing intricate wood detailing badly in need of a paint job.

He wanted to think of this house, this town, his mother—the faded movie in his head that comprised the first seventeen years of his life—as something unrelated to the person he was today. But it was becoming increasingly hard to do so. He remembered the smell of freshly laundered clothes, the creak the basement steps had made when he'd sat down, the weak light from a forty-watt incandescent bulb in the stairwell, the drip-drip-drip from a leaky utility-sink faucet.

He remembered the textured ceiling in his room, the bathroom with the pink tile, the way his brothers used to splash bathwater out of the tub . . .

The ambulance came to a stop. The driver engaged the parking brake, walked to the back of the ambulance, and pulled open the doors.

"We're here," said Mark.

Rad lifted his head and squinted as he looked out the rear of the vehicle. "What are you talking about?"

"We're here."

The concrete sidewalk out front was riddled with black dots—old gum, Mark knew. He used to walk the sidewalks of Elizabeth and instead of trying not to step on a crack, he'd tried to avoid the gum dots.

"Mark, Dad doesn't live here anymore. We moved when I was in college. That was like, over ten years ago."

At the airport, Mark had recited his old address to the ambulance driver as the government orderlies had been securing Rad. He'd done so because Rad had said to bring him home to Elizabeth, home to Dad's house. He'd said his fiancée was living there temporarily, while Rad was in India.

Mark had just assumed Rad had been talking about the home they'd both grown up in.

"Huh."

"I was wondering why we were going by the old station. Thought maybe you just wanted to see it."

"I kind of did."

Mark glanced at Rad, and then back at his childhood home. It seemed even smaller than he remembered. He thought of his mom sitting on the steps out front, waiting for him to come home from school, asking how his day had been when he showed up.

"Are you sure you're all right?" asked Rad.

"Yeah, sorry for the mess up. So where are we going?"

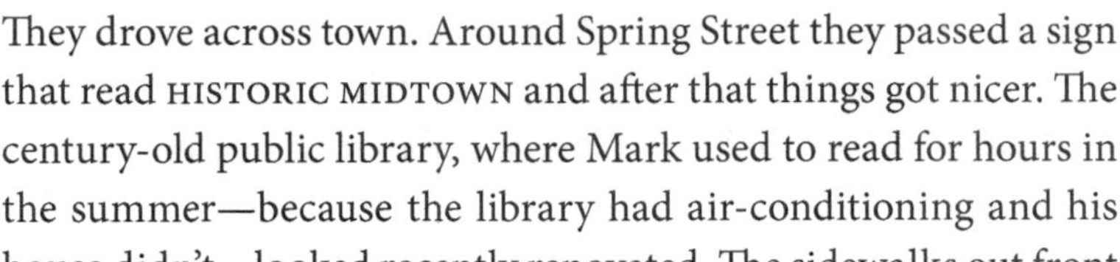

They drove across town. Around Spring Street they passed a sign that read HISTORIC MIDTOWN and after that things got nicer. The century-old public library, where Mark used to read for hours in the summer—because the library had air-conditioning and his house didn't—looked recently renovated. The sidewalks out front were paved with newly laid brick.

Mark allowed that things might have changed a bit more than he'd thought.

Five minutes later, they turned onto a street where decent-sized homes sat amid well-tended yards, tall old trees, and mulched flowerbeds. The ambulance stopped in front of a brick house that had an Audi Quattro parked in the driveway. It was one of the larger houses on the street, with wide front steps that led to a large double-door entryway, three front gables, and expansive bay windows on the first floor.

Rad lifted his head just enough so that he could see out the side window of the ambulance. "We're here." He sounded relieved.

As Mark was stepping out of the back of the ambulance, a pretty, blue-eyed woman with brown curly hair ran up. She wore a tight white blouse, tight jeans, and glittery flip-flops. Her teeth were white, and straight. And she smelled nice, Mark noted, as she pushed past him.

"Rad!"

"I'm OK."

"Oh my God baby, oh my God, I can't believe this happened to you."

On the plane, Mark had been listening when Rad talked to his fiancée. He knew that his brother hadn't told her much about what had happened. Just that he was hurt, and was coming home, and could she be there when he got there?

Mark extended his hand and gave her his first name. "Rad can explain how we know each other later. In the meantime, I think the best thing to do is to get him inside the house."

An older woman appeared behind Rad's fiancée. She had gray hair, a bit of a belly, wore big gold hoop earrings, a gold bracelet, and a velour tracksuit. Her eyes fixed on Rad. "Good lord! Did the monkeys do this to you?"

"It wasn't the monkeys, Mom. I was attacked. Well, shot."

Her hands went up to her mouth. She looked down at his leg, and then at the bandages on his shoulder. Blood had seeped out of one corner. "This happened in India?"

"Later, Mom."

Mark recognized her. She was the woman his dad had married after the suicide.

"Shouldn't you be going straight to the hospital?" she said. She cast a wary glance at Mark, not recognizing him.

"He's stable," said Mark.

"Oh baby," said Rad's fiancée. "This is crazy. If you think you need a hospital, we should get you there now."

Mark added, "He should be looked at soon, but you have time to pick your doctor and decide on the right course of action."

The ambulance driver and the orderly who'd accompanied him walked around to the back of the ambulance and started unfastening the clamps that held Rad's gurney in place.

Then the front door of the house opened.

Mark recognized Petar Saveljic at once—recognized the slouch of the shoulders, the wide-set darting, reptilian eyes, the hard jawline. His father had gone bald on the top of his head, but he'd always worn his hair short; no hair didn't look much different than short hair had.

The only difference was the way his father was dressed. In the seventeen years he'd lived with the man, Mark couldn't remember ever seeing his father in shorts. Typically, it had just been the soiled blue work pants he wore at the gas station, or the worn-out gray dress slacks he'd put on at home after he'd washed up. But it was unseasonably warm for early November—in the upper sixties, Mark guessed—and he was wearing shorts now, pleated khakis that came down to his knees. His legs were spindly and he wore leather Docksiders with no socks. His golf shirt was a bright yellow.

Petar Saveljic walked down to the ambulance, his eyes fixed on the driver and the orderly who were sliding Rad out of the back of the ambulance. "The Indians do this to you?" he asked. Though his tone was hostile, he mostly looked worried.

"It wasn't the Indians, Dad."

"We're going to need help getting him up the steps and into the house," said the ambulance driver.

At that point, Petar Saveljic noticed Mark. He stared at his oldest son for a few seconds, looking confused, and maybe afraid, as though he wasn't sure to believe what he was seeing. He took a step back, as if pushed by an invisible hand. "Marko?"

"I'll help bring him inside," said Mark. "Then I have to take off."

"Marko?" He squinted, incredulous.

"It's a long story. Rad can explain."

"I don't understand," said Rad's fiancée, looking from Mark's father to Mark.

Rad said, "This is Mark. You know—"

"You mean—"

"Yeah. The one—"

"Oh my God." Her hand went up to her mouth.

"Congratulations on your engagement, by the way," said Mark.

"Two of us are going to need to be on each side of the gurney," said the ambulance driver, taking a position near Rad's head. "Grab the metal bar underneath securely. We'll roll him to the steps, then lift." He turned to Mark's stepmother. "Ma'am, if you could get the front door for us?"

Petar Saveljic's living room in the new house was nothing like the gloomy living room of Mark's childhood, whose dark walls had been decorated with religious icons—medieval-style paintings of men long dead. This was a sunny space with cream-colored walls and glossy oak floors. Books with gilded spines, which looked as though they'd been bought for purely decorative purposes, lined built-in shelves that framed a gas fireplace with a marble mantel.

But then Mark saw the icon.

It was small, no more than six inches wide by maybe a foot tall, encased in a pine frame that had been painted black. Tucked into one of the corners in the bookshelf, it was the only thing in the entire living room that he recognized. The sight of it caused his heart rate to quicken.

There he was, Saint Sava, looking as dour and two dimensional as ever.

Mark tried not to stare, but he couldn't help himself.

It was an ugly painting, of a dead man who meant nothing to Mark. Saint Sava had been the founder of the Serbian branch of the Eastern Orthodox church. Although Mark didn't care about the man himself, the painting meant something to him because his mother had viewed it as her own personal good-luck charm; she'd even taken to rubbing the old saint's nose when she was in need of extra good luck—before Mark had a big exam, for instance, or when his father had been applying for a second mortgage on the house. Saint Sava's nose had gotten a little smudged from his mother's right index finger.

Even from a distance, Mark could see that the nose was still smudged, and it touched him.

He turned away.

His father didn't know he'd taken the name Sava. No one outside the CIA knew. And no one inside the CIA knew why he'd taken the name—that he'd done so simply hoping that it would bring him some luck. That's the way he'd thought back when he young. He'd been more superstitious then, more willing to believe in things like luck.

"All right then," said the ambulance driver, turning to leave after Rad had been safely deposited in the middle of the living room.

"OK, brother," said Mark. He'd seen enough. "I've got to leave now too, but I'll give you a call soon, see how you're doing."

"You're going? Just like that?" asked Rad's fiancée.

Mark's father hadn't said a word since they'd all entered the house.

Mark turned to her. "Get him seen by a doctor sooner rather than later."

"What should I tell BP?" asked Rad. "About what happened?"

"Tell them the truth," said Mark. "Or lie, if you'd prefer. Your choice. If BP insurance won't cover the hospital costs, the government will. Someone will be calling you."

Mark let himself out the front door, following on the heels of the ambulance driver, and didn't look back until he heard it open behind him. It was his father.

"Marko, wait."

Mark stopped. His father shut the front door behind him and walked down a few steps.

"Does Rad . . ."

His father's hushed voice trailed off as Mark locked eyes with him. Petar descended the rest of the steps, but kept a hand on the railing.

"Does Rad what?"

"Did you tell him?"

"No."

Petar Saveljic looked visibly relieved. "I just don't know how he'd handle it."

Mark turned to walk away again, when his father asked "And you? You're good?"

"Yeah, I'm good."

"Well, thanks for . . . for bringing Rad home, I guess. He said you helped him? I don't understand . . ."

Mark turned and began to walk down the driveway, but the thought of his mom's painting in there was gnawing at him. He turned back to the house. His father was still standing there, watching him.

"The Sava icon," said Mark. "I see you brought it over from the old house."

His father looked as though he didn't know what Mark was talking about. Then, "Oh, yeah. That."

"Give it to Rad."

A pause, then, "Sure, maybe I will. Why?"

"Not maybe. I'm *telling* you to give it to Rad."

Petar Saveljic's eyes narrowed as an angry, cunning frown formed on his face. It was an expression that was still intimately familiar to Mark—even after twenty-eight years of being away. Twenty-eight years ago, that expression would have meant something bad was coming. Not now, though. Mark had been in the spy business long enough to know when he had the upper hand. He didn't even have to speak the threat aloud. His father just needed a moment to figure it out for himself.

A long moment passed. Mark heard the ambulance backing out of the driveway. He'd been hoping to ask the driver for a ride.

"Yeah. Yeah, OK. I'll give it to him."

"Give it to him today. Tell him that his mother used to think it was good luck. Tell him you're giving it to him for good luck. As an engagement gift."

"All right." A pause, then, "Who the hell are you, Marko?"

"I'll be seeing you, Dad."

Mark walked out the driveway and kept going when he hit the road. The setting sun was shining in his eyes. He felt happy, but the lack of sleep combined with the beer he'd downed with Decker was catching up to him. He turned his head away from the sun, and for a moment felt lightheaded—so much so that he needed to stop briefly to keep the world from spinning.

62

Kyrgyzstan

Daria Buckingham drove from Balykchy to Bishkek in an old Lada she'd borrowed from the orphanage. The windows were rolled down, even though it was chilly outside, because she enjoyed the feel of the cold air on her cheeks, and the warm air from the car's heater blowing on her legs. She was looking forward to the coziness of winter, to the snow she was certain would make Bishkek feel like the lonely outpost on the steppe that it once was. The snow, she imagined, would bring people together, would make it feel as if the city was under siege. People would bond together to make it safely to the spring.

A text message came in on her phone from an unknown sender, interrupting her thoughts. She was about to check it, but then remembered how a family of Kazaks had recently been killed by a teenage driver who'd been texting while driving. She was going to stop for gas soon anyway, she'd check it then. She had to learn to be comfortable with less risk in her life. She had new responsibilities to consider.

Her period still hadn't come, her breasts were tender, she was tired, and the smell of onions turned her stomach in a way it never had before. It was happening.

She hoped the text that had just come in would be from Mark, telling her what his flight number was for his return trip to Bishkek. He'd finally called her yesterday morning to let her know he was in Dubai of all places, and that Muhammad was safe and with his grandmother. So good news on that front, but when she'd pressed him for details, he'd just said that it was a long story, that he needed another day or so to fully wrap things up, and that he didn't want to talk about any of it over the phone. He'd sounded distracted, and tired. But at least he was safe. After not hearing from him for over a day, she'd been worried.

She imagined that Mark would be home in time for a late dinner, that they'd be able to sleep in the same bed together that night. When she'd been hiding with friends in Balykchy, she'd thought of him often, wishing she'd been able to tell him her secret before the call from the orphanage had upended her plans.

She wondered how he was going to react when she finally did tell him. He'd be a good father, of that she was almost certain. For a moment, she even allowed herself to hope that the news would lead him to get out of the spy business for good.

Acknowledgments

ONCE AGAIN, I AM DEEPLY INDEBTED TO THE TEAM AT Amazon Publishing—especially Jacque Ben-Zekry, Andy Bartlett, and Alan Turkus—and to my agent, Richard Curtis. Their counsel, kindness, and support buoys me.

Christina Henry de Tessan did another wonderful job editing this novel. I'm also grateful to Corinne Mayland, David Mayland, Tim Gifford, and Scott Stone for helping with the copy edits. XNR Productions of Madison, Wisconsin, did a great job with the maps.

Many reporters, scholars, and ex-CIA officers lent insight to this novel through their books. An annotated bibliography can be found at DanMayland.com.

About the Author

Photograph by Corinne Mayland, 2012

DAN MAYLAND LIVES IN Pennsylvania with his family and frequently travels to the remote corners of the world that he writes about. His first book, *The Colonel's Mistake,* was the inaugural novel of the Mark Sava series.